The

Wandering

Ones

Tyler D. Kumaus

ASA PUBLISHING CORPORATION
AN INNOVATIVE OUTSOURCE BOOK PUBLISHING HYBRID

ASA Publishing Corporation
1285 N. Telegraph Rd., PMB #351, Monroe, Michigan 48162
An Accredited Publishing House with the BBB
www.asapublishingcorporation.com

Copyrights©2024, Tyler D. Kumaus, All Rights Reserved
Book Title: The Wandering Ones
Date Published: 12.15.2024
Book ID: ASAPCID2380921
Edition: 1 *Trade Paperback*
ISBN: 978-1-960104-70-0
Library of Congress Cataloging-in-Publication Data

This book was published in the United States of America.
Great State of Michigan

Message from the

Storyteller

————··⚡⬦◄⊕►⬦··————

Tyler D. Kumaus

"What's the point in living?
There is no point, none at all. But isn't that a good thing.
It's up to us to find our own reasons for living by focusing on
what makes us smile.
If you feel warm and alive, then you have your reason."

Table of Contents

The
Wandering
Ones

THE CLIFF

Waves . . . waves were all that the man could hear from the cliff's edge at the top. The sounds of the waves breaking against the rocks below seemed both terrifying and soothing, like watching a plane coming in for a landing. It's scary that this large object is hurling to the earth, but at the same time, the smooth landing is a unique sight to see. Hearing these waves below made the man recall the chaos of his life. This man had lost it all: his hope and his dreams. Soon, he would continue down the path, just one more step to close the book on his story. He looked up to gaze at the horizon just one more time; the light of the setting sun was a peaceful embrace for the man. The colors of the light blended together to create this warming quilt that comfort the man. At that moment, he closed his eyes in order to take that step.

Instead of the rough waves hitting below beckoning, he felt something soft and innocent. A small hand grabbing the man's hand before he even had a chance to move forward. Opening his eyes, he turned and saw a small blond-haired child in a white gown grabbing his hand and now part of his coat. To him, the grip of her hands was as if she was holding a teddy with such warmth and passion. A moment passed before she looked up at the man; gazing into her eyes, they reminded him of better days. "It's not your time," the child said innocently; the man didn't know what to say; he didn't tell anyone where he was going, and he certainly didn't know this child. "I've been watching; I know what is happening to you is rough, but . . . there is still time to change things. You can start again and make a difference. I feel it's important to remind you that you're loved by someone. Even if you don't know who they are or have nearly met them, or even if you think they don't care about you. It's important to remember that if you do this you wouldn't be another light gone. What you'll leave behind is more painful than what you're experiencing right now. Step back and move towards a brighter future of your own making, but please," she begged, "don't give up."

The man looked forward, letting the words of this 'child' sink in for just a moment. 'Can I really start over,' he thought, only to realize that this kid was right. That hope can always come back, that new dreams will form, and that we are the masters of our own destiny. Even when we are lost in the dark, the flame can be set anew. It's up to us. As the man turned around to thank her, he saw that no one was there. No girl, no footprints. The only thing that he saw was the field of grass that he was standing on, which was blowing back and forth, going with the winds that were taking them. Now, with this new wind underneath his wings, he took that step forward towards a new story. Leaving the old one at the edge of that cliff.

THE DARK VOICE

It was a dark and stormy night in the Boston area, worse for that time of the year. It was 3:00 in the morning, and James was in such a deep sleep that if his sister had seen him, she would have thought that he died. The gray covers were everywhere across the bed, barely covering his chest and one of his feet. His pillow was somehow across the room as if he had already set it there by design, but in this state, he didn't even notice the pillow missing.

At some point in his deep sleep, he was awakened by the sound of lightning that fired off like a shotgun going off near his ear. And with the same intensity of a gunshot, James shot up in the air like a cannonball and flipped his bedside light on. It took James a few seconds to come around and realize that it was a storm passing overhead. However, it was hard not to notice through the dark, ominous shadows trying to reach into his soul just beyond the reach of the dying light bulb from his bedside light. After a minute or so, he was calm enough to turn out the light and try to return to his dreamland of wonders, which was so rudely interrupted.

Nevertheless, it never came to him; he just spent what felt like forever tossing and turning, like a hot dog on a grill, just sweating up the sheets. Sometime later, after what felt like hours, he decided to get up and get some water. Just as he was wrapping his damp fingers around the cord for the lamp, he heard a voice whisper in the dark, "Please don't; we like the dark." The voice came from nowhere and everywhere, like the dark waters of the ocean. Those few words were cold and calm but also mysterious and otherworldly. "Who's there?" James replied to the void, and the void coldly replied back, "Nothing, and that's how we like it . . . If you turn on the light and see us, well, you'll have wished that you had never woken up to begin with. For we are the unknown, always there, always watching . . ."

THE LAMB AND THE WOLF

T he forest is a place where things differ from the everyday lives of the modern universe. For most, it's a kingdom of nature where the goddess known as Mother Nature still rules, battling the tides of time that create destruction at her borders. Though for most, it is mysterious, but for the young woman walking through this kingdom, it's more familiar to her than most. Cause nature was her home as well, a primal place where mankind is a part, not the owner; as such, she respects it with the kindness it deserves. For her, she grew up in it; she lived for it, cared for it, and in return, it cared for her as well.

For today's odyssey, she decided to trek through a deeper part of the woods that was both ancient and otherworldly. A place where there was no path to a destination but a sea of wild green that covered what was in front of her like a soupy fog. A few hours into her journey into the unknown, she came across a thick hedge-like bush that seemed to go on forever. It was a literal plant wall that seemed to be reaching for the stars above, giving off a feeling of both chaos and order, just like her life. Curious and wanting to continue on, she saw no other alternative than to simply walk through the green ocean of possibilities. With every step, she was poked, slapped, and shoved through her passage. Eventually, after what felt like forever, she emerged through the brush like a child being born into the world.

What she saw surprised her could only be described as divine. Before her lay a clearing of a beautiful stream glistening with a godly smooth surface that sparkled like jewels. It flowed along a beach of stones that seemed almost perfect. Each and every stone looked as if it had been handcrafted by angels, and all were soft, round, and innocent. "Hello there, child," said a kind voice that broke her out of her trance, forcing her to turn towards its owner. Residing just near the water sat two beings that immediately and without question gave off a variety of different feelings: fear, peace, anger, sadness, harmony, life, and death. "There is nothing to fear, child," the one who first called out to her was a beautiful woman; she sat on a large boulder wearing a flowering white and black gown. Her dress was so long that at first glance, as it was flowing into the water, it was becoming water. Yet the most peculiar thing was the ceramic mask she wore that looked to be a lamb of sorts.

"There is always something to fear," the other individual said in a raspy tone as he stood against a nearby tree. This man, who seemed to be more rugged than anything, was in a tattered red suit. Yet the suit still seemed to hold onto him despite the rips and tears that seemed to have bits of bloody hair sticking out. Unlike the lamb woman, this man wore an old wolf mask that, through his hair, showed a number of cracks. At the moment of seeing these two, the woman wanted to run and flee, but she couldn't as something stopped her. The two before her didn't seem like they wanted to harm her; they seemed like they genuinely cared for her; they were the first in a long time, and that's why she started to sob lightly. "See, there is nothing to worry about," said the woman, "you know who we are; we are beings that are forevermore together. Your whole life, you have tried to forget us, but deep down, you know our names. For we stand as one, are one, a pair." The man stands forward and snarls at the woman, "Never one without the other, for everyone knows us in time, at some point in their stories."

It's at this point you have questions for the two, the lamb and the wolf. Before they gave her a chance to open her mouth, they asked in unison, "Would you like to hear a story?" 'A story,' the woman thought, and before she could answer, the lamb mask told her, "There was once a sick man who was very lonely. He traveled the world alone, not being able to interact with anyone. Yet despite that fact, all things must interact with this man, so he was shunned for his existence. Then he had an idea: in order to not feel lonely, he split himself into two, right down the middle. So that he would never be alone." "So that he would always have a friend," said the wolf; as the lamb told the story, it hit the woman to her very soul. The reasons for why she came to this moment replied in her mind just as fast as the tears were coming out. The woman in the lamb mask and the man in the wolf moved towards her; they placed hands on each of her shoulders and calmly said, "Most run, even flee until their end from us, because they stood still at some point. So, treasure all your moments, even the final ones. For we were that man, and we have and will always know your names."

"Beauty fades. That's why it is beautiful. All stories have a beginning and an end. Today you strive; yesterday you fell; tomorrow is yet another mystery."

THE DARKNESS

Before the universe became what it is today, there were two beings that fought for power in an endless war over the right to spread their influence. These two beings were Ignial, the king of the light, and Pelel, the lord of the darkness. Brothers, friends, rivals no one remembers how it all started. What's known is that the light king was a fair being that showered all in his light and warmth. He rules over his dimension of angels and lights cloaked in a similar light. The light king was a 'pure' individual, looking like an angel among angels, his long blond hair flowing with his white wings that expanded from his back. As king of the dimension of light, he was the light, as shown by the fact that his face contained a tridimensional light that couldn't be looked at with the mortal eye. In all his time, Ignial strived to bring peace and order to a chaotic universe. By helping those embraced in his light to fight against the demons of the void, making the people of the light the sole rulers of the universe.

His adversary, the lord of darkness, is still a mystery even to this day. There isn't much known about the man that rules the night. Rumors say that those who have seen him say he is a demon that just wants to engulf the universe into the preexisting nothingness. Though those are just rumors, the reality is completely different. The dark lord, lord Pelel, is accentually a soft-spoken man who wants to protect his people. Allowing them to rise to new heights so that they can create a paradise for all, even alongside those in the light. Despite his peop e being seen and treated as demons (as per Ignial's views), the people of the void are always under threat from the people of the light, just due to where they come from. As their ruler, Pelel was looked at no different from the rest. For Pelel was no devil; in fact, he wasn't even a warrior; he was just an ordinary man. He spent his time not in armor or fancy clothes but dressed in a long black coat with a hood covering his face. He chooses to cover his face, not because he is an ugly man, no, not at all. This man was gentle; he just wanted to hide from the world, the same one that he had looked at with those sad eyes. The same eyes that lost hope long ago, for no matter how hard he fought for equality, for peace, it never came. Age after age, eon after eon, he watched as his people suffered, and they looked to him to guide them. At the very least, he could do was hide the weight that he carried and the pain it caused him, every day, from everyone.

One evening, he was sitting alone in his room overlooking the sun setting over his land (or their verse of a sun). The sky was changing before him, filling up with different shades of purple and white as one being set and another rose. "Why do we keep fighting each other," he voices out loud as he reaches for the bottle of whiskey next to him. The smell was as strong as its taste, and he began taking slow swigs of it to drown his sorrows. After the last swig, Pelel sings, "Why? The universe is infinite, but they wouldn't stop until they wipe us out." Realizing the emptiness in not just his words, as he put down the now empty bottle, he reached into his coat to pull out a smoke. "We are the same, yes, with different origins, backgrounds, and cultures, but the same. So why is it that the proud and arrogant need to be right when it's not the right choice to make." After placing the cigarette in his mouth, he pulls out a box of old matches and strikes one up. As he held the match between his fingers against the end of the roll, watching as it burned into nothingness, he let out a long puff as the cigarette burned his fingers. "Ignial, we were born from nothingness and wanted to make something for ourselves. Right?

So why . . . what changed in you?"

Though no answer would come, even if it did, would it even make sense to Pelel? Probably not. So, he just sat there listening to the nothingness of the universe, of the planet, of life. And for a few brief moments of silence, he let it out before t had to end. In the distance, the sound of bells ringing reached his ears; the cycle was about to begin anew. "It's time, isn't it? Welp, no use waiting around to dual on the past; I better get a move on." Throwing the cigarette into the dirt of a long-dead plant, he started to move towards the door. "I hope that we can still have that drink before this is all over . . . though will it ever be over? Will find out soon, wouldn't we . . . brother."

It doesn't matter where you come from; we are people. We aren't born with hatred in our hearts; that is something that we learn and try to surpass, forget, and survive . . .

. . . for as long as we walk this world.

THE SHOT

"Why is it always me . . .?"

Bang!

In a flash, my shoulder exploded with the heat of a thousand suns, but suddenly it was just cold. It was so cold that the pain, shock, and blood running down my body were all numb. A literal whirlwind of feelings hit me all at once as the hole in me just grew, forcing more out of me. The force of it all is too much to bear. Though, why do I feel so cold? If I had to guess, it's just my mind's way of coping so that I don't panic still, even if it's just the mind I am rendered as helpless as a new babe. No matter what I did, the pain just wouldn't stop. It was sapping the strength from my body. I could barely stand; my legs felt almost brittle, forcing me to brace myself against anything that could support me. Which so happened to be one of the last old stone columns that were still standing. I tried lowering myself to the ground as best as I could given the circumstances, yet what little strength I had to stand was about gone. With the column crumbling against my back as I slid down, I couldn't help but think that this was funny. Here I am, trying to support myself for more time, yet with each motion, time was eroding the very support behind me. With tiny bits breaking off of the main body and falling to the ground with grace. Along with others spreading into my jacket.

At last, I was on the ground, still bleeding, still in agony. All I could do was sigh of relief, laughing as the pain seemed to dull even just a bit. Taking a chance, I pressed my right hand against the hole, putting as much pressure as I could on it. It was a long shot since so much was already around me, but it was a chance if I could slow the bleeding. Regardless, it didn't matter. The shot came from somewhere. "I needed to protect myself, or what little life I have wouldn't be for long," I thought as I tightened the grip on my pistol, raising it with the hope of where I thought the shot that hit me came from. As it so happened, I was close.

Emerged from into the light of the busted-up window next to us that seemed to span across the large room. She stood there with a large rifle aimed at me with the tip of the barrel smoking from the recently spent round. Swinging the weapon to her shoulder, she loudly said, "Well, hey there, love. What brings you to my neck of the woods." As she started to approach from across the room, I could see through my painful haze that my gun started to shake. I knew what that meant. I had Mear seconds before my arm gave out, and I would be left defenseless. So, I took my shot at her and missed completely; then I watched in terror as my trusty pistol fell to the ground, as lifeless as my arm. "Well . . . well . . . well, ain't that an S.O.B.! You came here for me, but you'll be flatlining soon enough."

When she finally reached me, she dropped to one knee and leaned in so that she could whisper in my ear, in a soft though crazed tone, "Listen, friend, this chaos will never end. You can try to run from the reaper, but she's in cahoots with fate. I live alongside the insanity of this world, with all its blood, death, and bullets. Though for you and those 'peaceful' people that think insanity is wrong, that can't be further from the truth, boyo. Here on the battlefield of life, we are all insane, for sanity is an illusion. And I'm here to prove that when you accept that, you'll be much better off, friend." Finishing that line, she stood up, swung down the rifle, and ejected the empty mag at our feet. She then reached behind her, under her long coat, removing a fresh new mag while, in the same quick motion, slapping the new one in. After putting a round into the chamber, she pointed the barrel just inches from my forehead. In that instance, I knew that the reaper was near and was ready for me. That the time was near and that all that I fought for was coming to a close. Within that second, there was a feeling in my chest that felt like something broke, and all I could do was laugh. I just laugh with a malicious smile on my face, knowing that all the while that the questions I wanted to answer will never come. "Well . . . well, I guess there is hope for you yet, love." And with that, I closed my eyes, and all I could hear was the sound of the pillar breaking.

FAITH?

This one is my node to the character Joshua Graham and those who need help.

You are in a church and in need of advice from a higher authority than that on this plane of reality. You move down the aisles of pews in order to find the priest. After spotting your local priest, you move towards him, where he is taking in the light of god on this day that to most seemed like any other day. "Come forth, my child, and tell me your problems, "the priest says without even moving to look at you. Without even thinking, you move forward, sitting next to the father; that's when you realize that he is the man who can help you. The father was dressed in the typical priest attire that all of them were, but what made him unique was that his body was covered in bandages that barely covered the burns on his skin. Feeling the sense of unease from you, he turns and says, "Don't mind my earthly appearance; you came here for something else." You work up the courage and ask him, "Father, I need advice. I feel alone in this world, and I don't know how to have faith in it. Is there hope for all my troubles, depression, and travesties that always seem to happen to me? I don't know if I can believe it anymore."

The father, in a calm, comforting aurora, leans over, putting his hand on your shoulder in order to let you feel god's love and voice through him. "You know there are many different travesties and troubles in the world. It's all right to be skeptical of if there is any hope, but what surprises me is that not many people believe that things can change. For those like us, the road is a difficult one with a path to the end that we may follow. Regardless, sometimes you fall off the path and end up somewhere much darker than the light that you are used to. You may ask, 'What is the point?' when that happens since you may not be willing to climb back onto the path from which you fell. Naturally, even the light of a single soul can't burn away all the darkness that surrounds it. So, no matter what happens, when the walls of darkness come tumbling down upon you, ask yourself, "What do I still have to keep the darkness back." The father leans back, pulling a cigar from out of nowhere, and continues saying, "When you have nothing left, there will always be family there that will support you." He started to look at the burns that showed through the bandages on his hand, "The light that once saved me was that of love, their love, God's love." The father lets out a light chuckle, "Right, it's okay to not be certain; fair enough; I guess dough is something that god did give us. Though I remember this before I go, it gives me great comfort to see that light in all that darkness. Don't give up on faith in yourself, the world, or others because he hasn't given up faith in you."

THE SWORDSMAN

In the Twilight of the night, the winds are as calm as a flowing river and as quiet as death itself. The fire before the warry swordsman was a calming one, with its flames dancing around like a barrier. One that was keeping the darkness at bay . . . his darkness. After the day that he had his body drained, it was as drained as the cup of sake beside him. He was tired with his mysterious, short white hair being caked with mud and his brown shirt and jeans torn and worn from the day they had of fighting. Feeling the need, the swordsman removed his shirt in order to showcase to the dancing embers around the flames the scars of his battles. The new ones hurt with bits of red peering through the tan bandages around his body, still crying those red tears, but the old ones . . . those were a different story altogether. They were not made through a dance of death with fire and steel; they were made from the fires that created him. The fires of pain with a dash of despair, that to him were the closest thing to hell on earth. The price of that pain also cost him his home, his honor, and, more importantly, his family. Unwrapping the red-soaked rags, all he could feel was despair for his enemy, the ones who did this to him. In his heart, he knows that not all men are made to be evil; it's just the nature of circumstances. The people he has been fighting may have their own reasons for unsheathing their swords, whether that be for money, pride, or even family.

However, to the swordsman, that emotional side of him doesn't come until after the fight, after the rush is over. At that time, he doesn't concern himself with the ideals or feelings or even the lives of those around him. When the time comes, he will do as he must, as any who carries the blade. The swordsman gestures over to his sword, sitting next to him in its worn, though comfy, black sheath. He reaches over with the demeanor of a parent, grasping the handle gently with one hand whilst the other was carefully holding onto the sheath. Slowly, he removes the sword, showing its void black blade to the cold night, making the dark shadows almost come alive. Each time this blade was unsheathed, there was usually a feeling of dread in the air. As if the blade weren't just a sword; it was the embodiment of the reaper of death. The swordsman felt a connection to it, as if it weren't a tool of death in his hand but an extension of his very soul, trying to clear this world of the evil of his enemies. He didn't care who got in his way, be they man or beast, demon or god; nothing would stop him. "Well, time is short. The morning will be here soon," placing that piece of him down, he reached into his sack, pulling out a loaf of bread from the last town. "I know you are there . . . come on out from the shadows, it's time we had a chat."

THE LOVERS QUARREL

It's been months since we last saw each other, and she still looks as radiant as the day we first met. Standing at the other end of the field, in her long crimson cloak covering her beautiful armor and skin. As I looked at her, she always seemed like an angel to me, one who was ready to either deliver comfort or pass divine judgment. Though considering the latter with the magic she has been using the last couple of attacks, it seems she is still pissed about that incident. Ever since they locked eyes in the field, she has filled the void between us with creators of ice and fire, along with the ruble that used to be my golems. Those were the only defenses that I was willing to use against her, though I couldn't help but feel a mixture of emotions for this situation. Yes, I need those golems for the job I was hired for, while at the same time, I don't want to hurt the one that still holds my heart. "Dam you, Beni, Dam you! I will never forgive you for what you did to my brother." As she said those words, I couldn't help but feel the guilt resurface. I had to kill her brother because he was going to slaughter an entire town of innocent people.

All because of one guy that pissed him off, but I could never tell my beloved that it would crush her to the point that she wouldn't recover. Though now was not the time to be living in the past, as my attention focused back on her, I realized that I had to move. Her beautiful black hair started to rise as she spoke another spell that would undoubtedly be the end of me. However, what struck me to the core was not the blazing anger that was aimed at me; what really surprised me was the pain she was emanating from us as if she really didn't want to fight anymore. That's when it struck me; as she raised her arms to finish the spell, I could see the flame runes that bonded her. As someone who has lived for quite a long time, I knew what that was. It was the flames of rage, a spell used to bind someone to their rage until it consumes them, even when their rage is nothing more than a flickering flame. I only know one way to unbind the spell. In order to do that, I removed my coat so that I could have better access to my arms and the wounds. Digging my finger into one of the wounds on my arm from the ice shrapnel, I extracted enough blood to perform the unbind ritual.

At the same time, in order to have a second, I threw up a few barriers between us, knowing full well that it would only last a few seconds. When I began the ritual, her attack would be coming. So, with the speed of the gods, I drew a blood circle in the air and aimed it in her direction, hearing the first barrier shatter. Two more remaining barriers remain. The circle grew in strength and brightness; I just needed a few more seconds, and it would be done. Another barrier was destroyed, the heat from her attack grew closer now. The chant was almost complete; I would soon remove my beloved's hate, her pain. As the final barrier broke, I was able to finish the chant and lock eyes with her. "I love you" was all that was able to come out before her attack hit me dead on, and everything went a painful black.

I don't know how much time had passed before I came to, but regardless, I felt at peace. Yes, I also felt quite a bit of pain with what felt like a hole in my chest, along with both an arm and part of my leg missing. But as my vision started to come into focus, I saw her holding my head in her lap in order to pour some sort of liquid from a metal tin into my mouth. "Hold still, my love, you will survive this," was all I could hear through her tears, "I don't blame you for what happened; that spell, that bitch, twisted me to the point of a rabid beast. I will save you, and we can continue from where we left off." Feeling a sigh of relief, I told her, "Thank you . . . I. I," "Don't speak, my beloved, let the healing waters revitalize you." Knowing that, I closed my eyes, and as I began to pass out again, I said to her, "My angel, I will always just go into the darkest pits of damnation in order to save your light."

WHAT IS GOOD AND EVIL

The fight between the two warriors that day was almost over. On one end, a dark warrior clad in black who, to the other spectators of the fight, could still feel the aura of darkness and death emanating from him. The right arm of the dark warrior had been cut deep, with a long gash pouring out an unsteady amount of blood from it. "How about that? You can still stand, can you? Though I still have plenty of power to finish you off." The other warrior, well, he has seen better days, to say the least, clad in grey clothes that were torn from the fight, a partial cloak flowing behind him, and one of his arms was missing from the last blast attack he took. Breathing heavily, he answered the bastard that took his arm, "I told you . . . you are not walking away from this." In anger, the "hero" of this story limbed forward and grabbed with his only arm a piece of rubble to support himself. "Well," the dark lord said, "It looks like the battle between good and evil has to come to an end."

"Good . . . evil? What the hell makes you think that I'm the good one in this fight!!" Finishing that word, the piece of rubble under his hand turned to ashes. "Well, yeah, I'm fighting to protect these idiots, but that doesn't make me good. I've abandoned those childish concepts a long time ago." Hearing that, the dark lord's face showed a bit of dread in his eerie smile as the hero spoke. "You define them as sides, but the truth is they are jokes that humanity created to make themselves feel better in the face of dark shit. All that exists is a void of possibilities, and we fill that void with morals, choices, and actions to justify our beings. For beings like me, who used to be human, I stopped

carrying and embraced it all. My reasons are my own, and they are neither good nor evil; they are just my own insane visions of me." By now, the spectators on the side were filled with fear that the two demons in front of them were both equally dark. Though one had hope, in her heart, that her love, the hero, would save them all and that they could be together at last. "But that wouldn't matter to you anymore," raising his arm to the dark lord, he pointed at him and said, "Cause, as I said, you're going DIE!"

The eyes of our hero glowed like that of hell itself as he started to speak the most powerful spell in his arsenal. Knowing what was coming, the girl yelled for the others to run because she had seen that spell before and knew when he used that one, the gloves had come off, and there was about to be one hell of an overkill. Though it was not the girl that only knew, the dark lord laughed and started to chant his own spell, with his eyes turning a voiceless black. "It's time to put you in the ground," he said, letting a blast from his arm go in the direction of the dark one. It was stronger than the others that she had seen him cast. Also, she thought her mind was playing tricks on her because her love's arm seemed to be back, but more like an arm of magical rock on fire. At the same time, the dark one sent his own blast out, colliding with the fiery blast directed at him. As they braced together, they formed a hurdling ball of possibility, outcomes, and futures, but there was only one possible outcome that was certain. The ball expanded as each one poured more and more power into their own attacks. Until it exploded in a flash of light, blinding the girl who was barely out of harm's way. She couldn't see with her eyes, though within her heart, she knew that it was over. That good or evil didn't win that fight; only those who make fate their bitch and laugh when the universe bits back. As the smoke cleared, she saw the outcome, though without saying anything, she burst into violent happy tears.

THE FIRST SIBLINGS

In the beginning, before people, before the creation, before life, there were two siblings that existed before it all. With both being equally natural and feeling that their lives were fair. Though, in retrospect, they may have felt that life was fair to them, their appearances gave others a different story. One was peaceful, yet most who would see him flee, for he was always a young man dressed in a black cloak that seemed to cover his whole being so well that apart from his face that was always full of sadness, he would have seemed like a living shadow. The one thing that made him stand out was his dark oak staff, which was curved at the top in a way that looked terrifying to most. The other sibling was a gentle one, though some would start arguments with her for things that she had no control over. Similar to her brother, she was also wrapped in a cloak but more in a fabric of blissful light. It covered all except her face of joy, making her appear to be a star, for she was always happy with her big brother at her side. She was the beginning, and he was the end. She got to be happy, and he carried the greatest and the saddest burden of all existence with him. Their names were Life and Death, and they were the first siblings.

As time passed for the siblings, they each grew further and further apart. Life was happy creating and expanding their empty universe: boring planets, stars, creatures with thoughts, and just about everything. She thought that she was helping her brother, creating happiness in his ever-saddening soul. Death, however, saw what his sister was trying to do and pretended to smile. For he knew that if she was happy, then the burden wouldn't be that horrible to take. Since it was he who had to help the souls of Life's creations move on after they had expired. He talked to them over the eons, with some thanking him but most blaming him for taking the time they had. He dealt with the anger, sadness, rage, and devastation that time gave to these people. Life never could know what he was experiencing; he was the older one, the brother, the protector. As time passed, the souls of the deceased would come to him in small droves, although there were periods where souls would wash over him, drowning him in a pit of despair, crushing him until he couldn't bear it. For he would and always protect his sister from the horrors of her creations, even when they tried to destroy themselves.

A while later, there came a point where fewer and fewer souls came to him. Taking this as a good sign for a well-deserved break, he went to his favorite spot. An old hill that has spent a long time overlooking a calm valley of change. There on that hill is a rock that has never moved its spot despite how long it has been there. Death rested his old bones on the stone, setting his staff against a nearby tree. He leaned back, taking what felt like his first breath in ages, then started to cry silently. "Is this seat taken?" Death looked at the voice; it was Life with her pleasant smile that always seemed to be the one thing that could warm him. Wiping the tears with his sleeve, he croaked out a low "No." Sitting down on the rock next to him, Life leaned against her brother, placing her head on his bony shoulders. "Brother, are you ok?" "Yes," he said, wrapping his arm around her, "I just needed a moment of calm. You have created such beauty, and I . . . I don't know, just forget it." "I know what you do for me; you deal with the sadness of this world. If you need to talk, your baby sister will lend you her ears." Breathing out the weight he carries, he inhaled a grasp of hope and told her, "I'm just tired; for the past eons, I have dealt with the passings of the innocent and the guilty. I noticed that the souls of the living were appearing before me less and less, and I saw this as an opportunity to make a change. Would you mind if I helped you, sister?" Looking over to life, she could see that her brother was suffering for her. He not only wanted to make a change in his life but also needed a change. "You know, brother, judging from the state of things, I believe we should just start over and try again together, just the two of us." Realizing what she meant, Death smiled, for he felt grateful for raising such a compassionate sister who cared for him. "Ok," he yelped, with tears starting to pour down his sickly cheeks, "let's do this together." Life smiled with joy, for not only was she ecstatic that she could help her brother in addition to taking on some of the pain that he held onto for a long time. She got to see her old brother again, that one who was always smiling, the one who always protected her, the one who was free to be himself. The two siblings then just sat there in silence for a long while. Watching the chapter close on the sense of violence in creation. I hope that the next attempt will be better for both of them. Less anger and less heartbreak, while at the same time, more compassion and peace.

A DEMON

In a time of random conflict, there is only so much that an individual can take before they become susceptible to the evils of this world. They feel themselves becoming weighed down by their pain, their anguish, and their own self-worth. Welcoming an old powerful demon to a weak spot on an individual's shoulders. In some cases, the demon appears before them as a small bird, barely making an impact on them, when it lands on them. Other times, it is a winged man resembling an angel of darkness, and all he does is place a hand on your shoulder. That is when it happens: not only will you never be the same again, but he makes you feel like you need him forever. For this demon whispers horrors into one ear, telling you, "You're worthless, you're unloved, you're a monster of your own making." Despite how he makes you feel, somehow, he also makes you feel comfortable. This demon will sometimes whisper into your other ear while wrapping you in his wings of darkness, telling you, "Do not worry yourself; those in the light will never understand your darkness. We may be demons, but they are the real monsters." This equilibrium of kindness, yet decay, is the demon's way of preserving the minds of those he visits when he takes the form of a man.

This old power comes to all at some point in their lives; for some, they can get rid of him. For others, he becomes a part of their very being, making them become demons themselves, falling from the good graces. Take, for instance, a young lad who was a social outcast in his early years. He tried to find his place in the world through an awkward outlook on life and a smile on his face that never seemed to fade. However, at one point, that awkward outlook changed, and that seemed to crush him. To the low point that invited the demon as a man, telling the lad, "It's ok to feel like hell, for you see what I see." The lad looked to the dark being with a sign of happiness, saying, "What took you so long? The light hurts so much . . . I am ready to join the darkness, for it is more appealing and accepting than the insanity that those in the light call 'normalcy.' Will you have me?" The demon was surprised, for those who see him in this form know that they can never go back to what they used to be. In some recent cases, they have learned to deal with it and try to fake the pain with a mask of normalcy. However, there have been a few recently that accept the hand of a demon despite the urge to feel the same again. Those few who are willing to fall into darkness are already consumed by their own darkness. The demon and the young lad gave each other a dark smile, along with a death grip on each other's shoulders. "Well, should we get started then," the demon said. "I thought you never ask, you depressing bastard," snicked the lad.

THE WRITER

It was late evening, but for some reason, the fog that rolled in made it feel closer to dusk, with darkness being carried in with the fog, similar to a stowaway on a ship with such a malicious presence. The writer was worried; looking out from their cabin window, he felt that presence coming closer and closer. Almost as if with each step the fog made, it devoured the surroundings of the forest, creating an island of darkness that only became smaller and smaller. Among other things, the light from the nearby lamp was becoming all the more fainter as if it were connected to the amount of time the two had before they had nowhere to go. Worried more for his wife's safety than his own, he grabbed the flashlight from the nightstand as his weapon. So that when the time came, he could defend them against the dark spectators who were just beyond the void. Leaving the room, he started to calmly call for his wife, "Alex . . . Alex." With each flicker of the lights in the house becoming fainter and fainter, his calls became more and more frantic. "Alex . . . Alex, where are you?!"

Then came the scream from what sounded like a nearby room, so he ran over to the sound. Until he came to a complete stop at the door, where all he could feel was a cold, dark future of possibilities that awaited him on the other side of the door. Slowly opening the door, he stared in horror as the room started to disappear the further it went from the door into nothingness. The only visible thing in the void was a small dirt path moving forward into the black. Further in the void, just off the path, there was also a small table with a small boxed TV on top of it. As the writer started to enter the room, something told him that he needed to go down the path, for his beloved was at the other end. With the courage of a lion, he slowly made his way down the path until he just made it to the TV. When he closed the distance to it, the box TV turned on, showing a version of him rambling. The TV version seemed to be disheveled as if he hadn't gotten any sleep for a long time. He was pacing back and forth in front of a desk filled with paper, talking. It was hard to make out, all the same, it seemed like the TV version was trying to talk to him. The rambling warnings came through as,

"It's not too late for us to fix it, not too late. We can stop it, we can stop it. It wants us, our body, our mind, our soul. It wants us to create a way for it to escape from this dream world. Just like the old stories of Lovecraft, it needs someone to open the door. We knocked on the damn door stirring it awake. Now, it wants out; it wants us to open the door and let it out. It will use everything it can to get the door open, and that includes Alex." Looking directly at that writer on the path, the TV man looked scared, like he had almost no hope left. Nevertheless, he had one more thing to say, "I have delayed it for as long as I can, and now it's up to you, my friend. You have to make sure that the beast stays caged if you let it out . . . it's all over. However, there may be one card that I haven't realized could have been played. You know it, too; the same thing that it wants is the same thing that can stop it. You need to close the book on this story, save her, and end our nightmare before it gets worse. You may not know it, yet this nightmare is something that you have dealt with for a while now; you just don't remember it still."

And with that, the TV powered down, and his memory started to come back in pieces. At first, it was a slow trickle similar to a calm river, though as the memories were coming more and more, they unleashed a madness that almost broke the writer. Wrapped up in these images along with the feelings, a sense of unease came over him that felt like a repeating record. Where he could remember that each time he went down the path in front of him, a different nightmare came and attacked him. As a consequence, the nightmare would start over. Regardless, that didn't matter to the writer; he would do whatever he had to in order to save her. No matter how many times he had to suffer or die, he would get Alex out of there. So, he took a cold, deep breath, seemingly inhaling the black nothingness, and decided to keep moving forward into the unknown.

DIARY ENTRIES

As the soldier moved s owly through the building with grace, he carefully checked each room for hostiles. Giving each room a sweep with the light from his rifle, showing only old rundown rooms. Where in these sweeps, he only noticed walls peeling, ceilings starting to collapse, and a few pieces of furniture that were burnt slightly. The only life that he could see was the rats running out of the rooms into the hallway, right out the front door. Finally, there was the last room, the room that he was here for, where the signal was coming from. Slowly approaching the room, he took one hand off his rifle, slowly pushing the door open. The first thing he noticed was that this room was completely different from the others. Unlike the other rooms, this one remained well-kept and as white as a padded medical room. All that was in the room was a desk near the window, with a computer, monitor, and a device that was blinking blue. As he entered the room, he shifted towards the monitor, which was in low power mode with a post-it note on it saying, "Play me." As he reached for the spacebar, a wave of dread entered the room from the open door, creating a sort of dark presence that the man could feel behind him. Hitting play, the screen came to life, starting a video of a young woman sitting in the room that he was in. She seemed like the doctor that he was sent to retrieve, but she seemed almost disheveled, tired. Looking into the camera, she spoke with a professional tone, saying,

"It's been 78 hours since communications have been lost with headquarters. Everyone is scared of what this could mean since we are a good hundred miles from anything that resembles civilization. Some people are worried about what this could mean; some have speculated that one of the containment sites was breached, and others are observing the surroundings of the complex to see if this is one of those ends of the scenario. The armored presence is talking about sending someone to the closest base a few hundred miles away." Taking off her glasses to rub her eyes, her professional expression changed, showing the tears that she was trying to hold back. "If we don't hear from someone soon, I fear for what might happen to us . . . Along with . . . her. Since the resupplies were supposed to be here five days ago, and the levels say that there is only a week's worth left." The video ended, moving on to another one. This time, she looked worse, with papers scattered behind her on the floor. "It's been four days since the last entry, food rations are running low, and containment supplies are almost out." Pausing for a while, she stared at something that was out of view, terrified of what she saw. "We are all on edge; with containment supplies at these levels, she is starting to stir. Some have started to hear and see things that aren't really there. Those who are experiencing symptoms are showing bruises in the form of hands, such as little girl hands. We tried to quarantine but realized very quickly that it didn't matter . . . I can't believe he was right. Our armored presence took off in the middle of the night, leaving the handful of staff to fend for themselves." Pausing again, the doctor reached out of the frame, pulling a syringe with a tube of some liquid in it. "This in my hand is the only thing that can help us . . . we need to block her out before her power full awakens." As she went to inject herself with the liquid, the video cut out to the next entry.

This time, she seemed like she was up for days; her clothes were torn, she was covered in cuts, and she was hyperventilating like she was just running from something. As she tried to calm down with her head now between her legs, the soldier saw some words and symbols in what appeared to be blood behind her, along with shadows moving. After a few moments, she took her head up, and with a deranged look in her eyes, she began to show how much she had unraveled. "It's happening now, NOW. She's free, She goddamn FREE!!! . . . tearing her way through the facility, with everything that is touched decaying, burning its time away. The darkness is her home . . . She wants to bring us into it, into her home. Most of my colleagues are dead or just gone . . . I think . . .I think I might be all that's left." As the doctor stared into the camera, a little girl emerged from the corner shadow. "If anyone from the organization is seeing this, don't come here; there is no one left to save. She owns this place now!" As the doctor says those last words, the girl behind her lets out a small laugh. The final thing that is shown before the camera is cut out is the doctor being dragged away by something, with her screaming, "GOD HELP ME!!!" Then that was it. The entries were over, leaving a lasting thought in the soldier's head, 'If she didn't want help to come, then who sent out the signal?' Alas, the universe finds a way to always answer one's questions, even the bad ones.

As he finished his thought, a voice spoke from what seemed like everywhere and nowhere at the same time. "Hello there," the voice said with an expulsion of evil. Taking up a position, the soldier flipped the desk, sending the computer equipment all over the floor. He readily checked the magazine, flipped the safety on his rifle, and aimed at the door with the speed of a professional. This was due to his many years with the organization's training and development that he took part in. Regardless, he felt that all those years of experience were about to be amounted to nothing. As a small hand was placed on his shoulder, that same voice whispered to him, saying, "You're not going to leave me too, are you? My other toys broke so easily when they said they didn't want to play anymore." Slowly looking over his shoulder, the whole room started to fill with a darkness that began to envelop him. With the shadows starting to suck him in, he saw where the voice came from in the form of a little girl floating above the ground. She struck the soldier with such terror with her dark, yellow eyes that she began to giggle. "hahahahahahaha . . . I like you," she said, and all that was free was his head and one arm. "You're going to be my special project." Those were the last words the man heard before being taken to her realm, her home, never to be seen again.

LOW POINT

It was a cold day in this hell of a life for James. The sky was filled with clouds with no sign of the sun ever popping out, ever again. The trees surrounding the path were glooming and dark as if they were trying their damnedest to hide from the world. Even the path beneath his feet was a rough one; for each and every step he took, the pain was digging into his soul. Though he continued walking, every step he took was a harder but relieving one. Finally, he reached his destination, a calm field where his long journey would finally end. The trees, the animals, and the grass surrounding him would be the womb of his death. Pulling his bag off his back, James carried it to the center of the field, reminding himself the reasons why he wants . . . no has to do this. When he reached the spot, he pulled a knife from the bag. Dropping to his knees, he knew the pain would be over soon; he just needed to slice his neck open, and it would be over. Placing the knife up to his neck, he closed his eyes, listening to the cold nothingness that was blowing through the wind, telling him that he was ready to do what needed to be done.

"Hey there. What are you doing over there?" Surprised by the voice, James opened his eyes and looked in utter disbelief to see a girl under a tree. She was leaning back against one of the dark trees, her white hair glistening in the cold breeze, holding a book in one hand and glasses in another. "Sorry, I didn't know that anyone was here. Can you please leave," looking down at the knife, "there is something that I need to do." "I can see," said the girl. "By the way, I'm Alice, and I can't. This is where I come to be alone, separated from people. What do you plan to do there?" Tears started to form in James' eyes, "I'm tired and alone. No friends, no family . . . no one to love me. I spent so long trying to find a reason to fight on, but I'm a disgusting, ugly freak. I want the pain to stop." Closing his eyes, he raised the knife to jab it into his neck. Nevertheless, the pain was still there.

Opening his eyes, he saw Alice standing over him, her hand gripping the blade of the knife. With blood dripping from her beautiful cut hands onto the cold, serrated steel of the knife. Staring in utter disbelief, James noticed the multiple cuts and slashes all over her wrists and arms. "You aren't the only one that has felt pain," Alice stated, "We are both freaks of this world. You have just been walking alone for so long that you think that's all there is . . . loneliness." Taking the bloodied knife from James, she threw it into the darkness of the tree, where they swallowed the steel forever. She took a knee so that she and James could be eye to eye, where he could see the same pain, suffering, and darkness in her soul that was in his. "How about this: we both start over together. People like us just can't be alone, or this is what happens." Getting to her feet, she ripped off a piece of her coat in order to make a makeshift bandage for her hand. After she finished in mere seconds, she looked at James, smiling and saying, "Now, how about you tell me your name." Just in utter shock that a beautiful girl . . . no, an angel was able to pull him out of this hell and save him was an understatement. In his heart, James knew that he found a new reason to go on; through the tears, he whimpered, "James." "Well, James," Alice smiled, "How about we go, get some food, and talk? There's got to be a decent joint around here." With an outreached hand from her, he couldn't help but cry more. Since to him, help, love, or kindness has never come. So, James wouldn't waste this opportunity; taking her hand, he said, "Yeah, I know a place." And they walked away together, both leaving broken pieces behind and creating something unimaginable from the ashes of all their combined pain.

NOT ALONE

In this world of a few billion people, there are times that we feel alone in the universe. People separate, divide, or just make themselves stand in their own darkroom, comfortable, safe, and protected. Regardless of the strength of that darkness, there are few who manage to find each other in order to create their own light. It could be as simple as a boy and girl who protect, love, and enjoy their days together. This boy, John, always feels the need to protect her from the dangers of the world, for she is the only one that he can bring that smile back to his face, along with his heart. John did this by using his strength of character, in addition to the rifle that he carried with his backpack. Every day that they were together, the good days, the bad, and the downright ugly. John would wrap his arms around her, saying things like, "You are the light of my life. I'd never let anything happen to you. I love you."

The girl, Emma, would always feel the same way as John did. She has always felt alone in this world; there is not a single person with whom she could share her thoughts, dreams, and true feelings, for the two, Emma and John, were like those separated heart necklaces that made one whole heart. Separate, they were fragments, broken down to the bare minimum, lost in the void of sorrow. Though together, they were one whole, completing each other, along with everything that was one another: their hopes, dreams, and happiness. In addition to the good, the two also accepted their darknesses: pain, scars (mental/physical), and the deep sadness that each held. Regardless, the two didn't care about such things. They were destined to walk down a long, broken road together, hand in hand, heart to heart, soulmate with a soul mate, regardless of the number of steps that their journey through hell would take them. And with each step they took, no matter how light or heavy, they would look into one another's eyes, hold each other close, whispering to each other, "I love you," in a way where it would come from the depths of their souls.

Life is a chaotic, messy, and dark path that we all take. We may feel that we are alone on a path to avoid. Though that can't be further from the truth, there is someone for everyone. They say that the most broken thing can be fixed with a little duct tape, and I feel that's true for people like us. Even the most messed up people, lost in their own anguish, can find that other half of the necklace.

Have faith that you will find that the other half.

No matter how messed up . . . No matter how damaged . . . No matter how weird

There is someone who will embrace your darkness . . . bringing you the sliver of light that you need in your heart.

LOCKED UP "VILLAIN?"

In the darkest pits of hell on this plane of existence, there is a hole. A hole that seems to have no bottom from the surface could be very well described as the express elevator to hell. However, it was only hell for the inhabitants who lived there. Or should I say the one inhabitant who was imprisoned there? At the bottom of this hell pit, behind a set of large stone doors, was a large room that they called his cell. Around the room, there were chains everywhere; some were attached to several stone monoliths, and others were melted into the floor, walls, and even the ceiling. It's these chains that led to the center of the room, where on a circular platform lay what looked like an average man connected to these shackles. Dozens of chains were wrapped around his wrists and ankles, restricting his movements. At the same time, several were connected to spikes that were jabbed into his arms and legs. These wounds, along with others, constantly seeped blood from them, draining from him onto the platform, finally down holes that went God knows where. Another important fact to add is that there is only one light in this dark room. A small fire that will forever burn, too small for warmth. Regardless, it somehow creates enough light for the prisoner to see the chains that contain him. I also barely saw the demons that would leak on the edge between the small light and the vast void beyond.

I know what most would think: that no ordinary mortal man could survive this long, abysmal nightmare. You would be right; this is no ordinary man, for he has been deemed a villain of the world. The prisoner was a pariah, a charlatan, and a demon for those whom he chose to oppose. For the world above will forever know him; know me as Dark Drake, the half-blood demon of the abyss. What they don't know is the truth behind his incarceration. Well, this is my truth.

I don't know how long has passed here as if I had a choice in the matter. All I could do was think of my revenge on those that put me down here. Watching the ever-dancing flame of my hope in front of me, warming the stiff wounds on my body with their light. It was all I could do from going insane down here . . . actually scratch that, I'm already crazy; I just don't want to end up going mad. As if on cue, HE appeared again in front of me, Asmodeus. Who is a demon that has been hiding in the void down here for some time? Unlike the others in the shadows, Asmodeus is capable of walking in the light, which is a mystery. As he approached the platform and into the light, I could see his tattered black cloak that had never once shown his face. Even one time, I tried to strain my eyes to see his face, but all I saw was literal nothingness. "Hello again, brother," he said as he stepped onto the stone, "May I sit with you?" "Sure," I said, "As if I have anywhere better to be." He has stepped out of the shadows a number of times to chat since his arrival in my cell.

As if I cued, he sat in front of me, pulling out a bottle of booze and uncorked it; as he took a swig, he said, "I want to ask something: Was It worth it?" The question came around often since I am the great "villain of the world." So, I decided to finally answer him, for the sake of my own sanity, yelling, "Yes, it was worth it!" Surprised by my finally answering, he gestured the bottle towards my mouth, and with a nod, he gave me a swig. "Well, my friend, tell me why?" Asmodeus didn't know the true story; no one did, and that's why I'm the villain of their story. "If you want to know, I found out the truth. Of the church, the kingdom, this whole goddam mess of a world. For that, I was betrayed and branded a traitor to my people." Taking another swig of the bottle, Asmodeus asked me, "What would you do if you could claw your way out of this hell?" I pondered for a minute; I didn't know what I would do. Would I disappear? Would I cause pain or live a peaceful life? Now, knowing the answer, I reached the bottom of my soul in order to say with a smile, "I would end those who created the lie and destroy it all from the ground up. I was a hero of the people, and in discovering the truth about this world, I was named a villain. Well, to hell with that. If they wanted a villain, now they got themselves one. I just hope the world is ready, for once I get out of here, there will be hell to pay." Again, he pondered with curiosity, and he asked me another question: "Then what . . . what will you do after you destroy the charade that they created?" That one was easier to answer than the last one, though a little more painful, "I want to start fresh in some remote town in the middle of nowhere. Maybe start a business, meet a nice girl, and start a family. Though before that can happen, I will . . . no, I must destroy the lie, destroy the betrayers." My demon friend stood there for a while; even though I couldn't see his face, I could feel his unique smile on me. "Well then, may I join you on this quest then?" he stated, "You are a powerful individual Drake, and I'm curious to see what comes of your rage. How about we forge a pact as master and servant?" Surprised, I didn't know how to answer; I spent so long fighting alone that I never considered the need for companions.

Regardless, though, there was something about Asmodeus that I felt that I could trust, not as an underline, but as a friend. "I'll gladly accept the help. Though it may be difficult in my current position." Even though I was held by chains, the constant blood loss sapped my power. Even if I were to escape, the creatures that blocked the path outside of the cell and to the surface would be a challenge. My friend, though, felt differently; grabbing my hand, he cut my finger with one of his nails, drawing a small amount of blood. He then took my blood and drew a crude magic circle on his arm while at the same time, he chanted, "With this circle on my arm, I am bound to you, master. With your blood, the pact will be forged anew. As the higher demon Asmodeus, I pledge my life and soul to you and you alone. My power is in your hands, master." With those last words, a bright light shined, lighting the whole room. It took a few seconds for my vision to return; regardless of when it did, what I saw was quite interesting. All around us, the chained pillars were destroyed, the metal in my appendages was removed, and the wounds that they created fully healed.

Taking the opportunity to stretch, I stood up in my tattered, bloody clothes. Asmodeus was now kneeling before me, "I am glad to see that your wounds have healed. Also, I noticed that our pact has made you impressively more powerful than before, master." He was right. My already immense power had grown to extreme heights, along with the feeling that there was still room to grow more. Wanting to test my power, I prepared to unleash a fireball at the doors to the cell. Previously, it would take me minutes to cast the spell, but for some reason, I felt that wasn't needed. As the fire grew in my hand, it felt different than before, almost pleasant. "Fireball," I yelled as the fire was released from a small condensed ball into a mass blaze that melted the door to ashes. "Listen, Asmodeus, don't call me master. After all this time, just be my confidant, my friend," I told him as the smoke filled the room from the magic explosion. All I could see was his head raised, seeing a young demon beast man. That's when it hit me: he wasn't a mysterious entity; he was just like me. Alone, powerless to his fate, scared of what was to come. I would help him change that; he set me free, knowing that I wanted vengeance. I will return the favor, for he is now my friend, and I want happiness for those I care about.

We feel that we are heroes of our own stories. With villains to vanquish and monsters to slay, but that can't be more wrong. Even the villains see themselves as heroes of their own stories. It's when they are hit with pain, sadness, and betrayal that they become the monsters that the world sees them. For people aren't born evil; it's the cruelness of this world and others that destroy their light.

UNLEASHED

The dream always starts the same way, with me lying in a wide-open field. Always leaning against my favorite loan oak tree at the foot of a hill. My hat is down around my eyes so that I can nap in peace as I always do, with the wind blowing through my hair and the greenery giving off an otherworldly malevolent vibe. It moved in a calmly warm motion through the grass into my hair, then slowly up the hill like a farmer guiding his fingers through his crop of refined wheat. At the same time, the wind was striking the branches of the tree with such force that the leaves fell, reminding me of those cherry blossoms in Japan. As I enjoy the day in the shade, I hear her approach from the house, "Hey . . . Hey . . . Hey Big Brother?" Seeing her feet under the brim of my hand, I moved it up to see my kid sister standing there. "Are you ok? Still sleeping? Come on, mommy's waiting for us with lunch." She was always like this; even though she's my kid sister, she never stopped worrying about me, her older brother. "Ok, Ava, ok, I'm coming," I said, slowly getting up from the ground, "I was just resting for a minute." As I got to my feet, I rubbed her head and told her, "What would I do without you, Ava." Those words seemed to go to her heart, unleashing a beautiful grin that was unleashed. It was moments like this that made me wish that they could go on forever. With words exchanged, she grabbed my hand, pulling me back to the house. Though I couldn't help but feel like something was wrong, as we moved away from the hill. That's when I noticed the sky started to turn into night as if a dark blanket was being dragged over our eyes. Ava got frightened, grabbing my hand harder and whispering, "What's going on, big bro . . .?" Out of nowhere, a tentacle suddenly wrapped around her, yanking her away out of my hand. It took every ounce of strength, together with my willpower, to keep up with her as she was being dragged back towards the hill. The tentacle kept moving back towards its host, which appeared from the ever-growing hole that was forming on the side of the green slope. Revealing a larger imaginary creature that looked like a man with multiple tentacles coming out of his back, grassy bread, and dirt-black skin.

As I continued to run towards it, I felt as if something in my chest was trying to be uncaged. It keeps repeating the same phrase in an animalist tone, "Let me out; this bastard will pay! Let me out; this bastard will pay! HE'LL PAY!" Each time the phrase repeated, I felt myself slipping, but this didn't stop me. I needed . . . No, I had to get my sister away from that creature before the worst cases that I could think of became reality. With each stride, I forced myself forward, with no place of action and no hope of defeat. That's when my sister, now hanging in the air from the tentacle, looking like she could barely breathe, almost lifeless, screamed in pain, "Big Brother, help me!" Those words hit me to my core so hard that it should have made me feel terrified for her fate. Yet I didn't realize then that I had stopped fighting the beast in my chest. For in that moment, all I could feel was the red glow of rage through the light that was emanating around my body. Along with hearing the now calmer beast tell me, "Yes, yes, release me. Just let go and let me take over. This creature is MINE TO DESTROY," through the continuity of these words, I couldn't do anything. All that I could do was feel my consciousness slip away as the devil within me focused its rage on the beast whilst telling me in an ominous tone, "Do not worry . . . I'll save her."

That's when I awoke from my deep sleep. Sweat covers me, especially where the scars are.

It took me a moment, as usual, to gather my bearings. I was in the cabin that our family used to go to in the summers. "Man, were those better days," I thought as I swung my feet over the bedside, where they ended up on a variety of rubble, bottles, and another garage. As my glance moved from the crap on the floor, I looked at the old burnt photo of my sister. Reaching for it with my burned arms, all I could feel was regret for what happened. That's when he appeared in his spectral form, which resembled a man with some of the characteristics of a grey wolf. "Master, are you all right," he asked, knowing dam well what was going through my head, "Was it that dream again?" I didn't want to answer since I partly blamed him for what happened that day, but I blamed myself the most. "No, Asano. I'm fine. I just need a moment," I told, as I took my hand away from the photo. All I had now was my drive to move forward; despite the pain, despite the loss, despite the end of the world, I had to keep moving. For as many great heroes have a phrase, "push on with the burden. Yet don't forget to smile on its face, for that is how we keep it in check.

DARK SIDE OF THE SOUL

As an unspoken observer of the realms, I have experienced many dark and terrible things on my travels. I have come to learn that people are not all that cracked up to be. Since I usually travel alone and work alone, I thought it would be of interest to interact with individuals where I could. Regardless of my intentions with my hopes for kindness in the world, I have been stabbed with several sharp objects, poisoned with unusual intentions from mischievous people, and have lost those to the spirits of the dark void that plagues these worlds. For as I travel the realms, I've discovered that the once malevolent darkness has stepped out of the shadows into the hearts and souls of men. When a person has become bonded with the darkness, I have noticed that there are two different outcomes to the invasion of their souls.

On one hand, there were people like Joseph, the guardian of a small village here in Midgard. During the time that I was present in the village, I was told that he was once a great man. Who protected the weak of the world and the village for years until he was given a higher call to war. That is when the dark entities that afflicted his soul came into contact, somehow unlocking the always-existing cage of his more demonic side. Ever since evil has been unlocked in him, one that caused the deaths of innocent women, men, and even children, all the while, Joseph smiled, knee-deep in bodies. When I saw the atrocities that he committed, I was forced to look into the eyes of madness while hearing these words, "Why are you looking at me like that." It was as if I wasn't looking into the eyes of a "guardian," more like into the eyes of a soldier with battle fatigue, cursed to relive an endless cycle of violence and death. This was one of the many instances that I can recount where men were torn apart in order to leave empty shells in their places.

Though I can't say that this was always the case, as I wrote down earlier, there were two outcomes to the invasion of the soul. Beings such as Joseph, who bonded to the dark entities, were turned towards madness, destruction, or the wrong path. There were those who didn't become that; instead, they accepted the dark shadows of the void and interacted with them. Creating a different relation from their counterparts. In cases like this, the dark spirits grow from pain, suffering, and loneliness in order to intertwine within the light of the soul. If you were to imagine what this form feels like, it's more like a weight that always presses down upon you. Wounding your soul in order to create this new mixture of light and dark that will never change. I know this well because I have a bond with the darkness, accepting it as a part of me. It reminds me of my failures to protect, save, and defend against those who seek harm against the world. It reminds me that due to these failures, I'm worth less than nothing.

All the while, at the same exact time, it gives me a different strength, identity, and outlook on the world than everyone else. It reminds me that people are cruel, conniving, and destructive in the pursuit of their own selfish goals. It reminds me that though there is kindness, happiness, and genuinely good people in the realms, I can't be a part of their reality. Nevertheless, I still try despite realizing that I can't show that dark side to anyone, for fear that one day, the lie I put up, this mask of a kind drifter, will be exposed even a little bit, showing the real me underneath. This is why people like me and like us are so focused on separating ourselves from civilization.

For it has been some time that the idea of "civil" has been a part of our beings. We just want to move through the world without fear. With the terror that someone kind, someone nice will look behind the curtain, seeing the real us. The beings of light in the darkness look through the world with both sets of eyes. One set of lights from the flame was a being of kindness. One set from the dark being that has become one with the flame. Both are equal, while at the same time, one is heavier than the other. Both are troubled while accepting of the shadow that is shared around the light. Not in order to devour, though, to create a messed-up equilibrium, a messed-up persona.

THE THINGS WE FILL

I don't know how long I have been traveling this path toward peace. The days seem to blend together so easily that it's hard to tell them apart: day, night, day, night, rain, snow, and nothing at all. This one was a rainy day; well, it was more violent than that, as if the heavens themselves were in deep grief with winds cutting to the soul. When I finally reached what seemed like a clear patch, I noticed what looked like an inn. Realizing what was in front of me, I decided that it would be in my best interest to stop for the night, rest, and get some food. As I appeared with tired limbs and an unset belly, it was then that I noticed the sign, "Other Worldly Inn." Happy for some quiet at this hour, I entered the old inn with its cozy furniture and people. "Hello there," a girl said behind the counter, "Welcome. How may I help you at this time?" Walking towards her, I realized that she was a cat demi-human (half-human, half-animal) with the ears and tail of a feline. "Hello there, Ms. I would like to use a room for the evening. And perhaps get a fresh meal; it's been quite some time that I have had either." The girl looked at me, the dirty traveler, with an old sword on his hip, a storm cloak that was so torn that it provided no protection and a series of claw marks through bloody clothes that were from the local dire wolf packs. Through all that, she just said with a smile,

"Of course. Give me a minute to get your room ready, and I think I can help with your clothes."

"That is the most kindness that I have received for a while now," I said with a smile and a tear, "Thank you."

"It's no problem. If you want some food, Father is in the

tavern through there if you're hungry."

And she was off down a hall; taking the opportunity, I motioned towards the tavern. As I entered, the room looked like your average tavern. A few wooden tables scattered around the room, some interesting artwork, a fireplace just about to die out, and a bar with whom I assumed was the father. Who was an older man who looked like he had been through some battles himself, with scars all over his face and arms? Just as I was watching him, he was already watching me, even without looking at me, "You in here for booze or food, friend?" I gulped, not knowing how to answer despite having been through enough battles myself. "Food, sir," I said as I approached the nearest bar stool.

And with that, I just sat there for a while, desperately trying to fight off the fatigue. Finally, he placed a bowl of stew in front of me; it smelled great since I had spent the last few weeks off of dire wolf meat. It took me a moment to realize that I already was eating it without a spoon. I didn't even remember picking up the bowl, let alone even attempting to grab a spoon. "Listen, son," the old man said from behind the counter, "why are you in this neck of the woods." Finishing up my bowel, I motioned for seconds; taking the bowel, he scooped up a large chunk of stew while I told him, "I'm looking for a new start. I heard that there was a town on the coast where no one would bother you. And nothing happens there . . .," As I started to trail off, I gripped the necklace that was under my shirt, twisting it with my thumb and index fingers. The old man placed the bowel back in front of me; it was then that I saw straight into his eyes: the pain, the hacking, and the heavy burden he cared about. I was terrified, too weak to react; that was when he took the opportunity to tell me, "I can see that you are a burden deep within side you. Am I corrected," Not wanting to answer with details, I nodded, "I thought so; it's all over your sorry face? Listen, son, can I give some friendly advice?"

Waiting for a few seconds before I decided to answer, I whimper, "Sure." He then leaned back against the table behind him, and with a grim though saddened expression, he said, "I know that burden, that pain that you carry. When I carry the same thing, it weighs me down to the point that I feel like you are almost nothing. You feel like you can't rely on anyone but yourself. For you are the only one who can prevent yourself from drowning in your own sadness or loneliness or whatever your poison is. So, when you meet people that you grow to care about, you decide to put all your problems, past and future, into a 'jar' with the hopes that you can contain them, letting them die slowly. Regardless, the problem is that they don't die; they never do. The jar just grows and grows until cracks form, causing them to break out. I broke once long ago; I was ready to walk away from this world, disappear, and vanish until there was nothing left that existed of me. It was then that I met that girl's mother; she helped me rebuild myself. She helped me understand what was inside of me in order to accept it. That is why I don't have to worry about walls breaking; I could let go just a bit so that I don't find myself in the deep waters again. They always are there in your heart and soul as a permanent reminder of what happened and what could come."

As I digested his words as well as the food, he moved closer so that he could put his hand on my shoulder in order to say, "Don't fight alone, boy. Find someone who cares enough to stand neck to you." Not knowing what to say, I stood up to say, "Thank you, sir. You gave me some food for thought. Ha, both literally and metaphorically." And with that, I started to walk to the room I was assigned by the girl, all the while thinking to myself, "I know he's right, but now's not the time for my own happiness or self-worth. I need to focus on survival; then, I can start over. I need to focus on money, food, and shelter when those are all in order. Then and only then can I truly begin anew. Maybe even start some sort of business . . . I still remember the stories I used to read to her as a kid, where the hero became an herbalist or pharmacist, I can't remember." Again, twirling the necklace, I thought to myself, "There were only two people that I could trust before I had to start over. My sister, god rest her soul, is back in the village waiting for me to visit. With the only reminder of her in my hand. And Ryi, that beautiful girl who I traveled with for the longest time before we had to part ways. I hope we see each other again, even if it's just for a moment."

With that, I turned in for the night, wrapping myself in the blankets. I am hoping . . . just hoping that the new start will find me some peace.

THE MYSTERIOUS DUO

"Come one and all," the old soothsayer spoke to the passer Byers, who stopped to look at the madman dressed in rags whom no one seemed to recognize, for this was a small coastal village that had nothing significant about it. With absolutely no reason to visit. "And let me tell you the story of the black twin wolves and how their story started. For a long time, this land was peaceful, with people just minding their own land. The five races of the humans, beast men, elves, dwarves, and the dragon folk lived in unity until that fateful day came. Where a crack of otherworldly light started to form across the land, and they started to fall. Warriors cladded in obsidian and hellfire, fighting against winged beings of fire and brimstone. That turned our once peaceful land into a war so massive that not a living soul could have fathom the scale. No one knew the reason why the two sides hated each other so much, but we came to know them as the Demons and Valkyries. For decades, they battled, with cities around the land falling under the banners of each side. This caused the races to choose sides in the hope that they would survive the end of this world war.

It was in the middle of know where that two enemies collided in a battle that nearly destroyed an entire forest and each other. Who were these warriors? Ignial the flame Valkyrie general and Merlin, the higher demon of ice. They were both highly respected commanders in their armies. They battled day and night, through blows and cuts. Until they were both out of breath; by the end of the fourth day where, all they could do was laugh as well as finally begin to talk. For it was only through communication that they realized that they were more alike than they originally thought. They were both tired from the constant fighting, from losing people and watching the senseless violence destroy the land. So as they talk, the two decided to disappear to somewhere far from the fighting, the cold Frontier Northland.

Through their "discrete" travels they got to know one another. And as they got to know one another, by the time that they reached their destination, they began to develop feelings for one another. It was within those feelings that a more than imaginable union was formed, birthing the first ever Nephilim; children of legend, sisters with half demon and half Valkyrie blood in their veins. With the names of Kai and Haca, twins with hair as dark as the night sky. Now while their union with children was a secret, it was a secret with a price. For Nephilim, children have the power of both sides, and that terrified everyone. Would they bring peace or death, harmony or chaos, War, or annihilation? It was with this in mind that they couldn't be allowed to live. Regardless of the outcome, the commanders prepared their children for the endlessly dark future. Upon their wishes, the twins received weapons from their parents in order to protect them. Kai received the frost blade, Revenant, while Haca was given the Hell sword, Nightmare.

Not a living soul knew what happened next during those years. For the last sighting of the family was of the parents at the family estate. The father is trapped in the family home, wounded, while it was engulfed in an inferno. And the mother, who was badly wounded fighting off waves of enemies, sent for them. Their screams still haunt my memories till this day. And the twins, they were gone, ran off like a wounded animal. Nevertheless, that is what they became. It was years later that a pair of hunters attacked with ferocity like a pack of wolves. Came down from the Frontier Northland, craving a path of death and destruction against the armies of light and dark. Taking down leaders, crippling champions, and defending cities of the neutral. Forever marking their territory with the signal of the wolves." After finishing his tale, the old man looked amongst the crowd, hoping that they believed him. But to no avail, they took him for a madman as others did. Again, he knew that he couldn't stop; he needed to spread the word of these two to the people. For only he knew the true chaos they could ensue.

"Hey, old man, is that you," he heard amongst the crowd. Watching in awe as two hooded women stepped forward as if they were different than the others around him. "We've been looking all over for you. We heard you moved out here and decided to pay you a visit, maybe even get some of your kickass brews," the woman in an ice-blue hood said. "Stop that sister. You and I both know that he is tired of your shenanigans," the other one in the flame red hood said, "Sorry about her rudeness uncle." It was then that his heart dropped and he realized who was in front of him. He started to cry, seeing the two pups that he took in becoming such fine and famed predators. "Hello children, it's good to see you too."

THE JOB NOBODY WANTS

Having the job that I do is tasking on the mind and soul, wearing my body down to the bone. For I deal with angry people putting their last frustrations onto me. I deal with the tears of those that don't want their journeys to end. Though rarely do I deal with people who have accepted their shortcomings while saying goodbye to this world. Regardless they all hurt to deal with, but the accepting ones are the most kind to me. For my name is Death the caretaker of souls and this is about one of those stories.

It all started like any other day, I got my coffee, combed my silver hair, and put on my coat so that I could go to work. First off, I know there are some questions coming to mind, such as, "Death has hair," or "I thought he wore a black cloak." Well, I needed to update with the ages, since people are more receptive to someone with hair, than a bald man that looks like a skeleton. And that cloak was destroyed in the wash long ago, and I found that a long coat makes me look cooler. Apologies, I'm getting off-topic in my story; as I was saying in updating with the ages, I received tech that allowed me to be transported to souls that needed my assistance in moving on to the other side. Since in the old days, I would just wander the land moving from village to village, dwelling to dwelling. Now, mind you, it is a lot harder nowadays since people believe more in atheism, cellphones, and fighting with people on the internet than each other, faith, and love. Though like I was saying this story is about one of the kinder people that I have dealt with in recent ages.

It started on a rather cold afternoon; rain clouds were

looming in the distance, and the surroundings looked more like Lucifer's paintings of hell than a cemetery. I appeared near the entryway of the grounds, since in these cases I don't want to appear in the middle and scare the dead, not that they wouldn't mind. For a while I wandered quietly up and down the variety of graves, with some looking new, while others were barely legible. It was near one of those that I saw the soul that I have come to help. He was a young man in a white button-down and jeans, wearing thick glasses under his shaggy hair. At first, I thought that he didn't notice me, but I was mistaken as he turned to me, smiling and said, "Hello there, sir. Are you here for me?" "Yes," I answered, "It's time that you moved on to a better place." As he absorbed my words I was expecting him to yell or to start crying, but he did none of that, he just sat there smiling. "May we sit for a moment, drink some tea perhaps, she'll be here a moment," he questioned pulling out a flask which I assumed was something stronger than tea. "Sure," I decided sitting down next to him, "Who are we waiting for may I ask?" And without fail, he pointed to the end of the aisle where a woman turned the corner carrying a bouquet of flowers. As she approached, I noticed an old ring hanging around her neck, when she finally reached the grave that the man was sitting in front of. "This is my wife, sir. She has been coming here daily for the past few years," he paused for a moment, putting his ghostly arm around her, "when I died in a car accident, that was my own fault." He took a swig of flask and then began to tell me, "I was a fool; I thought that I could speed home during a storm when the roads were slick.

I ended up flipping on a turn, wrecking the car and my body." I was surprised by him; this emotion that was radiating off him was more of grief than sadness. "I knew it was my own arrogance that caused my death, but I just couldn't leave my wife and our newborn son yet. Do you get it now," turning towards me to give me the flask. I accepted that, for it's been some time since I have had a drink with a kind person. "But you do know that the longer you stay here, the more the pain of your death weights on her," I told him, since I have seen this many times from souls that refused to accept their deaths. "I know sir, but I just wanted to stay by her side just a little longer, providing what little comfort I can. Since when I go, I wanted to make sure that when I go to the other side that she'll be happy. That they'll be happy with their lives. At least that's what I hope for," he told me as his wife finished tending to the grave, and began to walk back down the long path, on her own. "Can I ask you a question sir," he asked me with warmth in his eyes, "Will they be able to find me . . . in the next life?" This again surprised me a bit since I didn't know how to answer him properly. Regardless I tried my best to answer his question, by telling him soft y, "You know what I don't have the answers when it comes to the next life. I was put here on this planet as an immortal being that was created to help ferry souls into the next stage. So that means that even if someone like a primordial spirit tells me of the next one, I can never be certain of if that's the truth. For I can never die. However, that doesn't mean that I don't have hope for what's next, if my time ever does come. So, when you ask if 'they'll be happy to find you,' my answer is I believe so. Since isn't that all we have when you break us beings down to the basics? Hope, just have hope, my kind sir, and be at peace."

As he listened to my words, a single tear rolled down his cheek, as he looked at me to say, "Thank you." Then he started to fade into the afterlife, and for some reason my heart wavered for a moment. As I looked down, realizing that the man's flask was now in my lap. For it was a gift, from a kind soul hoping that when they see each other again that they'll be able to have another drink.

THE IDEA OF TIME

You know as I lie here watching the sunset begin to set along the beautiful mountain range. Trying to unstiffen my back that was against an old tree that had long fell over. When my mind began to wander, thinking about how time has treated things like this tree, and me. In my 37 years of life, there are only a handful of times that I can count that have had an interesting impact on my time on this planet. Such as the bullet that I caught in the shoulder and stomach. The ceremony of marriage to my beloved, along with the births of my children. And the death of all of them in a single instance. But what are these moments in the time that I have spent on this earth, then mere moments, mere glances of a single life. Do they matter in the grand scheme of things? For there are millions of creatures on this planet, so does what I do, what we do matter?

Dam right, it does!

Now with the sunset a bit lower, my legs started to feel numb for every movement I made. Such is the nature of time and this 'grand scheme of things,' which I think is all crap. We as individuals hope that our stories matter to others more than ourselves, but that a lie. No one cares about your story, that's exactly why the only person that should care is yourself. For it is your story, your beginning, your bits of tragedy or happiness, and the ending chapter that we never see coming. Which is why we, as individuals need to use the time in those middle chapters to live our happiest, whatever that may be. Make, do, or experience something unique, something beautiful, something that you can say, "This is mine and no one else." Do not be afraid to write a story that is different from the others that you see being written before you. For the ideals like happiness during times of sorrow, need as much strength to get through them.

Be your own strength when none is left.

This day is almost up, the sun is about a few moments from going behind the mountain. And I might be joining it, as the knife wounds on my torso continue to gush blood through my hands. Running down me, like the sands of the time. Therefore, time is an important thing, for we think that we control time through its concept. Though it's the opposite, time controls us through just about everything; technology, ideals, politics, capital, war, and age. It is things like this that take our time and twist it into something that makes us forget the most basic concept. Be human. For the time of a human being is short, were born, we live, and then we move on, hoping that the next group can get it right this time.

Appreciate the time, for despite its concept, it will never change. We just get a little better at valuing it, little by little.

As the last flicks of day appear across the dusky sky, I hope that the next group gets it right. Don't fight our petty ideals, conflicts, or grudges. Try to work towards peace, unity, and happiness in order to create a utopia that the likes of the imagination have never thought of.

For it's through the valuing the idea of time, that one can value the happiness of one's own story.

Now mine is done.

THE PAINTER

It felt like a recurring dream to the man, even though it was more like a recurring nightmare. He would be standing at the canvas, preparing for the task at hand. A set of paints laid out before him, with his unique dual brushes in both hands, as the unnatural hand came from out of the shadows into the mind of madness, causing him to paint. And paint he did, through strokes of bright and cold colors, thin and bold lines, with each stroke becoming more and more erratic as time went on. Eventually, a series of words would enter his mind, in order to voice to him in a feminine, "Create the seven, Create the old seven." By then, the final stroke would be done, revealing a different being for each day of the week, with a different name being told to him, and by the end of the week, the cycle would start over.

For Monday, a being made up in shadow armor with bits of flames shooting out from the cracks in the helmet would be made. It would be wielding an obsidian mace of flames with it raised towards the painter. The voice would tell him its name over and over until he wrote it onto the canvas, "Wrath never incur the will of Wrath."

On Tuesday, the painter created a monster of oversized pride using the colors of the sun. Which it looked like a lion beast man, with the body of a human but the physic and tail of a lion. The creature wore armor that glistened like that of the setting sun, whilst duel-wielding maces that glowed like that of high noon. Its name was told to him with that of gusto, as its color rose from the canvas, "Pride-Pride, for your fear is his Pride."

For Wednesday, a portrait of a mage was forming with

feelings of malice and jealousy radiating from each stroke. From how she sat upon a throne of books, she was envious for power and knowledge, even more than the books provided could saturate. As she sat there, it could be seen that the being was an intellectual, wearing a robe that left little to the imagination along with an overwhelmingly large witch hat that barely covered the marks over her demonic eyes. As the painter finished with those eyes, another name was given to him, "Envy Envy for this is Envy."

From Thursday, a feeling of laziness emerged from the painter, as he used tired motions to create the next one. This creation was a tiny woman that appeared to have just woken from a nap. As she stood there looking as snug as could be expected, draped in a large blanket like a cloak, that barely covered her night dress. This one was different as the painter used soft colors and tones, a feeling of sleeplessness came over him. The voice spoke to him again, this time she sounded as drained as his creation, "Sloth Sloth Sloth."

As Friday hit, the man hungered for a challenge one that would enrich him. So he created one, a being that would collect all in order to satiate its lust for wealth. That's how he emerged with a combination of soft and hard colors, he was dressed as raider. This being stood on a pile of crates, wearing pelts of different animals over its shoulders, waist, and arms, while wielding a long spear with a tip that glimmered with the shine of the prettiest jewels. And as the painter worked on the finer details his eyes crossed the canvas, and he hear a name that made him feel warmth along with a dash of averse, "Greed for he is Greed."

When Saturday rolled around, the painter felt drunk with fulfilled emotions as he made this mad creation. That took the form of a nobleman, wearing a worn-out tan suit, black hair slicked back, and glasses that covered the voids where his eyes were. And in one hand he held a flask of sort of liquor, where in the other there was a dagger. It was as sharp as the painter's will for more, in which it seem to provide with blood and other liquids on its hilt. Through its absorption of all the different colors into one, the painter looked forward as if he was watching a pig gorge upon its feed. Disregarding the chaos that was the canvas, he hear her speak the words, "More More, For this is gluttony, and it will always want more."

Finally on Sunday, a day of peace, a day of love, the painter looked to the setting sun, wanting to create a being for this romanticized moment. It was in those dying streams of light, thin lines that the final and most dangerous one was brought into being. For she was a succubus of mortality, as she appeared to be seductively walking through the lonely painter, straight to his very being. Dressed in a leather corset that left little to the imagination, a long dress skirt, and her short hair flowing through the tempting colors. Regardless of her beauty, her verbosity was just as elegant as the magic flowing from her eyes or even her fingertips. The unimaginable beauty of this one was something to lust over, and it was in that moment that both the painter and the voice said in unison, "She is lust lust, for power, for knowledge, for love."

And this was his penance for what felt like forever, creating repeats of the same creatures, asserting their power, until one week came to an end. That's when everything changed, the voice spoke to him, not with any sort of emotion, but with a sad monotone feeling. "It's time my love . . . You're about to bring our children into this world, and with that its renewal," the voice said, as the beings in the paintings started to crawl out into being. Like a child being born the room began to glow as the voices of the seven spoke in both synchrony and dysfunction.

Wrath spoke with the commitment of a soldier, "The fire burns within me to make a change to this damaged world. It is time."

"Time to start over."

Pride was more brazen with his words, "None can stand against us. We will make a change for our father."

"Time for change."

Envy was more angry than wrath as she expressed, "ya things need to change, but the ruler of this world got rid of our ancestors. The only reason that we exist is thanks to our father."

"Time to get back what was lost."

Sloth was asleep on the floor, but she still tried to speak through snores, "It's . . . our . . . honor . . . to be . . . a part of . . . this family. I will . . . do what I must . . . in order . . . to . . . protect it."

"For our family."

Greed looked around with avis, such as his being, "I don't know about the rest of you, but a little chaos might be just what we need. After all we are the descendants of the original seven sins of old. So paying back the bastard that destroyed them might be fun."

"For our people."

Gluttony look as if he was already making plans, "Sorry for the delay father, we are ready to serve. Despite how some of us are just brute strength, some of us have plans to offer."

Lust stood before the rest, ready to take the lead of her brothers and sisters, "We are finally here father, the long-awaited light in our darkness. We will carry your fire, your will with us as if it were our own."

"We are yours to command. Father."

It was in that moment that the painter knew. That despite being plagued with visions and voices from this mysterious female voice, he was alone for a long time, isolated from the civilization that rejected him. Now not only was he cursed to make changes to this world, he was given a family of his own, one that he hopes to protect and make a better world for. And with that in mind the only idea for moving forward, was voiced to his children.

"Let us take this jewel of a world and make it our own," he said to his new family, "The civilization that lives apart from heaven and hell, will be our utopia.

And as the words left his mouth, the painter thought to himself, "If I may be a monster, a sinner, I will rationalize my pain into bring happiness to my family."

THE BIRTH OF NOTHINGNESS

I don't remember how I got to this point of my life. Cladded in armor that doesn't protect me all that well, whilst giving me more speed. An old short sword on my hip, along with pouches of potions and a small round shield attached to my left forearm. Surrounded by strangers who are all preparing for battle, knowing that it may as well be their last, judging from the hundreds of beastly roars and cries in the distance. They were all just beyond our barrier of ruins and hastily thrown together debris of wood and stone. The man standing next to me was a mage, dressed in the school of the spirits, looking as if he was ready to turn tail and flee, but to where. As he was shaking in his robes, he turned to look at me, asking, "Hello there, may I ask a dumb question? That shield on your arm, will it protect you in this battle." "I don't know," I answered him, "This shield is small and light for quick movements. A large shield may provide better protection, but at the cost of movement." As I answered his question, he looked at me terrified, since we might die, he must have been looking for solace in a comrade. Though that is something that I can't provide, for all I seek is the destruction of those that are on the other side of that wall, the race that I have sworn my wrath upon, the race that took everything from me.

As I looked around at the faces of terrified swordsman, mages, and rangers through the vertical slits in my helmet. I hoped that I would find people that were prepared or aware of what was to come. However, all I saw were the faces of scared people, terrified that today was their last. And I know I should feel sorry for these souls, but I feel nothing. Those feelings that I had before that day are almost completely gone, and with every passing day, I feel less and less human. Regardless I didn't see the point in being human, things such as emotions and feelings got in my way.

"I rather be a war-torn shell of my former self than the scared child I once was," I thought.

Through my wandering I heard the horn from the captain of the guard. He was standing in the center of the courtyard, standing on some crates like a king on his throne. The captain looked around wearingly at the terrified faces of the men and travelers that were under his command. Seeing a rag-tag bundle of armored men in both new and nearly ancient gear. While he stood up there, in armor fit for a captain, you couldn't help but focus upon the falcon that was on the breastplate as he boasted his chest in order to raise morale.

"Listen up, men," he shouted, "those of you that have fear for what comes next should be afraid.

Control it!! Take control of your fear for it is more powerful than courage. Courage is a false hood that will be the death of you out there. For courage means little when your arms are ripped off by a hellhound, or torn apart by those dam hobgoblins, or bleeding out on the battlefield. For it is fear that keeps you focused, fear keeps you moving forward; fear will be the catalyst that brings down your enemy. And if you fall on the battlefield, know that you gave others a chance, at living, at a future, no matter how long. And when you meet the reaper, look him in the eyes and show him real feeaaarrrr!"

It was in that rag-tag speech that my shabby comrade's spirits rose, but mine didn't. Cause I saw firsthand what a hellhound does to a person, the horrors that the goblins do to people, and those beings that crawled out of the pit do to the human soul. Disregarding my own experiences, "They don't know the truth, that while monsters are real, there are things worse than monsters that exist," I thought as the horn blew again.

That was it, the signal that was meant to signal our march . . . our deaths. "No matter," I said as I drew my weapon, "I'll take them all, then I'll meet death with a smile." And with that, I was charging far faster than the rest of them. I did not know if today was the day that I would see my siblings again. Tyr, I hope that I have measured up to your expectations. Freya, my kid sister, I hope you're ready to see your big brother again.

THE LONG YEARS

I don't know how many years it has been, but I'm tired. I've spent so long down here in the master's domain that I have trouble remembering the sky, the trees, the vast plains surrounding the dungeon, and the master with that smile of his. Where are my manners? I am Violeta, the head guardian of the master's home of Dragnual, as well as his protector, his confidant, his oldest friend, and the one who he cares for the most. I also lead the others under the master's command, our family, though his presence has been gone for so long that most of us feel broken, lost, empty these days.

Mel and Nel, the twin children, have done their best to buy their time through raising their demons. Last I saw of them, they were on the eighth floor, trying to create behemoth golems that could not only carry mountains, but be the pride of Dragnual. Nevertheless, that was some time ago, so I don't know how they're actually doing. My best guess is that they want his approval when he returns home. Since, after all, to the master, they are the closest thing to actual children in his domain, so he spoils them like his own kids. There are times that I envy them for that reason; they are so carefree, kind, and childish, and despite that, even I can't help but treat them like children myself. I just hope that they are happy with each other. I feel helpless when I find either one of them crying or lonely.

Then there's the fallen angel, Raphi, who leads the armies of our great lord and master, as a proud warrior. Now, she has fallen so far that she has become a shell of her former self to the point of destruction on the fifth floor for some reason. Last I checked, she was training so that if and when he calls his armies into battle, then she will be ready. Though Raphi has been going so hard at it that her body has fallen into disarray. It was when I last checked on my friend that I saw her, covered in cuts and bruises that she refused to let heal, arms that were so weak that they looked like the gelatinous form of a slime that could barely hold a cup, let alone a blade. Then there were her wings, god her wings; for as long as I could remember, they were her pride; she once told me, "I want these babies to be the thing that crushes an opponent's spirit. Where one ook will tell them that an angel of death is here to reaper their pathetic souls." Though these days it's a different story, since Raphi's once great wings of death, now look as though they have died as well. As she seemed to lose her pride, all that remained were a few dozen feathers that could barely get her off the ground. While they could regrow over time, like her body, she has refused to take proper respect for herself, for loyalty, for hope, for her purpose as a warrior.

On top of those three, there's also the brilliant Beelzebub, or Bell for short. Now I haven't seen him in a long time since he locked himself away in his private space, not letting anyone else in. This is the most saddening since Bell was such a great strategist with a vividly cunning imagination that loved to be around people, as well as the master. He was always so gluttonous when it came to craving for admiration and knowledge. I can recount numerous times when he created plan after plan that not only benefited the master but Dragnual as a whole. In addition to that, he always took great pride in his otherworld collection of books: never allowing dust, dampness, or decay. And now, the only one that has had the chance to see him is Azazal, his right hand, and she doesn't say much about his health.

As for me, as I said, I am tired of being alone down here, trying to hold our demented kingdom and family together all on my own. It is why I spend every night in the cold darkness, drinking myself into a coma with a blade just mere inches from my grasp. first bottle. I hope to ease the pain, for it's been so long since the master disappeared before our eyes, with little we can do but watch. I feel like he knows that we tried to help, though all he could respond with was that smile at the time. Second bottle. We just . . . I just

..need him to make me feel like I am worth it. Worth being the person to stand by his side. Worth being more than just another member of his family. Worth being me. Third bottle. This is always the point when the walls holding the tears back, started to break.

Though, this time was different. Through a haze of sadness, the door to the room opened, illuminating the room with a square of light in the darkness, revealing the pitiful version of me. And in the doorway, I saw a figure wrapped in an old torn cloak, but I couldn't see their faces. So, they stood there for what felt like forever before he said, "Hey there, Violeta, it's been a minute." "That voice," I thought, then I drunkenly mumbled, "it can't be? My love . . . my partner, is that you?" It was then that he slowly dropped his cloak, revealing a figure covered in fresh scars and bandages, in addition to a new magical prosthetic left arm. As he began to limp towards me, he began to say, "I'm sorry it took me so long to get home. Where I was sent was worse than hell, and I clawed my way out back to all of you." When he finally reached me, he got to one knee, placing his hand upon my cheek, and looking into my eyes, he smiled and told me, "Violeta, I'm home and I will never abandon any of you." All I could do was cry, cry into his chest as he rubbed my back.

THE GUNSMITH

Ping . . .Ping . . .Ping . . .

In the fires of a forge in the depths of madness, a man worked with every ounce of his being. With each swing of the small hammer against the metal, sparks flew, lighting up the man's dark face, showing the determination to achieve perfection. He needed to make sure that each and every piece of its being was nothing but perfect. For it needed to achieve its function, as shown by the numerous containers of broken, blasted, and smoldering pieces next to a table. On top of that table lay a series of metal pieces of various sizes. They were the organs, the veins, the very being that would bore his device. Though it would be pointless if he couldn't get this part right. Wiping the sweat from his forehead, he managed to unconsciously clear some of the muck; though that mattered little, he gritted his teeth and furthered his resolve.

Ping . . . Ping . . . Ping . . .

Now, you may think that this story sounds familiar. A gritted man on the verge of insanity lets everything go in order to achieve the goal. And some might see the man as just that, but that's not the whole story. For one, he is only seventeen, with no muscle mass to speak of to swing such a mighty hammer, or even come up with the idea for the device. It was his drive, his resolve to destroy, not kill, those that took everything from him. As he worked, the spirits of his loved ones watched on, dammed cause of him, and he knew this. For they, his mother, father, sister, and girlfriend, were the victims of the monsters that tore the very souls out of them as well as the very essence of what made him.

The smith in front of the fiery inferno used to be a happy, go-lucky guy, not a care in the world. Now, all that he cared for were carved out of him, leaving him with only rage.

The type of rage that would consume anyone else, bathing them in the aurora of a mindless beast. One that wanted to charge in recklessly, with the only hope of taking out the prey before he became one. Regardless, he was different, the rage and anger that swirled within him was what forged the new him, giving him a purpose. For it was that anger, that raging inferno that burned as bright as the forge, was all he had left. Even at times when he tried to show a fraction of his former self, it was all a mask that hid the monster in him. A monster that would not charge but stalk its prey, waiting for the opportune moment to strike.

Ping . . . Ping . . . Ping . . .

As he strikes away through the pain of each swing, focused on the task at hand, he never noticed that he wasn't alone. Standing in the background of his work, in his mind, there was a being that took no form through that of a shadow, and it wanted to chat. A conversation of sorts that wasn't spoken through traditional words but more within the spirit. It was there that the uncaporial being asked the smith, "What is it that you are willing to give me for my help?"

Since it didn't want to walk away with nothing, it was, in fact, this being that came to the smith, laying the groundwork for the both of them. One was in it for revenge and his own hopeless gamble that he could be redeemed. The other wanted something more sinister, something that any being of his caliber couldn't get. The smith, still deep within his craft, like a god making the first man, told the being that he was willing to give anything and everything that he had left. The being then smiled, glad that he found a human that fell so far. No, not a human; the being looked at his new partner, seeing a monster from the depths of hell walk the surface.

Ping . . . Ping . . . Ping . . . Ping . . .

The smith then stopped, pulling up the goggles from his eyes to hair, revealing clean circles around the eyes with an eerie grin. Realizing that it was finished, the attempted piece that he spent the last few days on was complete. It bore a black steel color about seven inches in length; it was the frame of the weapon; all it needed was the rest: the six-cylinder chamber, the hammer, the barrel, and the lock that would keep it all in place for what was to come. He then took what he believed to be his hand, which was now intertwined with the shadowy being, creating the bullets that would deliver judgment.

1 . . .2 . . .3 . . .4 . . .5 . . .6 . . .1 . . .2 . . .3 . . .4..5 . . .6 . . .1..2..3..4..5..6 . . .1 . . .2..3..4 . . .5..6 . . .

With each bullet forming the metal in his hands from what seemed to be his own bloodlust. As the spirits of his loved ones watched, they saw that the shadowy being in the background was now behind the smith, guiding his hands.

"Let me help you feed that rage so that we both win."

As he worked on creating more and more bullets, placing them in a leather satchel. He smiled, knowing that even before it was tested the device was complete. Somehow, he knew, however still wanting to see the results he loaded the chambers one by one. "So this is how it begins," he quietly said. Click, the chambers were full, and he took aim at a photo on the other side of the wall. Then Bang, a 2-meter large whole, was created, with the epicenter being where the bullet hit. The gun worked

And with that, he was off, gun in hand, and followed by a dark aura of bloodlust and hell that will follow.

THE MULTIVERSE

Hello there, my name is Professor Alister, and I want to take a moment of your time in order to discuss a theory that isn't well discussed. That theory is known as the multiverse theory, or sometimes parrel worlds, and it's been the subject of my studies for the past twenty years. Now for those of you that are not familiar with this interesting scientific theory, it goes like this:

There are a multitude of universes out there consisting of different timelines. With each one having some with similarities, some with differences and some completely different from the original. These universes/timelines are like a tree branch, existing in the same space and time. The branch starts with one event, even if it's not important, such as a simple decision of what route to take, left or right. The theory is that whether you choose one or the other, the branch separates into the opinions available. And it doesn't stop there, it goes and goes until the branch has split so much that the original idea/universe is almost nonexistent.

If that is too general of an idea, let me give you a more specific one. One that I feel is a classic among scientific theorists is the Nazis during World II. Now, in our timeline, the Allies dropped the atomic bomb on the Japanese, and the Russians tore their way to Berlin, confirming our victory. Though, what would happen if the Allies didn't make the atomic bomb or the Germans developed the tech first? Theorists believe that given the wrong choices, the Axis would have won the war, in turn destroying the Allies and occupying the United States. There are also thoughts to consider when it comes to the Americans and the Russians joining the fight. Would the outcome still be the same? As a scientist, it's our job to consider the unthinkable and imagine the unimaginable in order to see the whole picture.

And that, my friends, and theorists, is a look behind the curtain at an undiscussed topic in the community.

THE THREE FACES

J ournal entry 349, Dec 7, 2241

As time progresses, I have come to learn that we are different when it comes to our situational awareness around people. For whether it's a traveler, a mage, an inn keeper, a bar owner, a friend, we all forced ourselves to don different face masks in life. Now when I talk about this I don't mean in the form of beings or in the literal sense, I mean the masks that we use to present ourselves to the world, our friends/family, or even our true selves.

In regards to that there's a proverb that I like to refer to in cases such as this,

"There are three faces
The first one is shown to the world
The second one is shown to close friends and family
The third one, is never to be shown. For it is the truest reflection of who you really are."

-Unknown

And this is what I want to inform the average person on, for you can't pour all your energy or time into a specific one, after leaving out the others. Take me for instance, I had spent the early years of my life focusing on the first two faces. As such, I molded the face that the world saw as this people person, molding the face to radiate kindness and a sense of trust and worth. In addition to the same soft-spoken yet loud, kind person that I show to the people that I trust, ergo, my family and friends. Now

I have spent so long on these first two that they were starting to wear down.

If I were to regard these faces as tools or a weapon, they would be in bad condition from years of abuse. Such as the nature of tools, but if you neglect one as I had for the third face, then you end up neglecting all your tools. They start to develop rust or weathering, cracks start to form where there were none before, and if not given the right care to grow accustomed to their wielder, they can not grow in harmony.

It was only years later that I had realized this fact, since for so long I have been the person that moves through the world like a ghost, no identity, no personal character to speak of. And it's through this disrespect of the third one, the truest one that reflects me, that is to be at fault for the carelessness of my own character. Due to poor oversight on my part, that face is just a ghost of what it should be. In fact, it's fair enough to call this the true ghost of what it should be: little to no urge to take care of the face, to mold it into that truth, as shown in the only feature on it, the eyes. Eyes that reflect the spirit of a dying fire about ready to dissipate into a cold withered, along with that breath of being burned out. It is only upon a second glance that I can see those sparks. The hopes that I can still be true to myself, and myself alone.

Regardless, I need to find a way to reignite that flame within myself. Maybe I just need to find a way to accept not just myself, but that true self I have neglected for so long. I need to make the choice to pick up that face in a darkness of my own volition, and make a convent. One that not only lets me know the truth, but discover it, too.

See the truth within yourself. Care a fire within yourself, not one out of hate, but one out of love. Love for yourself, for it is something that people have come to forget. If you are reading my journal, try not to rationalize my words, take them to heart.

Look inward at the face you never show anyone, and ask yourself, "Do I take care of that true reflection of myself, or am I focused on what civilization and what others want me to be?"

That's enough for today, I must save my energy for another one.

THE MONSTER OF THE MIND

As we walked down the marble halls, I couldn't help but feel a sense of unease. My happy, carefree family was quiet as we walked down the hall, giving off an aura that I couldn't quite recognize. It turned the once vibrant hallways, into ones of change as the setting sun filled the way in front of us. Chiron walk ahead of us in silence, as if he was breaking the bits of darkness that were expanding from the shadows to our destination. As we walked behind Chiron, I couldn't help but wonder where Arti, my daughter was. When I asked them in the medical tent, surrounded by faces I trust and cherished, all bandaged and cut up. I was met with looks of sadness and grief, since we lost so much I thought it was because of that. Though Chiron walked into the tent, and all he said was, "Follow me." And that was how we ended up here, in my house on Market Street, surrounded by the critically injured and the dead. The majority of the injured were in the rooms, while the dead were carefully laid out in the largest room.

As the founder and leader of our small town, I told them if they ever needed room in an emergency, to use my house. Since it was a gift, from a corrupt broker as collateral and too big for just a few of us, I saw it as a good use of space. Though as we walked down the halls further away from the injured, my worries began to grow, "What is she doing here?" And that thought was something that I was frightened to ask any of them; Chiron, Tashia, Riley, Magi, and Deo. I could tell from the looks on their faces that they didn't want to tell me, except Chiron, when he stopped at the room on the end. He looked down at me, into my eyes, eyes with such sadness, in order to tell me, "In here," as he opened the door.

When I walked in, I first realized that this was an unused meeting room, with a few couches and a coffee table off to the side. And it was clear at first glance that someone was sleeping in here as shown by the blanket and the poor pillow. In addition, there was a desk and some chairs for one-on-one meets on the other side of the room, near the window. Though instead of an empty table between the chairs, there was a cover with something underneath it. My mind froze while my body moved forward as Chiron moved towards the sheet, and the rest of them filled in behind us. Reaching for the sheet, he put his head down, and without saying a word or even giving me a glance, reviled her, my daughter, Arti.

Then everything went black. It was as if I was pulled out of my body into a room, one with no door, no windows, just nothing. A room that was just pure absence of existence, even sound. For as I tried to scream, yell, cry, laugh, and all the emotions, nothing happened.

That's when I heard voices, "My lord . . . Father . . . Master?" And then I was back in my body, in the room, with my daughter. As well as the rest of my family that looked nervous, even though I didn't see their faces. I knew they were scared as the aura I started to emit was one of power, rage, and grief that was ready to swallow them whole. So I did the only thing I could, I shoved it all back in, straight into the deeps of my soul, where it would stay, forever. "I . . . I'm sorry. Can you all please leave," I asked them, even though I could tell that they wanted to stay with me, cause that's how long they have been with me. They just told me things like, "Take all the time you need," as well as, "If you need me," as they slowly shut the door, I pulled the hood of my overcoat over my face so that no one could see me or my expression. Then I was alone, on my knees, with my daughter, not being able to shed a single tear.

"What's wrong with me? I know I should be sad, this is my child after all, but I feel nothing. It's as if a raging beast of a storm has grown inside of me, unleashing all these different emotions at once. And they are all fighting for the right to control while at the same time destroying the being that is me. Breaking me down to a beast, a monster that can't do anything but just sit there, gazing at the physical being of my child. I told her mother, my wife, my love that I would protect her for long as I had breath in my body. When I look at her, I don't see the cuts, even the final one, the only thing I see is my child. My child, the one I couldn't save." And as I turned to look out at the last shards of the day, I couldn't help but feel like a monster. One that would not only protect his family, but also bring oblivion to those that would bring them harm.

THE OTHER SIDE OF STORYTELLING

As I sit here in my dark space surrounded by continuously growing shadows, shadows that tried to confuse me; my senses, my body, and my mind. I can hear them speaking to me, trying to destroy me, make me lose myself in their shadows so that I would drown for all time immemorial. My only solace, my lighthouse in the darkness being the small light in front of me, where my computer to another world was. This other world was of my own creation, I gave birth to people, the land, the ideals, while at the same time creating a foundation that people can stand upon, filled with their own morals. For it is the job of a storyteller to create the plot, and that of the reader to fill in the blanks, but this darkness was trying to change that. It tries to change the story so that it had somewhere to go. See the dark space, the shadows that surrounded me were stuck here, same as me, trying to escape from their home, that also served as their cell. Though it looks to me as a conduit, one that can shape a path that can allow for it to escape through my pages. Allowing it to wreak havoc upon our world, so I must give it my all to slow its progress.

The sound of knocking in the distance, 'Knock, Knock, Knock.'

Regardless, I find myself losing it more and more with each passing moment. With the strokes of my hands becoming more erratic as time passes. Whatever time is in this place, as I have lost touch with things such as that, in addition to reality. That has become more chaotic, like a storm raging, the voices I hear yell and scream, they tell me things, dark things, in attempts to break me. Just like him, my warden, and the apparition of the darkness that surrounds me. From time to time, he emerges from the shadows of my ever-sinking island, dressed from head to toe in a black suit with his hair slicked back. The first time that I saw him I thought he was the reaper, ready to claim me when the time arrived, but he looked like me. In our first conversation between us, he made it perfectly clear that, "I was him and he was me." The darkness that surrounded us, that made him into reality, came from the depths of my soul, and it would get its way.

The sound was strong this time, more like a pounding, 'Knock, Knock, Knock.'

Again, I must slow its progress, through my haze and try to hold on. There are times when I dip into insanity, where I lose consciousness, and it takes the wheel, desperately trying to hold me down. But I still try to fight; I leave myself notes, complicated ones that are unique and familiar to me. So that in my moments of clarity, I have some idea of what needs to be done, even when I don't recognize the person writing me back.

"Go back, it doesn't want you to go back." "More conflict, the hero needs the opening to escape." "It wants the hero to lose, it wants all of them to lose." "It wants out; I need to extend the points." "WHAT'S THE POINT? HE WILL BREAK US." "Make the Story yours."

That last one, "Make the story yours," it gave me an idea. I have been trying to bid my time, giving it the people and some points in the plot, but what about the surroundings? If I can just give enough detail then I will be safe. Similar to other stories that I have read in the past, I will create a setting that is as vague as possible. I need to set the stage, give enough information that will allow for the reader to fill in the blanks. Yes, this is my way out; if there are blanks and gaps in the story, then that will be my chance to escape.

The sound was now in my head, beating me into submission, 'Knock, Knock, Knock.'

No, he is coming again; he's been trying to drag me down into the darkness of the future and beyond. Like I'm drowning; being pulled down into the cold deeps of this new circle of hell. The light grows dimmer and dimmer as the beating gets worse. If I fall, I'll make sure that they can never leave.

VOICES OF THE MIND

*V*oices . . . the voices that come to me in my dreams, now come when I'm awake. They don't stop. Please let them stop. I hear the voices of members of my family and friends. I hear voices that aren't even close to human, almost monstrous. They're drowning me, slowly killing the person that was once me. I don't even recognize myself anymore. Am I even human? Am I still ME? Please help . . .

As I sit here in the depths of my own hell, the thought of madness is something that seems to become more pleasing as time passes. For it's been two months since I've fallen into the depths of the labyrinth, alone, armed with only a dagger and my thoughts, which have been no help. The constant monster attacks and the side effects of eating them, have been the only thing that has kept me alive and on guard. Since down here they rule, kill, or be killed, if you are not careful, then it will be your end. That is why I eat them, they help me, they heal me, but they hurt me. I lost a good amount of blood once after a battle with a giant spider when a pack of wisp wolves descended upon me, tearing me a new one. If not for my abilities and my will, then I would have been dead time and time again.

Regardless, that's not the only threat down here; the isolation in the darkness that surrounds my little fires would devour me whole if I let it. Which doesn't seem that bad in my current state; I'm on level 18, and who knows how many more floors there are before I actually reach hell if I'm not already there? And I have already have sustained more than a number of injuries across my body that the average person would have died from countless times. If not for the waters I found and the monster meat, then I probably would have killed over long ago. But the shadows attempt to gnaw away at my mind, which hasn't been hard as the meat is changing me, though the voices it uses have left me troubled. Voices that are from friends and family alike, as well as those of other things in the dark. In my fits of madness whilst eating monsters, I hear whispers like, "You need to push forward, big brother," from my sister, "Man up for crisis sake, are you a man that gives up," from my father, "You can make it out of here my child," from my mother, "Don't die ok idiot," Hinata yelled. It hurts so much. Hearing their voices again hurts . . . cause their dead. Long dead, about ten years since they died in the fire, that claimed my village. Starting me down into a hell worse than this, depression.

God it hurts, please stop. I get it . . .OK . . . I get it! My soul is reminding me that I have to keep moving forward if I want to retain any sense of myself. But why? Why do they have to be reminders for those who are no longer here? It just reopens old wounds, making me want to vanish down here even more.

Another month passes, as the voices of the abyss grow infinitely worse, worse than I could of ever even imagined. They don't speak to me the way the others did. Rather they delve into the inside of my skull, weaving a tapestry of unnatural doubt within me. Making me distrust myself, making me feel lost, displaced from reality where I am me. Showing a version of me where I could be more colder, more *alone*, more monstrous.

"Kill, Kill, Kill!!! Survival of the fittest is the rule of law of the land in this world. You need to grow stronger if you want to live. Let the weaker version of you die. Let the pathetic die; let the loser fall into darkness forever. The beast within needs to be unleashed, it needs to become the new you. Let it devour your emotions, and your morals; new ones will be made. When the new you is born."

I believe I'll reach floor 39 in a few days. Before, I would feel happy that I have made it so far down that I have survived. Though the voices are getting stronger as time passes, I begin to feel like I am on an island. One that holds the essence of my true self that can't escape anymore, trapped, surrounded by the enemies that now hold onto him tight with all their might. The new me is a shadow of my former self; he is excited for battle, expected to survive, not to live another day, just survive. I have killed many obstacles to get to where I am now; my clothes are in taters, and my knife broke, but I don't care. I'll make new weapons and new clothes, I'll carve my way through this nightmare like Dante and escape hell.

"Hahahahahahahahahahhaah," laughter starts to reverberate off the cold walls around me one night; Cold, maniacal, insane, sad. I can't pinpoint where it's coming from in the darkness. It wouldn't stop, like a wounded animal, it seems to let it out for comfort. Then it started to sound like it began to cry at the same time as well.

It was then that I realized where the sound was coming from. I saw it, in the reflection of my weapons, the water, and in my soul. It was me, laughing, now crying at the fireside, alone, surrounded by the enemy around me.

I don't know what tomorrow will bring, but my soul is cold now. The voices of my friends and family are still there but can't reach over my sorrowfully dark ocean. Where I now sit on that island, alone, afraid, mad. What reaches it is the new me, the one that will survive this and claw my way out of here. I must keep moving forward, I must SURVIVE, I WILL LIVE FREE.

HERO TURNED VILLAIN?

Long ago, I stood on a snowy wasteland in a fight for the right to live. The cold air swirled around me, with the malevolence of an ice spirit, freezing me down to the bone, making it harder to breathe. It beat me to my core, with every clash of metal against metal, beast against beast. It is times like this that little tells are given, allowing death to strike us with little hits towards our own mortality from time to time, and this was no different. The snow fell before us, touching our skin like the grace of a feather; despite the conditions, looks can be deceiving. It was these exact types of crystal beauties that were despite to clear the board before me, one of blood that has fallen onto this frozen land. Scattering like fallen petals in patches of red all around us. The blood was coming not only from me but also from the man lying before my eyes.

Dying on the ground before me, desperately trying to clamp as many of the holes and tears that he could, across his torso. At the time, I looked down, tired, thinking, 'Is this what you wanted, this pointless squabble? You have been trying to kill me for years. Now I can't help, but try to feel sorry for you, to help you.'

It was then that I noticed the blade in my hand; cold, worn out, and down the length of the blade, red, red that seemed to flow to the very tip, allowing it to drip. It was then I decided to look up, and not meaning my eyes connected to his. If I didn't mention, his name was Leo, and it was in that moment that I didn't see anger or resentment. All I saw was a man, not a friend in need of comfort, someone who, in these final moments, wanted to feel accepted, loved, and forgiven. Asking for me to extend my hand into his.

These feelings were difficult to comprehend; he was just trying to kill me. Though we were once comrades, I would even say friends for a long time, Surviving numerous battles and trials that forced us to grow closer. The blood and tears we shared for the good of the people took their toll on both of us. Regardless, we were together, at least I thought so; Leo never revealed much about his past to me. Until that day when he betrayed our code, took our secrets, and killed so many innocents. Even so, I was never angry with him; I never wanted him dead. I still see Leo as my friend. No, he is my brother. So, I decided to lean down on one knee next to him, grabbing the hand that he was extending. When I grabbed it, I noticed that the wasteland around us seemed to grow much calmer, almost silent; the wind died down, and the flakes flowed even more gracefully than before. "Hey . . . Listen," Leo weakly said, "There is something that you should know. Will you let me show you?" "Yes," I said confidently, "show me." It was then that my mind was melded into his emotions, thoughts, and memories.

What I saw came all at once, like an arrow flying at full speed at oneself. I saw Leo's life all at once; there was so much pain. From a noble family, he was the first in line for the head, but he was a bit of a black sheep. Not living up to the standards of the family name, he was tossed aside and sold for cheap to elder scientists. To then be cut up and beaten on for usage as an experimental test subject on new military enhancements. They did so many horrible things to him, took out body parts, replaced them with experimental ones, sometimes just trying out crap for a laugh, sadistic bastards. At Night, he would go insane just to escape the constant torture, laughing at the bits of moonlight that crept into his cell. He would tell them his dark desires for revenge and chaos. Even then, that wasn't enough; he would always manage to come back around to sanity. See, the things done to him had pumped magical elements throughout him, causing near-constantly excruciating pain. Like before, insanity was an escape, but this time, he tried to seal those demons. A box was created in his heart in order to hold them, with the only hope that it would never be allowed to open again.

Years later, when they were done with him, thinking he was a failure for a test subject. My friend was tossed into the wilderness with the rest of their failures. A pit of enhanced bodies and broken machines that was meant to be his grave. As fate would have it, he still persisted, crawling out of this grave; broken and bloody. He swore to the heavens, to hell, to whoever would listen that he would make them all pay. So, he wanted the land for a few days, just trying to stave off the evils that lurked in his heart. On the fourth day, he collapsed near the order's home, where he first saw me, finding him actually. A boy about his age, tired, bloody, and bruised, while at the same time, eyes that radiated kindness. It was after that he felt safe, a family that cared, a brother, a purpose. So safe that he let that box in his heart disappear, into the deepest deeps, never to be seen again.

Or so he thought. It was a few days before his betrayal that he saw them. The order, making a deal with those scientists from all those years ago, right before his eyes, not recognizing him at all. In that moment, the box that resided deep in his soul broke, unleashing a demon that thirsted for the souls of those bastards that would remember him. Leo didn't want to hurt anyone, especially me, but the anger got the better of him. This caused him to spend the next five years in a red, full haze of fire and brimstone. With that version of him, the one that wanted to make a difference, to be a hero, to fade into memory. And the path of revenge and blood was the new one that he chose to take.

In those dark years, he would force himself to cry. If only to remind himself that he was once a good person, once a human.

Not the monster that was born through pain and madness.

. . .Then I was back before my brother, still holding onto his hand, with tears forming in both of our eyes. "Can you forgive me," he said to me, "I've been so angry with the world that my heart became a void of darkness. I wanted to right the wrongs done to me, but I created more myself. I just . . .I just didn't want to hurt you." With both of us crying now, I told him, "I never hate you. I still see you as my friend, as my brother." It was then that I saw the man that was lost all those years ago, right in his eyes. The eyes that no longer held the hatred of a demon, the eyes of a child, lost, alone, wanting someone to hold him.

Even when the light went out. Even when the wasteland around us started to come alive again.

The evil died and the good saw the light for the last time.

What makes a villain? They are just abused, forgotten, lost heroes that have fallen so far from the light. That the only way for them to survive and adapt is to accept the darkness in their hearts. For it's sometimes the only thing that they have left.

OLDER PROTECTOR

Today's the day, even for a somewhat sunny day I walked up the hill towards my destination. The grass was blowing with the grace of that wheat from the Gladiator movie. The trees were blowing ever so gently despite the high winds that it felt almost otherworldly. It was as if nature itself had looked into the depths of my soul seeing a being in recollection, and decided that it needed to give me some peace. No, not just the promise of peace, it was just a thing of innocent purity. In losing thought I refixed my grip on the bouquet of flowers I was carrying in one hand and a bottle in the other, the weight of both seemed to increase. I began to reflect on why not just these things are important, but my own being as well. Everything that I am, the good, the bad, and even the downright ugly, is all for my younger sibling, my sister.

It's only people like me, like us that understand the gravity of being an older sibling, or brother in my case. You need to present a strong front to them, for it is our job to be the wall, the protector. One that is there to keep out the bad, keeping the innocent light of good safe inside. Trying not at all to break down, showing any weakness or cracks, despite trying to stand eternal, we are human too. Regardless, the cracks can still show now and again. I can recall numerous times when my sister asked me the most simple question, "Are you okay?" And no, I was never alright, but I wanted to make her feel ok, so I would always tell her, with a smile so fake, "I'm fine." It never was to lie to her, I hated to lie, I was the older brother, and I didn't need to burden her with my problems. I always wanted to protect her.

Protection . . . . . .

As I continued down the path, I decided to untie my sweatshirt from my waist and put it on. I still don't know why I'm doing this, I'm not cold. I just want to not feel like I'm alone today as I walked through the wooden gate in front of me. It was this feeling of loneliness and isolation that I had come to know, that would allow me to tell her about horrible friends, horrible people, and evil creatures. I would give her the good advice and thoughts as the wiser sibling, but most of the time it fell on deaf ears. Since she was younger, she seemed to have that weird confidence of whatever she did, it would work out mind. There were times when I would tell my younger sibling, "Don't do anything stupid." And like a man with the worst luck possible, she would tell me events that happened with a smile. Like everything worked out as it was supposed to, whilst I was in the corner of the room having mini-heart attacks from her "pleasant evening."

Now as the open fields of grass started to turn into this cage of metal and blocks of stone, I couldn't help but feel like a failure. All I ever wanted to be was an older protector, a guardian to my younger sibling. I want to let her know the rights and wrongs that I have made and how to justify them. Despite well knowing the fact that she needs to learn her own mistakes. Even so I must try, for a stationary being is more rooted than one that blows with the wind.

The wind . . . It started to pick up again.

This is it, I'm here. "It's been too long," is what I thought as I sat down in front of one of the stone blocks. I gently placed the flowers on the worn surface, whilst making sure to wipe clean the area. "I hope that you know I cared and still do," I said as I uncorked the bottle, taking a swig. "It was my job to make sure that you were safe. You knew that there was someone in your life who wanted what was best for you. To protect you with their life . . .hell even go to prison if the situation called for. But you're gone now. I failed . . . I failed you." I didn't realize till then that tears were falling onto the stone. "I just hope you are happy now, even if I can't protect you anymore. I want you to know that I'll always be here." And as I finished those words, I put the rest of the bottle on top of the stone next to the flowers. Leaving behind the hope that when the time came for me to do my job, then she would look up to me.

As she always had . . .

Remember to respect your older siblings. They hold onto the hope that they can protect and provide wisdom to the younger generations. For they hold back the abyss so that they can swim free from it.

WHAT IS . . . HAPPINESS

It was not that long ago, in a dark backroom, where I conversed with a man that would soon be my enemy, but first a chat. In an old room, the light of the dawn trickled in through the blinds, illuminating the table between us, with a smell of air fresheners used to hide the smell of musk. At one end was the man, well dressed and groomed, all signs that he was an authority figure, as he stood next to a rather large cushioned chair. Whilst another stood on the other end, clad in regular clothes (shirt and jeans), except for my overcoat that was as dark as night, with my twin revolvers strapped to my legs. I couldn't help but loom next to the similar chair at my end, realizing that they were both well-crafted yet worn out. Both of us have never met before now, though with the tension in the air, the man in front of me showed in his eyes the true error of this meeting.

"Please sit," the man said as he began to sit, somewhat unsure of himself on his throne. "Thank you," I said sitting down myself, readying myself for the moment of my departure. "If you want, I can bring in something to drink if you're thirsty. Water, Tea? I'm sure it took you some time to get here," the man said, trying to be hospitable, "Oh, forgive my manners, you can call me Cid." "And I'm Ban; it's a pleasure to meet with such a well-renowned man, and I'll take some tea." I replied, wanted to extend the kindness of pleasantries, but I could tell at that moment what he was trying to do. At the push of a button, a maid entered the room with a tray cart with tea and water. I could tell that the woman pushing the cart was terrified; her face, and her body all showed the signs, and even her hands were shaking as she poured the tea, but for some reason, I felt that It was directed towards me. I mean, yes, my eyes are those of a demon; regardless, it's rude to judge a book by its cover. "Thank you, miss, you may take your leave," Cid said, waving the girl off, "Now we can begin. The purpose of this meeting is to see if you would be willing to negotiate a peaceful end to this war. For it's been three months since you took the port, and your men seem very eager to move to the city." I get it, he wants me to stop my advancement on his land, with only his wits and flattery, humbling me so that he can survive, but that can only get one so far. I have a bigger goal in mind; for me, for my family, for my people, all of those that I hold dear.

"I can't do that, my good man," I told him.

"Why, just why! You have the power to do whatever you wanted. You can do anything, so why, why take it out on us. The people in these walls have done you nothing wrong. So why are we innocent beings who have done you no wrong?"

"You don't understand. Yes, I have power, but power in itself is pointless; it's merely a means to an end. Not for ideals, or for more power, but for the one thing that we all seek . . . Happiness."

"That can't be the only thing you're after . . .," Cid said with a confused look on his face.

"In the end, isn't that what all beings are after? We chase and chase after that feeling called happiness all our lives, having to clear tragedy, anguish, and the cold winds in order to reach it. Though, it's almost always just out of grasp, no matter how far one runs. What I want is to give those that I cherish even a taste of that feeling, to bask in its warm embrace." I then looked directly into Cid's eyes, the essence of his very soul and told him, "I don't deserve even the slightest notion of it, but they do. So, I will dash into the fires of hell, becoming the king of the demons, so that they can have a future where I am the only sinner."

As I finished those words, I pushed back from the table and started to walk towards the door. In opening the door, I turned back to Cid and told him, "I may fall from heaven for my actions, regardless this is the real world. So let me make you a coven, or a deal of sorts. Let's have a clean war; may the best person survive." With that I was on my way out of the building and to my people, whilst in thought, 'I wonder what true happiness is? I want it for my family, but have I ever been happy.'

The word 'happy' has two meanings. For one it means to feel the light of the world in your heart. For the other, for those that have fallen, it means:

H – Hopeless

A – Alone

P – Pain

P – Pretending all's right

Y – Yelling at the demons

LIVE, DIE, AND DIE AGAIN

I once thought that the idea of never being able to die, would be a gift from god. I mean, I have read all those stories in books and light novels about the 'hero' dying then restarting the day or reliving a specific moment in order to get it right. Though the one thing they forget to mention is the effects of a continuous loop that the hero can get stuck in, reliving a moment, day, an hour, a minute over and over again, for all time. Seeing the same thing happen over and over again, not being able to stop it. Yes, they can try and try and try, but in the end, the same things happen. And each time the loop restarts, all the pain, memories, and emotions are still there.

Right at the surface . . .

I once thought that a power like that would be a gift. Boy . . . was I fucking wrong.

The loop was about the battle outside of Brighton. The original day went like this, I would wake up in the village inn of Brighton, next to Ren, my girlfriend. Her beautiful smile was the first thing that I woke to with her telling me, "Dean, it's time to wake up," then the day would begin. We were brought there to help defend the village; me, Ren, her sister Ran, and my best friend Hajime, from a wave of demons crossing the old forest. We had brought enough ammo and supplies to sustain a long siege, and the reports stated that they were supposed to arrive in three days. So we were planning on spending that time preparing, making it easy to get to ammo and food stocks, fortifying lines, and training those who could fight before it was too late. Me and Ren were going to help with fortifying the defenses with earth magic, creating walls. Whilst Hajime and Ran were with the villagers, showing them how to fire volleys of arrows and where to set up the LMGs. Though as the day came to a close something happened, by the last flickers of daylight, the army had materialized out of nowhere.

All I could think about is why didn't the scouts report in. We had several of them out there, at least one of them should of gotten off a flare or two. But there was nothing, just the sounds of people panicking and a monstrous aurora on the move.

After that, everything went to hell. First, a majority of our ammo stocks detonated simultaneously for no reason. "Did they launch projectiles?" I thought no, none were seen, then the frontline was hit. Me and Hajime ran towards the front, while Ran and Ren tended to the injured and panicked, trying to directed them away from the enemy. When we reached the frontline, it was obvious that we weren't ready. Most of the volunteers and men were dead, those that remained did their best to hold the line, so we joined them. For what felt like forever, we held them back as best as we could, though we tried Hajime called for a steady retreat. That was when an artillery barrage flew overhead, covering the village in the inferno of hell. I then saw Hajime fall right before my eyes amidst the chaos, a series of bullets and arrows ripping through his body. The shock of seeing him fall forced me to just run in hopes of trying to find Ren and Ran, wherever they were.

It was in the middle of all this hell that I found them, torn to pieces whilst trying to protect a group of children. They were barely recognizable, it was in a single moment that was when I saw it, the necklace and satchel. At that moment, I lost it; darkness enveloped my soul, unleashing a demon.

Just like the blade that pierced my chest, killing me and the demon. All that which was me was released: my hopes, my personality, my feelings, my rage, and sorrow. Then I heard it from the abyss; it told me in a monotone voice, "This is not the ending that I seek." A light, and then I was back in bed with Ren as if the last day didn't happen.

I know how this sounds, shooting up in bed scared, and looking around to see the inn's room with Ren's beautiful sleeping smile. At first, I thought it was a dream, looking down not see any sort of wound, hearing Ren breathing. With the first lights of day trickling in, I couldn't believe it, they were all dead the town was burning. Yet here they were, alive, and everything was fine. I couldn't help but think that my memory had started to play tricks on me; I mean, I could still remember the feel of the fire, the blood dripping out of my wounds, and my girl's lifeless body in my arms. So, I did the only thing that I could do: I tried to play it off until it all happened again the same exact way as before, like a reoccurring nightmare that was coming true right before my waking eyes. The explosions around us, the army marching towards the deaths of the men, the fires raining down, Hajime falling, the girls together again, and me dying again.

Then I woke up screaming, waking Ren, who again was asleep. Concerned she asked me what was wrong, so I told her it all, the entire deal. I couldn't tell if she took me seriously or was just trying to play it off, as I talked, all I know is what she had said, "We'll get through this, don't worry, I believe you." That was a hopeful one, might be the last hopeful thing I ever heard. If she believed me then they would too. Sadly, no, my friends told me while laughing that I must have drunk too much last night. So I made a deal with myself and whatever being that would listen to a promise, 'I will fix this. The love that my comrades and I share is like a debt that I could never pay. Though I am already to a falling start into the jaws of the abyss to save them,' or that's what I first thought when this endless hell began . . .

. . . For I don't know how long, I've been trying to save them. Each loop, I wake up terrified, as always, next to my girl. Her concerned face is trying to ask me if I'm already, but I'm not - I've watched them die so many times that I've lost count. Sometimes even numb.

I've tried to stop the explosions from taking out the dumps, to no avail. Each time I blow up; can't defuse, can't move them, can't warn anyone, it always goes off. Sometimes I just let them get me cause I couldn't do anything else here. End result, they died, I died, I wake up terrified.

Then I've tried to warn the people about the enemy coming, instead of days from now. No one would listen, they said that the reports said this and that. So I tried to fake reports from scouts that didn't exist, they still couldn't believe it, an army of that magnitude couldn't have moved that fast through the terrain. I even attempted in one loop to completely bolster our defense from the army. The end result was the same every time: defenses didn't hold, and we all died, screamed.

. . . Rinse and goddam repeat.

I even tried to save all my comrades, no matter what it took. I memorized the movements of the enemies, from the weapons they carried all the way down to the direction and speed of their attacks, in order to protect them. I tried to convince them to escape, avoid the front lines, and even leave the village. Somehow, they always died, even when we managed to escape the cold steel of the enemy, more just appeared. 'In the end . . .the same dam outcome,' was all I could think to myself.

For a while, I even did nothing, just laid in bed all day, with her wrapped in my arms, waiting for death to knock at the door later that day. For so long . . . until it was too much to bear.

That was when I lost it, all sense of rational thought and reason left me. Abandoning my body so that a new reforged soul can take hold, a more cold one. I walked out of the village so many times that eventually, it felt like nothing. Ignoring the cries of my girl and comrades, I walked away into the woods, where the enemy would come from. At first, I tried to sneak away, I even brought them, it didn't matter. It was hopeless, we . . . no, I was little more than a blimp on their radar. It didn't matter how many I cut down, they just keep coming, and coming, and coming.

That's when I eventually broke down even further, violently screaming and crying to the universe, "When will this be over . . . I just . . . I just want this to be over . . . I've watched them die so many times that I can't even cry anymore . . . the blood on my hands is drowning me . . . ahaf..ahaf..ahaf . . . what did I do to deserve these . . . memories . . . please just let this end . . . I don't want them to die . . . I don't want to die . . .are you enjoying the show, you sick bastard."

THE DARK HEART

It's been some time since I have felt my own heartbeat. The days of a feeling in my chest were a thing of the past. It's just been cold, the cold heart of a lone man, one that has been ostracized from society. No, that's too general for this to be right, it's more like all the 'normal' people. For years I have wandered, trying to find my place in the world. While yes, there have been people and places that seemed to be accepting of me, they still weren't right. If I wanted to find a place for me, for a broken me, then I would have to go to the farthest edges of the known world. In order to get away, in order to find a place for me, in order to be . . . happy?

Is this something that I deserve? Is it still in the cards for me?

At the edge of the world, resided a town with no name, no political or military promise, and no care in the world. It was where I decided to start over; a new place, a new life, a new name. I would no longer be known as the devil of man, Ryder. The man that was 'picked' to be the scapegoat for the royal family. The man that 'killed' his traveling party, an innocent costal town, and even his own sister. ALL LIES. I would take this chance to start over, make new friends, a new life for myself, maybe start a business. I mean, I always wanted to help people with more than just the leather and steel; maybe this time I could try medicine, an apothecary sounds nice. When I discovered that in a town on the edge of the world, people don't like to ask why they are here. It both made sense to me and relieved me that if you're here, then you're obviously running from something.

Money troubles, famine, war, politics, business troubles, love

. . . Love?

That feeling has been absent in my heart for so long, after the kingdom killed my friends and my sister, they killed a part of me. They had reached into the very essence of my soul, ripping that part out. Now I don't feel anything, just the void in my chest where my heart used to be. You know, I used to think of love in the form of a quote that I saw in a book once.

> *Your heart is only one half of a puzzle*
> *You can try and try to find a piece to fit it*
> *But it will never stick*
> *It's only when you find the true other half*
> *That you can truly be whole again*
> *-unknown*

"Your heart is a puzzle," what a joke, the heart is just a tool that people use to get what their hearts truly desire. Love is for those select few that actually care for each other, like for my sister and for her. She was the only other person, along with my sister, who actually loved me; her name was Jess. When I met her, my party was tasked with helping to save a coastal town from an approaching goblin army. We were just outside of town when we were ambushed by a patrol of goblin riders. Outmanned, outarmed, outmatched, we did our best to hold them back. Then Jess emerged from out of nowhere, giving us a chance to push the enemy back. The whole time, I couldn't help but admire her beauty, and not just her looks. It was everything: her deminer, her skills with the blade, and that smile, they all seemed to fit her perfectly. A woman of class and style that fought for what she believed in. We spent the next few months together, fighting side by side to protect the town, collecting herbs, destroying the raiding parties, and just enjoying each other's company. It was during this time that I couldn't have been more happy, I wanted to stay like this, with her forever. Then one night . . .

A fire, a fire that released the demons of our sins onto this world. Men clad in unidentifiable uniforms set the town to the flame, killing everyone that could be a witness. At first, I thought they were mercs the goblins were working with, but I would find out differently later. They tore through everyone in their path, men, women, and children. They didn't seem to care. At one point, I had managed to lead a handful of survivors off the board, including Jess. I spoke to her near the edge of town, on the edge of the light of the fires and the dark unknown, "I need you to take these people and run for the mountains. Can you do that?"

"What about you?"

"I can't my party and sister need me to back them up."

"Well . . .just make sure you come back to me in one piece." And she kissed me, surrounded by bodies and blood, I never felt more alive at that moment.

"I promise, I will see you soon." And then she was gone.

Though happiness was something that would never come for this name. After leaving her to the civilians, I jumped back into the fires of hell; I thought I could walk right through it. That night, I couldn't have been more wrong, as when I reached the center of town, I saw the bodies of my party lying defeated, dead. One of them holding the torn remains of a uniform of an attacker for dear life; when I picked it up, I realized that it was the kingdom's crest. The same one that sent us here to help, the same that dedicated itself to equality for all species. Now knowing that we were betrayed, I then spent the rest of the night fighting for my life, trying to find my sister, just hoping that she was alive. But shit, I guess hope runs out, too . . . I found her . . . surrounded by dozens of dead soldiers . . . blade fallen to the ground, covered with blood . . .with fatal wounds. As she lay dying in my arms, she pledged with me through chuffs of blood and wheezes, "Listen brother . . .ahf ahf . . . please, I don't want you to blame yourself. We all knew the risks of being adventurers. Just..ahf ahf..please don't let me be alone . . .ahf ahf, and I know you too well so don't end up alone yourself." "Ok sister, I will." She died in my arms as the rain started to fall, casting out the fires of my own personal hell.

When it was all over, I knew I needed to go into hiding. It was in an inn not far from the rubble of the coastal town where I discovered the poster with my face.

'Wanted for the destruction and massacre of a village near the port. In addition to the sin of aligning himself with demons, through the sacrifice of his party and kid sister.'

So, I ditched my clothes, making sure to "borrow" some from a nearby clothesline, which also included a cloak. Score. Then I was gone not leaving a trace, feeling that piece of me being torn out, telling myself, "That I will survive this, I must look out for myself."

I never saw Jess after that, or so I thought. A few years after arriving in the village . . . on a quiet evening . . .

It took me some time and, more importantly, funds to get my shop. I've managed to set myself up as a respectable doctor at Greener Pasters apothecary. I now have money, friends, a business, and occasionally I take the odd job or two from the local guild, I'm content with my life. Though there is something missing, I've been thinking about the past a lot lately; I even bought a weapon or two just in case I get attacked. "Though I'm still alone," and just like that, the door to my quiet shop busted open with the elegance of a hurricane. Coming out of my daze, I looked to see a figure wrapped in a cloak, in the haze of the dim candles I couldn't see their face, but I quickly realized that it was a woman. "Sorry we're closed for the evening," I told the hurricane as nicely as possible.

"Well, I finally found you Ryder," the figure said, still not being able to see her face. Surprised I reply, "Who you must have me mistaken, my name is Lark." She then started to laugh, as she began to approach me and into the light. "That's not your name," as she entered the light I saw her face, it was Jess, "You do remember right? I thought I told you that you weren't getting away that easily." It was in that moment that I felt that feeling in my chest once again. A feeling that made me feel warm, almost alive again. And not wanting to let it slip through my fingers once again, I dropped to the ground on my knees. "Are you ok," she cried as she circled the counter to check on me. I couldn't help it, but I cried; I cried out my pain, I cried out my suffering, I cried out my rage, I unleashed years of emotions that I had bottled up for the last few years. Seeing the tears, all Jess did was hug me, crying as well. After some time, the candles died out, leaving only the moonlight that now brightened up the store more than any flame. It was in this moonlight that I heard, "I was so scared, you never came, I thought that I had lost you. When I heard from the local knights what happened, I knew that it was all lies. You could never have done things as horrible as that. You're a good person, you care about people, your sister, and me." She then took my head and guided it, so that my eyes locked with hers, then she told me, "I love you with all my heart, and I want to stand by your side." And in that moment, I felt the hope that I thought died on that day. Jess managed to see the real me, the one that was lost in the dark void of despair and lifted him up.

Once again, I felt more than just the need for survival or being content. I have the other half of my puzzle. The light in my abysmal darkness. "I once thought that a heart of loneliness and pain, would never heal. Like a scare across the body of the soul. It takes a strong light to save a heart that has been enveloped in the abyss of darkness."

A WANDERING HERO
OR A DEMON

Hello there, welcome to my dark little corner in this here dimly lit tavern. So, you came here for a story, is that it? Well, let me tell you the tale of the wandering man, oh, who am I? Well, you can call me the storyteller, but that's not important. Now onto the tale, they say in this area there is a being that has been helping people. Whether it be bandits or monsters, he manages to take on any and all strong opponents. Some say he is a hero, one that has basked in the glory of the gods in order to protect the innocent. Never disguising between social classes when it comes to the victims of the evil of this world. I've heard that some people say he looks like an angel, always flying in, cloaked with revolve as cold as the steel blades that he carries. One man told me that he tried to offer the man a reward for saving them, but he kindly refused, walking away with a smile.

While there are others that have seen this man as more malicious than heroic, like the tales of old. I once talked to a traveling merchant who was ambushed by bandits late one evening. He told me that after they emerged into the light of his caravan, threatening to kill him for just a few crates of vegetables. It was as if the shadows of the oblivion had come alive, dragging away the criminals one by one. He told me that from the safety of the light, he could hear the otherworldly cries of the men being dragged into the jaws of a monster, a sound that will haunt him to the end of his days. And when the cries

finally ended, a man, no he was more described as a demon. He approached the merchant, just beyond the faint hints of light, looking more like a shadow than a person. All the man would say is that he said nothing, he just looked at where he thought his eyes were, and watched as he melted back into the shadows of the night.

Do you want to know a secret? They're all wrong about him . . .

Now most can only speculate about the origins of this shadowy savior, though I myself know differently. I actually had a chance to talk to him myself. It was a few years back, when I used to live a day's hike from town. I was enjoying some tea when I heard a commotion outside, I looked with steel in hand finding a young man. He was in bad shape, his clothes and the grey ragged cloak that he wore were caked in blood, some not his, but it was hard to tell. As most of the blood was coming from wounds that were soaking the ground underneath him. In each hand were daggers, rusty as hell caked in red, while at the same time well taken care of. All I could do was bring him it, cause I thought, "I can't just let this kid die on my doorstep, especially when I'm the only person around for days."

He slept for five days . . . during that time I did all I could. I made sure to provide him with food, water, and proper medical help. Don't ask where I got my training from. I did all this cause on the third day when he was stable, I wanted to find out what happened to him. For a while, I followed the blood trail he left from my doorstep, all the way to a cave. This cave was hidden by the brush that looked like it was planted there. Till this day what I saw in the bellows of that abyss will forever haunt me. A whole lot of men were slaughtered like prey, and in the deepest part, I found them. A group of women and children were butchered by the man who lay at the entrance to their cells, knife still wet. They were still chained to the walls of the cells when I came around.

Except for one, a child whose chains were cut off, she was the only one that seemed to be at peace, a child . . . bastards. My whole time down there as I wandered through the stone halls, all I could feel was the mark of rage that was marked through it; rage for those innocent people, rage for the dead, rage for the unjust.

When I finally got a chance to talk to him, I began to understand. His name was Leo and when I asked him why he was injured, all he said was, "I hunt the evil of this world." Leo went on to explain that slavers, bandits, murderers, dictators, those that destroy the lives of the innocent, he kills them all. When I asked him why he did what he did, an air of calm came over his face forcing him to look away, showing the massive amount of scars across his back. After a moment he turned, that's when I saw that his eyes were glowing bright red. And in the few words that he said, I knew that he was anything but human; he said with gusto, "Because someone has to wipe them out."

A few days later, he set out, despite my best efforts to help him. He thanked me, and that was the last that I saw of him. Every now and again, I hear the stories of the shadow savior, the wandering hero, or the demon of justice. Regardless of me knowing the truth, this guy is nothing more than a beast with an unrealistic goal. ha, but I can't help but root for him. The man known only as Leo does what no man will ever do. He protects people from the threats that others ignore, for he doesn't want others to go through the same thing. Well, you might as well order a beer or something. It's going to be another long night, and I hate to drink alone.

Never judge the acts of one's character. Some are neither good nor evil, they are their own actions. For they have their own reasons and their own burdens.

A REASON

In a lonely room, away from the rest of the world, a man sits there in a chair behind a small table. A dark room with the only light entering was the trickles of dusk from the nearby window. These beams of light gathered like pillars through the window, elegantly and beautifully round. The sounds of the world outside of this room seem distant to this man, as if they weren't real, but mere memories. The sounds of people working in their shops, at the port, families eating together, people laughing, just pure happiness. He looked towards the light entering his black space, acknowledging it, "Let me tell you something spector," he stated to the light. Before his eyes, the natural phenomena of the changing light turned into a woman with skin as pure as the moonlight and clothes as beautiful as the prettiest flowers; she was light. Was he going mad, the man didn't care enough to even contemplate this. After all, it wasn't as if this was the first time that visions of his past plagued him.

It's been five years since his infiltration into the kingdom and their special armed forces. And in that time, he has committed a number of atrocities against those people, harming thousands of innocents. The same people that he even grew to rely upon, call comrades, some even friends. He was sent in to destabilize the kingdom for the empire's eventual takeover. They authorized him to do whatever was needed, using his position to obtain information. Along with committing so many acts of cruelty that were supposed to eliminate those that would pose a threat, his ambition took so much more than needed: men, women, and children; it didn't matter as long as the job was done. Some acts called for the misplacement of information, the death of one man with a blade, thirty with the cold steel of bullets, and even unleashing monstrous creatures unto the populace to create diversions. At that time, the man was inexperienced; he just wanted to prove himself and be useful to someone. It would only be a few years later that he would realize that he took so much for those that forced him to dirty his hands.

As he told the light what he did, the lives he destroyed, the faces that haunted him. He recollected those long days and nights when he saw things that came from his worst nightmares. In his sleep, the man is always in a bed, but something is wrong, movement is all but impossible. As much as he thrashes, he can't break free; that's when they start to show. From all the shadows that surround him, the faces of the dead start to make their slow crawl towards him, grabbing onto his arms, legs, and torso. The shadows then slowly rip him apart, piece by piece, and he feels every second of it. Sometimes, regardless of when he is either awake or asleep, he sees the faces of those friends. Constant reminders that he betrayed their trust in him, lurking in the recesses of his soul, telling him, "You did this." They even gave him 'suggestions' that come in the form of hallucinations.

"There are times that I find myself looking at my arms for no apparent rhyme or reason. Seeing that there are now long, jagged cuts along their entire lengths, deep ones that pour so much red out of them, Then I blink, and they're gone, as if what I witnessed never happened, like a dream. And the only thing that reminds me is the dark swirling void in my chest, reminding me of what I am. Though every time those visions come, I can feel a sense of . . .well bliss reaching into that shadow."

"There are other times when I look at a weapon, a sword, or a firearm. Then it comes a feeling that possesses oneself with no rhyme or reason, no voice, no soul. It shows you the emotions and memories that were buried so deep that you all but forgotten about them. That feeling then reminds you that if you press the blade to your throat, or the cold steel of the barrel to your head, all it would take is one motion."

The light woman never said a thing, she only gave the man a look of sadness. As if to say, "You know and acknowledge the evil things that you have done. It's ok to feel sad, but you need to make amends and move on." Though the man always knew that this was an option, the arrival of night's darkness made the decision more difficult. So difficult that he reached behind him, into the shadows for the cold metal of peace. That came in the form of a worn bolt action rifle which was a memento from his time in service. As he ran his hand along the rifle, the wood was smooth to the touch, despite the number of holes and jagged cuts, showing that a lot of care had been put into it. Then there was the metal, beaten down as if it was buried in the dirt, though still well polished, even in the glow of the moonlight. He then grabbed the bolt slowly pulling back, feeling like it was moving much lighter than memory serves. Even with a glance at that memory, he flimsy grabbed a bullet from the table in front of him. Sliding the goldish metal into the slot of the rifle, then pushed the bolt back into place. Locking in both the bullet and his last chance to back out. So, he places the barrel into his mouth for the quickest death, tasting metal shavings and oil from the barrel's tip.

A few seconds and it will be all over. The pain, the memories, the guilt, all of it will be over. And then he could rest; besides, he wasn't needed here anymore. Slowly placing his thumb onto the trigger, he could feel the other side. So, he closed his eyes, waiting for the release of death, whilst gently moving his finger.

Then, there was a knocking at the door to his little room, he was worried that he would miss this chance. Though when he heard who was there that all changed. "Uncle . . . Uncle are you in there? It's almost time to go. Come on, you promised that you would take me." "I'll be out momentarily, Sasha," the man told the young girl; putting the gun down, he ejected the bullet. He realized that this was not the right path; yes, he had to make up for his sins, but could he really leave his only family alone in this cruel world. Placing the rifle down back in the shadows, he emerged from the room into a new light. This light was Sasha, with his coat and hat in her little hands, "Here you go," she said with a smile. He then kneeled down and hugged her, taking his coat. As he got back to his feet, Sasha asked, "Uncle, are you alright?" It was then that the man felt the tears coming down his face, tears from emotions that hadn't been present for some time. "I'm fine now, actually," he said, now grabbing his hat as he told himself the new reason why he had to go on.

"It doesn't matter what I've done in the past. Yes, I've lived a rather crappy life and have done some horrible things. However, it doesn't matter she is the reason why I need to keep moving forward. If I can give this girl a good life, education, morals, and a full belly, then I can feel like I have done some actual good on this planet."

The gifts we are born with can be curses,
Though the curse of one can cause nightmares for many,
We must remember that it's a part of them,
They are their own person, not just the little things.

WAR IS HELL

W hen I was young my grandfather told me about a journal that he had found during his time in service. It was found deep within an overgrown and abandoned bunker in the mountains of Danderfall. He took shelter in it whilst separated from his unit after an ambush. While securing the depts of the old concrete bunker, my grandfather discovered the old remains of a dead soldier, basically a skeleton in just an old uniform. In its hands, the old soldier was clinging onto a weathered leather-bound diary and an old pistol. The following are a series of entries from the recovered journal.

January 5th

It's time, the government declared that we are at war with not just the Duchy, but also the Reichton and the Empire. I'm terrified yet excited at the same time. I've always wanted to serve my country, and now I get the chance. For guts and glory, for the country.

January 23rd

Finished my training and waiting for my deployment orders. I hope me and my rifle, Pepper, get a good position. I don't want to end up in some front-line spot but rather in an important position. The squad I'm with includes Jeff and Jin, the twin elves; Ryder, the muscle; Jessy, the most skillful and beautiful sniper; and Captain Donner, the most basic ones like Legion, the android.

February 5th

We are finally on the move and I'm so excited. We're being sent to a base in the mountains in need of men, for when the enemy attempts to flank the main lines. I've also heard that this base is so cool; best fortifications, the best equipment, and the best defense. It sounds like the perfect spot.

February 7th

I was so wrong, this posting is the worst. We were told "that we were to push back any enemy that comes through the mountains." So, you would expect that we would be well supplied, good defense. Nope, it was whatever you would call less than bare bone. The supplies here were meant to last for only a six-month basis, and the defenses were shambles. The walls and buildings were all falling apart, but the only inspection was the bunker and that was a few decades in need of repair. Though, I hope that with my squad mates, we can get through this. The twins and Jessy have set up patrols around the base. Ryder is helping Donner move supplies and armaments to good positions. And I and Legion are on the radio and look out from the tower for the 2nd squad to reach us.

March 15th

It's been a month, and I'm so bored. All we do is patrol the surrounding mountain paths, train, check supplies and listen to reports from the cities. Which is worrisome; the front line is pushed back to point Delta outside of Ferrna. That means we could be seeing enemy scouts any day now. Jeff and Jin seem worried, cause their folks are from Ferrna. But I think we should all worry, if the line keeps getting pushed back, then this country will fall.

April 2nd

We were attacked today during the resupply. They seemed to come out of nowhere; the 2nd squad lost most of their men in the initial attack. I just hope they were scouts and that's it. Since if we get hit by anything stronger, this place will become a meat grinder. For both us in this tinner box and them in the very flammable woods. Most of the squad are on wall watch; Ryder has been tasked with setting up the guns and bringing out the ammo for quick access. The command structure here wants to call for more reinforcements, but Captain Donner thinks that we will survive. I hope he's right.

April 21st

Jeff died from some animal on patrol. Goddamit, why did he go alone? Jin was the one that found him, why him, or what was left of him. I saw the pieces it looked like an animal went to town on it. Everyone is trying to cope, but Donner keeps trying to remind them of the enemy.

May 14th

They came back, FUCK, they came back. I thought that we would see the enemy coming, but not like this. Two weeks back, they hit us in full force. Night and day, it doesn't stop. Most of us haven't gotten more than a few hours of sleep, and It's destroying us. The only choice is to trust in each other and pray that reinforcements will come soon if we don't report in. Please, God help us.

May 25th

We're losing it, no sleep, no ammo, and little food. Ryder is dead, the ammo dump was hit from a stray motor round. Jessy keeps talking about running, but Legion says he'll report her to command for desertion. Though does it matter, our last report from the outside was that supplies were being dropped in from a base a few hundred miles out.

May 27th
The transport with our supplies, our food and ammo, was shot out of the sky. It was in view for all of 30 seconds and then it was a ball of fire. Seeing that plane fall, I could tell some people's hope burned away, too. Donner is trying to remind everyone that someone will come, that we have the bunker to protect us, but even his words seem false. Most of the weapons are out of ammo or busted, even mind. All I have is a pistol and a knife.

It's only a manner of time, they have numbers and supplies. I just overheard them talking about eating the plants growing off the bunker.

June 13th
They're all dead - they're all dead. I guess they got tired of waiting us out, they bombed us back to the age of the gods. Jin and Donner are dead; I watched as their lifeless bodies hit the floor; 2nd squad ran off a few nights back before we were hit. So It's just Legion and I that's left of the garrison. But I don't know where he is; he just called me "my brother," then shoved me into the bunker, locking the door behind me.

I guess this is it. They've been beating on the door to the bunker for the last few days. I don't know what will happen if I get taken, but I wouldn't let that happen. I'm low on food, and I only have one opinion left. Dad, Mom, I'm sorry. If anyone finds this, I just wanted to let the world know. We tried to protect what we held dear. God forgive us, forgive me.

-We tried.-

To the untrained eye, war is the battle of the money and politics. It doesn't matter who fired the first shot, but when the bullets start flying, hell comes to earth. And we are all its residents.

Never forget war is hell. There are no victors, only those that suffer at the hands of it. Respect your veterans, for they are veterans of a hell that we can never fathom.

A REFORGED SOUL

I don't know where to start, I just tried to do my best and it all ended up blowing up in my face. Now I'm in an endless fight for my life, on the run for what feels like forever. Bloody and bruised, and I'm pretty sure that my leg is broken, but that's not the worst of it. The hounds of the damnation, that is, the demon lord's army, are on my heels. Though I can't stop, or I'll die, I need to live. I want to live. Crap . . . All this is because I thought that I could make a difference with one simple job, but I'm so weak, so worthless.

Then, a voice within spoke to me; it radiated an aura of crimson bloodlust.

"No, it's not over yet. Survive young cub, release your claws and show your teeth. Kill them all!!!!! Nothing matters but your own path."

Kill, Kill, Kill, Kill, Kill, Kill, Kill, Kill, Kill, Kill, Kill, Kill, Kill, Kill, Kill, Kill, Kill, Kill, Kill, KILL!!!

STOP . . . You know, let's take a step back; I need to give this background some proper context.

It all began some time back, maybe three or four weeks if I remember right. I was hired by the Demon lord's army to escort a VIP from town to the capital. Well, more specifically, our merc group consisted of three fighters: a sage, an archer, and me, a reincarnate from another world with sub-average skills. Though that's a detail that we can focus on later. Now see, the area from the town to the capital was a wasteland of war, monsters, and bandits. The plan was to move quickly through the areas with the least resistance, breaking any obstacles within our path with quick force. I believed that we had a good chance, well-supplied comrades I could trust, and the VIP could hold their own. Especially since they were the demon lord's daughter, who I was told through stories, wanted to unite the races.

All seemed fine, or so I thought . . .

In summary, two of our fighters were killed by a swarm of the living dead; our sage was taken in the middle of the night, and that's not the worst of it. We ran straight into every small conflict and skirmish that we were trying to avoid. Every day was a fight for our lives, while every night was a mixture of paranoia, sleepiness, and blame, mostly directed at their fearless comrade, me. By the time we finally reached our destination, the princess was the only one who would tolerate me; the rest, well, I found out later.

Three days at the capital . . .

I didn't realize it until that day, but the men that were in my party, those that I have shed blood with. They were never my comrades; they were just using me. On that day, I was chatting up the demon lord and his family about business when we felt explosions all over the capital. It seemed that those I trusted wanted Demon-kind destroyed, and believed that if they killed the Demon royalty, they would be heroes. Heroes that would be treated like kings; riches, wealth, and women, anything to their heart's desires. Alas, they failed before they could even get close. Underestimating the Demons, they were captured by the castle guards who weren't caught in the blasts. When interrogated, my comrades had only one thing to say, "We were just following his orders. It was all his idea, not ours! We were forced, he said he kill our families." All lies, lies that the Demon lord bought hook, line, and sinker. I was arrested as the mastermind in the assassination attempt on the royal family. Though no matter how much I denied it, no one was willing to see the truth, even the princess who I thought was someone that I had grown close to.

I would spend the next six months in a never-ending nightmare. Tortured with water, fire, blades, and even drugs, they wanted me to suffer for my supposed crimes. Each and every day would be hell, I just wanted to die and they wouldn't let me. They would just ask me, "Will you admit to your crimes?" And I would just tell them nothing. It wouldn't be until when I was at my moment of despair that I would make my move. When death was about to come, I would escape through the unknown shadows.

I don't even know how many people I had killed, slicing them to ribbons that when I looked back, it was a maelstrom with me at the center. This storm would not stop; my jailors never would have thought that by keeping me down here, they would unleash something inside of the calm. By the time I got to the surface and through all that red, I was outs de of their perimeter. With an aurora of damnation that followed, making the once kind person become something else. Then I heard the alarm, so I ran . . . . . .

Now I'm so tired, I haven't been able to get much sleep in the last few days of running. I'm worried that I'm losing touch with reality, letting my lack of sleep drive me to insanity. Though something keeps pushing me, driving me. That aura of red that came out of me was something else, creating something else within me. Through the now incoming rain, I managed to find a cave to hideout in hopes that they would pass by. Huh, hope what useless emotion that is draining from me, along with everything else.

"Hahahahahahhahahahah . . . where is this coming from, whose laughing? Hahahahahah . . ." that's when it hit me, it's . . . me.

"Of course It's you," a voice said from the darkness. "Whose there," I replied to the voice, though two more spoke. I heard a timid voice say, "You, . . . you know who we are. We've been with you for all your life." Then the first voice spoke, "We are a part of your spirit, the essence of the very things that make up your soul. We are here to help you." "Cut the crap," the third voice chimed in, more animalistic than the rest, "He needs to know the truth!" Not understanding what was going on, all I could do was bury my face into my hands, hoping that they would go away. I spent what felt like forever like that, and when I looked back up, they were still there. The angry one started emitting that aurora again while looking more pissed off and told me, "Listen there, buddy! Do you really think you can survive with how weak you are? I . . . We are here to tell you that something needs to change." As he said that, the blood-red aurora moved down to his arms and eventually his hands, which were both on the shoulders of the other two. "You need to evolve. We . . . Will . . . Be One," they all said in unity, then the two warped into balls of light, one in each hand. From my seated position they looked like orbs of the universe, a collection of all the colors, as well as that crimson red swirling within. It reminded me of the eyes of both: someone who left our plane while at the same time being born into it. "Are you ready?" He asked me, looking down at me with the eyes of an animal, not a monster. A monster that wasn't standing there out of kindness, no, it was another reason; it wanted to devour its prey.

"........." Then he hit me with the orbs, pouring them and himself into my very being. The pain that came was nothing like I have ever experienced up until this point. It was if my body and soul were in the hands of a craftsman hold a blunt blade. I was being molded, remade into something else. Every time I thought it would be over, it only got worse; the crimson color began flowing through me in harmony. It wasn't a malicious hurricane like before; it felt more peaceful as if I was in the eye of the storm. Closing my eyes in pain I could feel it; all that was weak was draining out of me; if not for my own willpower, then I probably would of passed out. "I need to see this through," and with that

I opened my eyes to see a different person. One with fire in his eyes, with hair as black as the shadows themselves.

I couldn't help but smile, from ear to ear, with an unhinged grin I knew it was for the best. The old weak me was ready to die, now I have the will to survive. Like a cornered beast, I'm more dangerous than ever, "Time to slip the dogs and unleash a new demon," standing tall, I felt something else. A new voice, that angry voice telling me to live, telling me to survive, destroying whatever was in my path.

"An angel with its grace has fallen into the abyss, and when it falls, it becomes something else. Something that should not be messed with. In the depths of the abyss, something worse emerges."

BROKEN . . .

"**A** person is only as damaged as they allow for themselves to be seen. When they are young, they're full of hope and ignorance, it's only when they age they find out the truth. We are all damaged and broken. We wear these perfect masks to hide the truth from the world. That we are a fictional version of ourselves that we pretend to be. And if you were to pull back that mask, then you would only see the true you. As a young kid, I thought that people liked me, that they were my friends. It was only later in life that I realized that they were never my friends. They just tolerated me and my kindness. I didn't know, how could I? The blissful ignorance of wanting to be like tricked me into believing in a false hope. That's when I realized the mask I was wearing was so well constructed that I never bothered to look underneath." Don't get me wrong, I do have a better grasp on that now, or so I hope."

"Now, I don't know? With that ignorance gone I don't know me, I don't know what my personality is, I'm more of a divining rod when it comes to situations. And telling people that confuses them, as if to say that's my personality. All I do is judge the situation and analyze it. Yes, I can be outgoing, loud, and very social. At the same time, I can also quietly read a book and focus on those thoughts that never go away."

"One such, though is always in regards to those that I cherish, and not just family. I'm talking about true friends. I've never really had any luck with those. Don't get me wrong, I've made friends; I'm just talking about the ones that can peak behind the curtain and see the real you, you know. 'huh,' you know an old man that I once talked to taught me a few things."

He said, "Listen here kid, when it comes to understanding the truth within people and yourself, remember. . ."

> *"The Brightest eyes hold the most tears*
> *The Biggest smiles hold the most sorrow*
> *And the happiest people, are really the saddest."*

"See, am I really worth it? I've watched as people have given me false hopes and promises, but for what, happiness? I've watched people offer their hand in order to help someone who has fallen, only to pull it away at the last moment. I don't know what trust is, I don't know what true love is, I don't know who I am. I want the pain to stop, that ignorance destroyed my chance to discover . . . me." The woman in the chair across from me looked at me with sadness. No, not just that, there was something else in her eyes: pity. "You poor man. Is that why you're so broken down to your very soul? You can't accept help or happiness, even when you need it. Is this why you are the way, you are? Cause you feel like that you don't deserve it?"

I didn't know how to answer . . . "Huh," an answer. The only one that came to mind was one that was always there. One that I tried to ignore cause I thought that I could handle it on my own. Bear the weights of my own faults, my own dysfunctions, my own pain, my own . . . loneliness. Since for a while, I would say to myself every morning when I awoke, "You are fine, you can do this." Though was that the true answer? Or was that a lie? 'Do I feel like I don't deserve it,' that thought radiated through my mind, and looking at a truly pure, kind open hand, all I could say was . . . "Yes."

Remember, we are all broken. We hide the pain behind the mask of a fake smile. Though, t takes someone with similar cracks to understand to say, "It's ok. You are ok."

AN OUTCOME

Let me tell you something that each and every individual must know. We all carry a version of our own self-worth that we attempt to hide from the prying eyes of the world. Some may call it baggage or weakness or even that they are a person that doesn't deserve things like happiness. Though that's just how 'one' see ourselves, some attempt to change the outcome of this, most of the time in the worst ways possible. I have seen people who were the principals of strength and confidence of a predator turn into the prey waiting to be slaughtered.

The confident and strong person that is great with a crowd, is one of those people. They want to help and be a good friend. I witnessed numerous people act like older siblings; they care for their friends and listen to their problems. While at the same time, they feel like no one will listen to their problems, hiding the scars with clothes from where they cut themselves.

Those strong people hide the truth, their weaker sides that they want no one else to see. Aren't we all really weak?

The loudest smiling people are another one to look out for. It's easy to spot them; these people try to make everything a joke, so they can get a laugh. I've seen this group of people be at the four-front of most conversations. Though, it needs to be at the taken into account that humor is sometimes how one avoids their demons.

Those big smiles that people show are there is hide the saddest feelings. Aren't we all full of sad feelings that will never go away?

The caring, quite kind people who also try to get people to like them are the ones to look at the closest. Generally speaking, yes, most of the population can be grouped into this category. Though, there are some that are the most likely to fall. They see their own personality as something that they don't need to care about. As if to say, "No one cares about me, so why should I become someone, why should I exist?"

Those who stay quite, holding in the pain of being alone. They find themselves wrapped in their own overthinking that they are what's wrong.

We are all alone. Alone with our thoughts, our feelings, and ourselves. Though it's ok, cause there will always be people like this that manage to find one another. The alone - aren't alone.

All these people think to themselves that one specific outcome is the only thing that they can do to stop the pain. That if what is under the mask of falsehood is shown to the people they know, then others will see them the way they see themselves.

Regardless, this doesn't matter, it's all the fears and self-hatred that we have for ourselves that cause us to hide the scars. For it's times like this that I feel like, and like to remind people that, "No one is judging you," or "What you do matters to no one else, but you."

So be quiet and alone, be strong yet weak, smile and cry, it's all ok. What matters is your own happiness, don't try to hide to make others like you.

THE FOREVER MAN

You know a normal person doesn't stand that long. Sometimes, they make a name for themselves, they make a change for the better, or they do nothing important at all. Though at some point they still fall, the same goes for people in general. We all fall. Yes, sometimes names last a little longer after the person that owns it falls, but no one is supposed to stand eternal. If one were to stand eternal, it would be the most lonely existence there ever was. It didn't matter how strong or weak, good, or evil, a hero or a villain they were, it would never end for them. For the cycle that every civilization follows will always circle its ugly head back around, making it an addiction, and we all know how that turns out.

I mean, really, come on, no one can actually live forever.

"Huh . . . but maybe."

Actually, there is one individual, and I've actually met them. They are about as average as you and me. Sorry, but they're not some great person. There is, however, one unique thing about him: on his neck right below his left ear, there is a number tattooed on '05.' Now I can't tell you what the number means, I've had it for so long that even I can't remember. As for my age . . . I don't know, it didn't matter to me after a few thousand years. Huh, did I say me? Well, crap, you caught me; I am the eternal "hero" that stands for this little rock we call a planet. Can I even call myself a hero? When I was born into creation, I was weak and didn't have much hope for survival. I just fought for the sake of the fight; when I first awoke, I was told that was my duty, my purpose. A purpose to fight for the greater good, fight for the future of the planet, fight for peace, fight fight fight fight fight fight fight . . . As time went on, that's all I did, no matter the conflict, I just fought without conscious, all for the sake of peace. Men, women, children, human, beastman, demon, it never really mattered that much at that point. Over time, I came to develop a soul of my own, a conscious. Still, it didn't matter if they were causing harm; I would still fight until there were no more, until peace came, and I hated that about myself.

Don't get me wrong, I don't hate peace, I get to lie down on a beach, alcohol in hand, but you know. It's like that manga novel about the robot guy that was a hero. He fought for thousands of years for humanity until the orders in his head told him to turn on the very people he protected; it's like that. Instead of wanting to destroy, I just wanted to end my lonely existence; in my long life, there has been no one. Don't get me wrong, there were comrades that I've traveled with, fought with, and bled with. I've even been a part of a few adventuring parties and merc groups. Though there really hasn't been one person, not a single person that knows the real me. The guy that has been fighting for what is right, as well as just fighting for thousands of years. No family, No friends, No love, just the ever-standing guard watching time pass, civilizations rise and fall.

No one . . . to defend me . . . to save my soul.

Though it's not all bad, in addition to my own spirit, I managed to acquire a variety of cool stuff. I have weapons, armor, and souvenirs from all the eras that I've been adding to my arsenal. It sometimes might be a bit too much; I've been told that, on occasion, I don't look like a person. That I look like a demon that has clawed its way out of the pit, bringing hell with me. Though in an endless watch, it can't be helped. Time and humanity can be very cruel. Before I leave, can I at least tell you something, of course I can. We are friends, after all? It was, I want to say, around three or four hundred years ago, I met someone who gave me some good, friendly advice. If I want to be honest, he might of even been the first friend that I've ever had, even if it was for a passing moment. At a bar in some backwater town, I watched as he fought another drunk patron, poorly, I might add. So, tired of watching a one-sided fight, I threw an uppercut, knocking him out. The drunk guy was thrown outside, and he bought me a drink. We ended up talking for hours, it was the first conversation in a long time that I actually enjoyed. Though my new friend noticed the look on my face, asking me what was wrong. "Why do you pick fights, even when it's pointless? All it achieves is more blood."

He leaned forward in his chair and told me, "Yes, it's all pointless, an endless cycle of violence and bloodshed that will always be there. We are all a part of it, as people, both good and bad. I've watched as horrible people commit horrible actions, all in the name for peace. It's really all a joke; those horrible people are committed only to themselves and not an ounce of empathy for those who are hurt. And I've watched as kind people trust, accept, and even forgive those horrible people. They even think that what they do is just an act, a form of grace. It's a lie, karma is a bitch cause she is so delayed, never helping, only harming. We're on our own if we want a just future, where the word 'fair' isn't a lie used to deceive people from true. . . So don't stop fighting kid, you need to pick fights to make a change, even if there is no reason . . ." Then he passed out on the floor. The next day the town authority found his body, it was split into pieces, hanging in an alley.

I never got to ask him more, but in that moment I understood two things. That this endless cycle of violence will never end, creatures of all races will kill each other, and I can't stop it. And the other was that I felt like someone cared, they didn't want something from me other than a simple conversation.

How much longer will I have to continue? Haven't I lived?

A SLEEPLESS EXISTENCE

White lights, those damn white lights are all that I can see. They were so blinding that my eyes couldn't make out anything in the room except for men in white clothes standing around me. I can't hear them, it sounds like I'm underwater, and their hands are inside me. Then it gets hot; flames are everywhere, it's consuming the building, I need to get out. I'm trapped, barefoot, and hurting, and then I find her in another room; she's on the floor next to a table. She's not moving when I yelled for her, so I waddled over to check on her; picking her up, I held her in my arms, trying to wake her. Though it's hopeless, she wouldn't open her eyes, she's dead. I don't know what to do, I scream as I held her lifeless corpse as the flames began to consume us. Before her body burned to ash before my eyes I heard her voice, "Run, you need to get out of here."

Then I woke up, sweat dripping down my back and tears running down my face; I must have dozed off at my desk as I was looking over the files. "I need to get the doc to recalibrate the device later; that shouldn't have happened," I thought as I rose, grabbing my coat while looking around the room. On one side, there was a bed that looked more like a couch than a bed, a set of weights in the corner next to a full-length body mirror, and stacks of papers scattered around the room, with some stabbed to the wall. "I'll worry about this later," I again, thought as I put on my jacket, closing the door behind me. As I headed for the meeting room, I caught another glimpse of myself, seeing that there were still streaks from the tears. So, I used my sleeve to try and clear away the streaks, wiping away the burden. As I reached an intersection of the hall, I heard someone running, but it was too late.

WHACK . . .

"Ah, what hit me?" I looked up in a daze, and saw Mia, miss's partner, was also on the ground. She seemed to be ignoring the pain from the smack to the head, it must have been her hair buns. Mia looked as if she was in a daze and was dressed as disheveled as me. She lay there apologizing without looking up while trying to get the stuff that spilled out of her bag. "It's ok, Mia," I said as I started to help her, that's when she looked at me, "Kiro, I didn't realize that was you." As we collected her things, I couldn't help but notice a worried look as she stared at me with those sea-blue eyes, asking, "Are you ok? Are you on your way there too?" "Yeah, sorry, I'm just not feeling so hot today," I quickly replied, walking off, all embarrassed. When I turned to look back a bit further down the hall, I saw her still standing there, and I could have sworn that I saw a combination of worry and determination in her eyes.

Later that day, after the meeting I was at Doctor Geni's lab getting the device around my next and shoulder recalibrated. I was on the table with my shirt off, exposing my past, the past that I want to forget. As I got comfortable, the Doc and I talked cause he knows the truth, why I fight so hard, why I carry so much of a burden.

"I told you that you need to pace yourself. The tech is supposed to keep you stable so that you don't lose yourself. You can't rely on it to not sleep, it'll wear you down," the doc scolded me.

"I know," I mundanely spoke, "But I need to; it's not that I don't want to sleep; it's just I can't. Every time I close my eyes, I'm back there, surrounded by the flames . . ."

"Watching your sister burn," he bluntly said, as he worked on the device that was hiding a portion of the scaring. "I know kid, I it was there, remember? I found you, this animal of raging determination that almost didn't look human. I fixed your body, took care of you, and listened to your story. Kid, I'm with you if you want to strike back at this hellish society, but you need to share the burden." As he switched tools, he asked, "Do the others know? About your lack of sleep, the scars, or why you do what you do?"

The doc then took out a cigarette, and with a snap of his fingers, a small flame appeared at the tips, and as he started back up, I told him, "No, and I don't want them to; they all have enough to worry about. My past and my scars are burdens; they are the reason I'm fighting for a better future for all of us. Cause if this world doesn't want us . . . then I'll make one that will. I'll be the one to carry that weight, not them." With those words, that was it; for the rest of the time, the room was silent; the doc and I didn't end up saying another word, as if that was the end of the conversation.

I wouldn't know until some time later, but the cameras in the room, the same ones that were controlled by the Doc, were being tapped. And those that were watching us talk were experiencing a variety of different emotions; surprise, anger, fear, worry all at once. Though one among them with an angry smile and love in her eyes gave an eerie response to the group. "This needs to stop, he can't keep going on like this." The rest of them didn't know then that they should of said something, cause if they didn't then it could change things, but they didn't. The others sitting around just sat there in silence, as the girl walked off with two 'volunteers,' well it was more forceful. Really, let's just say that information wasn't exactly deemed relevant or important to the girl with a plan.

A few nights later . . .

"It's been a crash course of hell the last few days, though I can't help it," I thought through the sweat and expulsion of energy, as I walked down the corridor. The night air was pleasant for the task we accomplished; I even managed to feel relieved despite the risk in addition to the injuries I sustained. I mean, I did in fact come up with the plan for the missions, who would go, and even the fact that I would take the most direct involvement when compared to the others. Regardless, it was a success; we all made it back alive; I just needed to get to my room and continue my work. Most of the others should be fast asleep or about to, so I have little to worry about when it comes to visitors. As I continued to walked down the hall, my strength began to fade into more of a hobble. "Just a little further, I can see my door," I thought as repositioned my strength in order to grab the handle. It was in that moment as I opened the door to what should have been my room, that I felt something that I haven't felt for a long time, grief.

It was the house that I grew up in, before the fire, before her death, it was when the old me existed. Near the back of the house where our kitchen was, I could tell that there was someone there. I could hear the sounds of food being cooked before I smelled it, as well as the singing. It was as beautiful as an angel, and as I approached, I recognized that angel. It was Mia, she was standing there with an apron on, cooking up a hell of a feast. "Hey there darling, your home! Why don't you take your coat off and hop in the bath? Dinner should be done soon, and I need help setting the table," she smiled as she hopped along, "I made all your favorites."

I don't know what happened, I couldn't say anything, it was if all rational thoughts had escaped my head, and I was just there. Then she started to approach me with that smile, "Don't just stand there, say something . . . please." It's just . . . it has been so long since that I forgot that old version of me. The one that carried about comics and anime, that wanted to do right by his

family, to make his kid sister proud. Now that part of me is nothing more than a dwindling flame, leaving just the monster that I turned into. Not knowing what to do I froze, that's when I felt it, the tears starting to fall down my face. "Hey, are you alright," she looked at me concerned, that look, as if those words hit me, finally hitting me, reaching the isolated island that I'd been on for so long.

I couldn't help it . . . it broke me.

All that strength, confidence, security was gone, and it all went dark for a moment. In that moment I could feel that island, the one that I created to isolate those emotions, those same ones that needed to be locked away, or they would consume me. Everything around that island was an abyssal void, one that held the reformed me, and the one on the island knew it. In that dark, the monster that was also me patrolled, protecting the island that held the last remnants of me. And that part of me knew that as well, the island was safe, and even though the other part was a monster, it was one that would bring wrath to our enemies. Any intervention that affected the isolated me would be burned away by the darkness, but a proclamation of warmth emitted, suppressing the monster. It walked through the shadows in the form of a person, stepping on the black waves as if they were nothing, until it reached that part of me. As it moved in, its warm handheld my cheek, not burning at all. "It's ok," it said, "Let it out." The figure of light then moved it, placing its lips against mine, fully embracing all of me that was broken.

It took me a moment before I realized that my head was now on the cold floor between my knees, sobbing. I couldn't stop, all the time, all those feelings that were being held back, broke for with. Trying to hide my face, I lifted my coat up to cover my head; as I tried, it wasn't there; I gripped and pulled on my shirt, hoping that I was dreaming, it wouldn't move. Then gentle hands grabbed onto my arms, I stopped, completely forgetting that Mia was still here in this dream that was once my house. "It's ok," she said, "Look at me," as my head lifted, I saw Mia, who was now trapped in my coat. "Even when you're hurting, you still care about me," she nearly cried – I must of put it on her in my moment of darkness, - "Though you need to let us share the burden with you, all of it," It didn't register, the tears in her eyes now. "By the way I know, I know enough. I had the computer genius hack into the doc's personal files, I know about your sister." She didn't know, most of the files the doc has on me are purely based on files taken from the ashes of the lab and governmental servers, was it enough? "You carry the weight of the world so you can make a better one for us. When I realized that I was so happy, you care about outcasts and rejects like us. Nevertheless, when we discovered that your condition was that bad it really pissed us off. We're your friends, your family aren't we? You can lean on us if you need to, we are here for you . . . I'm here for you." As she said those words, I knew that I couldn't let her see any more of my pain. With my now red baggy eyes, I looked into hers, attempting to reassure her to hold up the mask, ". . .," and nothing. All I could do was cry.

As I lay there trying to hold the dam back, that already long since broken when Mia cupped my face. Her hands were soft and firm, just like the rest of her, "Now Listen," she stated, "If you won't say anything, I'm going take some of that burden." I was now in a headlock, how I couldn't even tell you, I still can't. One moment I saw Mia in front of me eyes filled with worry, the next she was manhandling me from behind, 'guiding' me into the sitting room. When we got there, I felt myself flipping over, my legs were swept out from under me, and now I was on the floor with a pain in my back. Mia then sat down next to me, grabbing my head she again guided me from the floor to her lap. "Now Listen again, Darling," in pain from being manhandled, I looked up, and for the second time in as many minutes, I felt a shift, as all that pain turned into fear. As I looked up from her lap, I saw Mia who was giving her same warm smile as always, closer showed more in her eyes, a beast, one that only ever comes out when she wants something, and those eyes were on me. "You are going to lay there until you get some rest; if you don't, I'll just knock you out," she calmly said, but the aura of her words gave another vibe entirely.

Not seeing any way out I thought to myself, "I better just play along. Less of a headache later." So, with my head on her lap, I closed my eyes for just a moment, before a voice started to sing,

"Little blue eyes, lights that still shine, I'll be right here,
A little star so bright, in the dark of the night, I'll be right there
Never forget you are never alone, I'll always be right here..."

After that point, the words phased out, and my body finally started to catch up with me, as her words caught up to me. Since it was the first time in so long that I could let my guard down. Hearing her tell me that she was there for me, made tears form again in my eyes.

"Are you ok," she conjectured, "Did I do something wrong?"
"No, can we stay like this . . . for a while longer?"
"Of course..."

Never forget that we all hold our own burdens close, demons that have possessed our very souls, bringing us down. We hide it as best as we can, but alas, the pain is more than most can handle. When someone is willing to shoulder the burden, then the pain dwindles, even for a moment.

CURSE BOTTLE 867

There are those out there that believe in the unexplainable, the mythical occurrences through history that serve no logic. In the shadows of modern-day society, there are entities out there that are more than just stories for the weak, willed, and scared. I'm talking about demons and curses, the evil that hides lurking around the corner, waiting for those of weak spirits so that they can take hold of you. I know, some may call me a liar, a crackpot, or even just paranoid, but I'm right. Even as I sit here writing in the dark with the only light coming from between the blinds behind me, I know, cause there is a curse upon my family. Its name comes from ancient times, drykkja, a demonic spirit that curses people who drink from its crystalic bottle chamber. In my travels, I learned that it entices people with the hope of taking away their troubles, whether it be grief, pain, or sorrow. Stories show that people that drink it are happy at first, before things change. At the same time it helps the victim, it enacts its own agenda against the person and their entire line. I found several legends throughout history of it destroying the very spirit of those it has a hold over.

Over seventy-five years ago, my grandfather found the drykkja's chamber during his time in war. He told me of how he was subjected to numerous horrors during his service. Losing friends and comrades left and right, even taking a few rounds himself. During an artillery barrage when he was stationed in the Rhine, he heard a voice call out to him. Above the cries of his comrades, above the near-constant bombardment, he heard it as if it were coming from inside his head. "Come to me." That's when he saw it, the glint of something glass poking out of the dirt. Reaching over, he grabbed it; it was small and felt fragile yet tough, and black liquid flowed inside. "What is this," my grandfather spoke, as if on cue, "I'm the one that will give you strength and wipe the board clean." The bottle spoke to him, "Uncork and drink from my everlasting cup." Not knowing what to do, he popped the top; thin vapors of red smoke flowed out, and my grandfather gulped them down. He was desperate. Can you blame him? War is hell, and a higher power was offering him help. Only he didn't know that he sealed the fate of us all.

His journal entries that I found later showed that he was deteriorating. He wrote that he "couldn't let it out of his sight" and that it was his "only sedative that would calm him." Even my grandmother told me that the man that left versus the man with that chamber were two different people. I did find one entry near the end of his journal that confused me, it stated, "It wouldn't stop. It wants and wants more of me and I can't stop. If I try to go without it I hurt, and if I give it then I feel infinity more worse the next day. It wouldn't let me go, that's what it says. Yesterday, I tried to throw it away, and it reappeared. It wants my soul, it craves the souls of people that have said yes to it. I don't know how much longer I have . . ."

Eventually, my uncle found it, and the cycle repeated for him too. Warmth, self-destruction, and death, it can't be stopped only slowed down. Now it wants me, it calls to me at night. The demon tells me that it can help me, it can make my depression go away. Though I don't want that, I don't want that demon to get ahold of me, to be in me. I will fight so that the curse ends with me, nothing related to the demon goes into my body. If the voices think they can break me, if the demon thinks it can break me. Then it better be prepared for a depressed, stubborn person that will stay themselves. "It wouldn't get me . . . It'll end with me . . . That cursed bottle will never see the light of day again."

LIFE, DEATH, AND THE ETERNAL

There once was a talented man who wanted to gain favor with the entities known as One's Beginning and Their End. So he played a game with them, in hopes of winning. Now, this man was no ordinary man; he craved everlasting power and the secrets of the universe. That was where the other two came in; the man, whom we shall call Adam, called them as they were the oldest of the primordial beings, the living embodiment of life and death. Adam believed that they could be the key to understanding everything and satisfying the hunger that plagued his soul. That's why he challenged them as soon as they appeared.

A mistake that would haunt him until the end of time . . .

"Interesting? Only those who fear their end want to gamble with me, but you . . ." Death usually stated, who appeared as a gently dressed figure in a black suit, slicked back white hair, and eyes as red as crimson blood. "Would you care to join us, sister? This is the beginning of something legendary?" As Death asked, he gazed over his shoulder at the beautiful woman standing next to him, Life. "Brother, you and these games are always troublesome. Nevertheless, this mortal doesn't want to die; I'm in." Life told her brother in a monotone voice, Adam couldn't tell, but her voice seemed to contain some excitement. Now Life was something else, a silk-white dress that seemed to connect to everything beneath herself, hair as green and lively as the trees, and her beauty, well they say all life is beautiful, but damn. "If you win, then you'll get your wish. If you lose, then you are bound to us as a servant. How do those terms sound?" Life told Adam with a curious grin on her. So, they played a game; as they began, Adam's smile grew vicious.

No one knows the specifics of their game, those records were lost with time, though some thought that it was a simple game of cards. Regardless, that didn't matter; all that was left of the record is that their game lasted four days and four nights, and neither of the beings nor Adam rested. It was as if all of creation was invested, whilst at the same time ignorant of their wager. Even other primordial beings kept an eye on their older siblings. Everyone and everything watched as a mortal would challenge two beings older than the universe, than everything. Then on the fifth morning, before it could concluded and a victor fairly decided. Adam, who wanted to achieve his goal for power, cheated the oldest beings in existence at the last moment of their game. At first, there were no words spoken, until Death, a master of games and experienced with liars and cheaters, knew what was going on. He rested a hand on his sister's shoulder, while pointing the other directly at Adam, "You thought you could cheat Death?" Life, who knew her brother well, evidently knew that he was telling the truth. The two rose from the game, knowing that this mortal needed to pay for trying to cheat both Life and Death. You don't do that . . .

So, they smiled knowing now that they needed to teach this mortal a lesson. The game was thrown aside, forcing Adam to try and flee. Really can one flee from Death? A wall of black flame surrounded Adam trapping him in the hell of his own making.

"So, it was the knowledge that you wanted? Well, I'm going to make it so that you can never die, forced to live forever. That will give you time for all the knowledge you want."

"So, it was power you wanted, was it? Then, you will regenerate any and all wounds to your body. You won't be able to die."

The two stated one last thing before tossing Adam into the bottom of hell. "Your life, your very being, is forfeit. We'll see how you're doing in . . . let's say about three thousand years." And then they were gone, leaving this man, no, this monster smiling in the very deep of hell. "You want to play this game, huh? I'm going to claw my way out of this hell and make the most of the 'gifts' that you gave me." As the rain began to pour, Adam looked to the heavens, in the very eye of the universe itself screaming, "You hear me!! I'll beat you bastards if it's the last thing that I do."

Two thousand years, that's how long Adam wandered the earth, taking in the knowledge, skills, and secrets that were discovered. Watching as civilizations rose and fell, cultures changing, people living, dying, becoming nothing. The endless march of time. For a while, he felt excited, happy that he was winning against the beings that had gifted him with these cursed powers. For a while it was enough to satisfy him, for a while. Eventually his humanity reminded him of the touch of people again, and again, and again. For several thousand years, all alone, watching the dust collect.

Then one day they appeared before him once more. What they thought would be a pleasant experience was anything but. Before them, the once talented man was no more. All that remained was a broken man in a chair, whose hair was as white as Death's and an arm that was more metallic than human. The beings, for the moment, didn't recognize the man since Adam didn't look like himself. If he couldn't age, then why was his hair white? If he could regenerate from his wounds, then what would have happened to his arm? Adam knew that they were curious about his appearance and his experiences, but all he could say without turning around was a broken "Hey there." That annoyed the two who were responsible for his long-suffering.

"Have you learned to appreciate the 'gifts' that we have given to you?" Death joked at Adam, "You should have never cheated in a game against us, your immortality is the price of your transgressions." Life stated as she stared down Adam. "Hey, we're . . ." Wack.

Adam then slammed his metal arm onto the wall next to him; it managed to create a rather large indent. Standing up, he turned to look the two beings in the eye, his metal arm twitching, trying to make a fist. The siblings were nervous, they were primordial beings that have existed since the beginning of time, and they were stunned. The mortal man standing before him, gave them a look of rage. Rage that has been festering for so long that it's all that the man knows; it's all he is left. Yet somewhere in those eyes of hatred lied a sad man who had seen the true face of the abyss. And he blinked.

Adam restrained himself, taking a moment to calm down, to unleash his crinkling fist. "You want to know how I'm enjoying eternity," he calmly told the two, "It's not the fact that I'm alone that doesn't bother me anymore. I've long accepted the monster that lies within, he and I are one. It's the fact that I'm eternal, I can never die, I never age. Do you want to know the number? The number of people I cared about that I had to watch die. 2,317 people, that's how many people I have watched turn to dust. Lovers, friends, children, I have watched them all grow, live, and die, and there wasn't a damn thing that I could do about it." As Adam started to approach the two, each step he took was like his first. It was as if they finally contained a purpose, a desire to move forward. "The times I've put flowers on graves is unfathomable. Sometimes there wasn't even a grave to place flowers upon. Do you know what it's like to watch that cycle on loop. Insanity isn't even close to the right words. It . . ." When Adam was more feet from the two, he dropped to his knees from what he was holding in. ". . . Its pure madness. I don't feel anymore; with each loss, my humanity seemed to slowly slip away." Tears started to roll down his face as he looked into the eyes of the two who caused this. The pain that they were after was only his, but the consequences of their decision caused the suffering of untold proportions.

As the two stood there, all that remained after that truth was the tears of a broken man. With the realization that sometimes a punishment can change people for the worse. Happiness and peace are finite, but pain and darkness are eternal.

BETWEEN ME AND HIM

As I looked at the sword that was before me supporting my weight. Watching as the blood from my arm started to run down the length of its steel edge, turning the blade crimson black. "I needed to move; if I don't, then all I've done would be for nothing." So I tried to reposition myself so that I could stand, thought the injuries were worse than I had first anticipated. My legs buckled and I was closer to the ground, coughing blood, "I can't . . ." I thought to myself, "If I can crawl or anything, then I still can." In that moment, I looked around seeing that the rest of my adventuring party was still fighting. Greg was missing an arm, though he still keep charging in with his mace. Amy was down to her last arrows and was preparing to pull her daggers. Kina and Kino were behind some debris, she was desperately trying to stop the bleeding from all over her brother's body, but he was long dead.

"Damn it . . . Damn it, why?" As I punched the ground, I angrily stared at what injured me. The best of the Dalatron, there has been little to no records of it since the city's downfall; even then, most of those were still rumors. Still I never expected that they were true . . . still. I was going to kill this thing, so much death has been caused by this creature. The rage burning in my chest was all the strength that I had left, the rest was just about gone. I again looked to my sword, a small puddle of blood was forming below it, connecting to the rest. Yet it still was the one and only thing that was keeping me from dropping. I mean, come on, it's always been the one thing to keep me going, keep me alive. As I stared at the dripping blade of crimson black through the blood, my eyes were reflected back at me. At least I thought that they were my eyes, it took a moment, but the ones that looked back were black with a golden hue. When I noticed the change, the eyes looking back seemed to know the truth, my soul, "That I was done." Though that was just the beginning, a voice then came to me.

"Are you really done," as it said those angered words, I watched as everything around me stop. Not slowed, stopped Amy's arrows were mid-flight, Greg's mace was mid-swing, and the creature just stood there. I was still mobile, the blood had stopped, but I could move. "What . . . what's going on? Whose there?" I couldn't understand what had happened. "I can't believe that you are ready to give up," the voice spoke again, as a black misted figure started to form in front of me, judging me with those same eyes. "Why," he asked, "why don't you stand up and fight?"

I struggled as I tried, but I couldn't; I was just too weak. My body was at its limits . . . no it wasn't my body, it was my very soul. Down to the very core of my being I just wanted to rest, to finally find the peace that I couldn't have in life. Though the figure standing before me just won't let go, he wouldn't let go. "Well," he angrily spoke, "Answer me. Why! Why don't you stand up and fight?"

"I . . . . . .uh . . .I....want," I tried to speak softly, but he didn't have it.

"You want? No, you need to stand up and answer me. Now!"

I tried again and again, but my body wouldn't listen to me. I've given it all I got and that wasn't even enough. Why can't I just die and leave the rest to someone else? Why does it have to be me? And just like that I felt the figure's hand on top of mine, gripping it just enough to remind me. Remind me of why I fight, he spoke again, this time a bit softer, "Do you remember now?"

Coff! Coughing up a bit of blood, smirking a little smile, "I remember, how could I forget." Now, this time, I tried to stand, and I could with a bit of trouble, of course. Though he was holding me up, cause he was always there, cause he was and always will be a part of me. The demon to remind me of the pain and suffering that *we* had to endure. He whispered in my ear, asking once again, "Why don't you stand up and fight?"

This time I answered, "Cause, I need to be the hero that people can look to . . . so no one experiences the pain that we had to endure . . . so we can finally unleash our wrath . . ." As I spoke I could feel an overwhelming power growing, despite the wounds I felt . . . power, "more I need more power." I took my sword from the ground, and as I raised it the blood burned into the edge, creating a crimson wave against the black. Unleashing the wrath with, my wrath, the hatred that I have let build up for so long.

"Let our enemies burn against our blade," I cried to him, letting him know that I was still committed. Even despite my injuries, I was ready to finish this. And as time began to start back up again, I readied myself for whatever came next.

The pain we carry is so that others don't have to be burdened by the same hardships.

Goblin Slayer, The shield hero, and Tanjiro the demon slayer

Beings who carry that burden, are purely good, yet hold a great pain.

OUR OWN FATE

Aaaahhhhhhh! Stretching out against across the grassy hillside, I couldn't help but unwind a bit. I mean, come on, not only is it an otherworldly evening, this is the one spot where I can feel everyth ng. Right now, as the sun begins to dance across the landscape, carefully avoiding the shadows of the unknown. The wind brushed its way through, marking everything and nothing all at the same time. Everything just felt right in that moment. If the universe can create places such as this to remind us of the harmony of it all, then I'm glad that I found this refuge. Taking a second to appreciate this, I closed my eyes for a moment to be at one. Before that moment had inexplicably passed.

"Hey . . .Hey, are you listening to me Kazuma?" A voice called to me; it was pleasant while anncying at the same time. I opened my eyes and saw her, Reka, my partner, standing over me, blocking the sun, her fox ears fluttering in the wind.

"Sometimes I forget she's beast man, I mean look at her. She's a beautiful girl who can pass for a human if it weren't for her fox ears and her three tails. Her bad habit can get to me sometimes, but I love her for tha:," I thought to myself.

"Hey . . ." As I tried to get up, Reka suddenly pounced like an animal on top of me. Her arms were holding down my shoulders, pinning me even closer to the ground. All I could do was look up at her in surprise. I mean, it's been a moment or two since we were this close. Reka stared down at me with a mischievous grin, her beautiful blonde hair flowing still in the breeze, outlining every beautiful feature. "So . . .," she said with a look of concern, "what's wrong with you?"

"Oh crap," I panickily thought, "Here comes her bad habit." For as long as I have loved her that habit of knowing when something was off with me has gotten a number of things out of me that I wasn't ready to talk about. Especially when combined with that look she gets on her face. Trying to play it cool, I told her, "As beautiful as always, you can read me like an open book. I'm fine, I promise." That got a smile out of her; that smile made this beautiful surrounding even better; I always wanted to see it. Though that wasn't enough to satisfy her, Reka snuggled up against my chest, "I know you are lying to me. You can tell me anything, ya know."

Rubbing her head with my now-freed hand, she said, "I know you have been and always will be one of the most important people to me." Hearing those words clearly made her happy; while I couldn't see her face, the way her ears were happily moving told me all that I needed to know. Despite that fact, I was still worried about telling her every time a problem came up since I tend to self-actualize. Working the problem so hard in my head that it gets to the point that I retreat into my inner world, ignoring everything else. Most of the time, people tend to deal with my personality, but recently, that all changed.

After that incident, I thought that the townsfolk would be grateful for all those monsters that I slayed. A few hundred, me, an old stone bridge, a full moon, it was a long night of blood and steel. I eventually lost count of the bodies and weapons that passed through my eyes. All in all, by daybreak, I marched into the town thinking that they would again be grateful. They just looked at me with a look of horror, a lone man covered in bloody wounds, a trail of red dripping off behind me. I, a lone adventurer, who just single handily annulated the army of monsters. As I walked down the street, the voices of the townsfolk who tried to whisper their distaste reached my ears,

"How can he fight so many . . . is he even human . . . so much blood is that all his . . . if he's that powerful then what is he . . . that monster . . ."

I couldn't care less, ignoring them was all I could do. Though it sometimes hurts when people are always scared of me. Their unwary feelings of a lone man who does whatever he can to help people was something not normal. Despite all that, a thought crossed my mind, "Should I change the way I do things? Like, trying to hide my strength, if even just for show? Does the world want me to be different and not me . . ."

"Hey . . . Hey . . . Kazuma," a soft-spoken Reka called, breaking me out of my haze. I looked back and again saw those eyes of concern that pierced right through me. "She doesn't know about these thoughts on my mind," I thought, "but I can at least voice them to her."

"Hey Reka, do you think I need to change?" I finally said out loud.

"What!? Who told you that you need to change? I swear I'll beat them until they're nothing but dust. Then . . ." As she ranted on my chest, I couldn't help feeling a mixture of love and concern. Though I doubt she would do anything that crazy . . . I hope. Anyway, I should push it out of my mind until the event ever arises. "No, No, No one said anything in particular," I rushed to say while trying to hide the fear emanating from my body, "It's just that people look at me like the very monsters that torment them. At first, I was fine with it. If people needed their own monster to come and help them, then what's the harm? Come on you've seen it too. After a while, it started to make me feel numb, like I've actually become that I've sworn to destroy. It all just makes me think . . ."

"That you need to change so people aren't scared of you." Reka's hand reached up to my face to cup my cheek. Looking down to give her my full attention, she chooses the perfect time, cause we locked lips at that moment. "You don't need to change. Cause you're the person that I will always love." With each word spoken from pristine lips, I took them to heart. "You don't need to change, 'cause when people tell you to change, it's for their own benefit. I mean, yes, you can choose to change yourself. Though really, isn't that just telling yourself that everything you are is worthless? And you my love are nothing but worth it."

"Ya, but what about . . ."

"No, no, you are worth it. Everything, the good and the bad, is what makes you, you. I've seen my fair amount of people try to change; it wasn't for themselves but for this cruel world that we are a part of." Still snuggled up in my chest, her fox ears moving with the breeze, she looked to reassure me, "So stop trying to deceive yourself, Kazuma, by thinking you need to change. You are perfect to me . . . and our family." Taking a moment for those words to sink in, I looked inward trying to take those words to heart.

"Ya, maybe you're right. I couldn't help thinking that I was a monster among monsters. Regardless if you're by my side, then all is well. Whatever happens, happens regardless of who we have to fight." I told her these words, realizing as I looked at the clouds that split the darkness and the light of day. That I shouldn't care what the world thinks of me, my existence is my own. If the world wants to pick a fight, then it's just a matter of time and place. As long as I have the people that I care about, then I'll be able to wage war against this world.

As we lay there for what felt like forever, with the setting sun sinking lower and lower, a thought occurred. "Hey Reka," I hoarsely chocked out, "What did you mean when you said, 'our family.'" At that moment, as the last rays of sunlight were falling behind the horizon, I watched as she locked her hazel eyes upon me. "That look," I panickily thought; as the shadows moved, encircling us for the new night, she whispered to me in the tone of a predator that was about to catch its prey, "The one I want."

At that moment, I knew I had lost, and all sight was lost on the two of us. I couldn't help but feel like the darkness was affecting me, forcing me to be lost to my more animalistic side.

We are the architects of our own destiny, do not accept defeat.

Relish in it, becoming the hero of your own story. While becoming the villain in everyone else.

DROWNING MYSELF

I'm cold, just cold.

How long have I been like this? Here in this empty void of darkness that absorbs everything that you are. Leaving a version of oneself that can't even remember who they once were. An empty, a great empty that is nothing more than a constant cascade of sorrow, bad luck, and the reprint of god's cruel jokes. I mean come on, how did I get to this point? I used to be able to fly in the sun, smiling without a care in the world. Now, I've fallen from that point down into the murky waters below. And that smile is now distorted by the waves above; sometimes it's a smile, sometimes a look of deep loneliness, and sometimes nothing at all.

'I'm drowning down here. The old me is struggling to get to the surface while the demons of the past try to pull me under.'

I can't recall how long this has been going on. Has it been days, months, or years? Who knows? Really, who knows how long this feeling can last? Then, one day, I heard a voice coming from the in-between, "Who do you want to be?" That point called the in-between is where the light of the world and the darkness of one's own hell meet, where there is only beauty through equilibrium. They're colors of light and dark mesh together to create something different, something new. It is neither a place of beginning nor end, but of rebirth. I could feel a gaze upon me as I struggled. "Who do you want to be?" I kept hearing it in my head. I couldn't breathe or speak back to this voice; I've been in this constant tug-of-war match between different versions of myself that I have long since lost my voice.

Though as those words kept repeating, I could feel that there was no anger, no conflict in its words. All I felt were the kind words of a foolish person that truly wanted to know the answer. So I struggled against the forces that have kept me interlocked for so long in order to answer.

All I could get out was, "Don..'t . . .kn..ow."

And then I saw a bright light focus upon me. I couldn't see, but I could feel myself moving. It was not like moving in a forward or backward motion; it was more caporal. Everything felt good, similar to the warm licks of a loving pet, kindness, and love. Even then, that was all I could feel; time seemed to slow down, or did it stop completely, I can't remember, or did I just choose not to? Eventually, the light began to die down, and I felt myself on solid ground for the first time in a while. Though it wasn't ground per say, looking around I began to notice some things. Everywhere I looked, it was as if the universe had come alive again; the stars, the colors of the cosmos, the emptiness of it all surrounded me. The colors of it all reminded me of paintings from the early renaissance. Standing there in awe for quite a while, I hoarsely said, "This is beautiful."

"Well, if it's so great, then why don't you join me."

"That voice again," I thought, turning around to meet its owner was more of a surprise than our surroundings. What was spread out in front of my eyes was a firepit with a small flame next to a small wooden table with two chairs on either end. With one of the chairs being occupied by a beauty of a woman; the scenery was one thing, but she was something else entirely. She sat there dressed in a long brown coat that looked like it belonged to a cowboy or armorer, long blue hair, and a pair of goggles on her forehead that held most of her bangs back. As I stood there admiring her beauty, I heard, "Well, don't just stand there. Why don't you take a seat," and with a motion of her hand the other chair pulled back. With no other choice and not wanting to return to my place in limbo, I was inclined to take the offer. The chair was something else as well; it may have looked ordinary, though just like everything else in this place, it was spectacular. "Thanks."

"Are you thirsty?" With a snap of her fingers, a set of glasses and an exquisite container of brown liquid appear. The container lifted gently, pour a finger into each glass; when it was full, one of them moved into my hand. I didn't know what to do; I'm in a strange place with a strange girl with a mystery drink. When I looked over, I saw that she had already downed her glass, bottoms up. As the liquid reached my lips, I realized that it was whisky, as it began to burn the back of my throat. Trying to keep it down, I kept gulping until, "Ack-Ack."

"Well, that's some good stuff," she said, "I take it you, not a whisky person; oh, the name Remi by the way." I tried to respond with my name back, her hand raised somewhat lukewarmly. "I know who you are," swirling her glass she looked at me with the look of interest, "I mean, I know the name you go by, but who are you." I was confused for a moment, she wanted to know who I was, but she already knew that. So, what could she mean? Did she want to know my hobbies, my interests, what I did in my free time, and my love interests? Not being able to take it, mainly since the question was too obscure, I turned to Remi, "What do you mean by that?"

"Isn't it obvious? I mean, who are you?" she then points the finger at me, "My poor sweet boy, you have spent so long being pulled in multiple directions that you don't even know your true self. You're drowning in doubt and can't find a way forward." Remi snapped her fingers, and the scenery changed; we were now in front of a large mirror. It stretched in both directions so far that I could barely see either end, as well as it only reflected . . . me. Nothing else was in the mirror, not Remi, not the table, just me. As I stood there in ignorance, Remi again spoke, "When

I mean who are you? What I meant was who is the person that you see yourself as?" Snapping her fingers again this time with an echo that resonated for a few moments, the mirror began to wave. Just like the drinks on the table when you put ice in them, the reflection was distorted. It all but obscured me, for a moment before I began to notice something. There were other people walking up to the mirror, and they weren't reflections from my side. With another snap of her fingers, the mirror began to clear, what I saw was again something.

"I'll ask you again. Who are you child with no name."

Standing on the other side of the mirror was a series of . . . me. They were all me, just different versions, like a series of weird. Before I could ask what the hell was this, Remi answered the question before it was asked, "Standing before you are what you could be. The ones that can take your place, becoming you, or the ones that will continue on in your stead." I turned around to ask about a million questions, cause it still made no sense. "Here in this place of in-between, I help forge the crossroads that people come to when they can't find themselves. Your case is unique compared to the others. Your crossroads are infinite; there aren't set paths but an ocean of possibilities."

"Possibilities?" I didn't understand at first what she meant; are they choices, consequences, or are they just their dimensional versions of me? Man was drowning in ignorance easier . . . "I don't think you understand," she continued, "you think that you are not enough, so change. These possibilities allow you to change to something else, allowing for the present you to sense. You are drowning in your doubt and ignorance, so you can choose to become something new, something that will take your place." Again, I looked around at the different versions, and just like vehicles or weapons they were all different. Some were for strength, some were for intelligence, some were built for faith, they were all different and unique. "They are all so different," I sadly voiced, "which one should I choose?" Remi looked at me, not with sadness, no it was deeper than that, it was pity. "I can't make that choice for you. Only you know who you desire to be." Walking up the line, staring at each version conflicted, thinking, "Who I desire? What kind of crap is that. I don't feel anything." Then I heard another voice. It was quiet, but I could tell that it wasn't mine or Remi's; it felt familiar. "I know that voice," as I looked toward where the voice was coming from, a light started to come from one of the versions. I cautiously approached, beads of sweat dripping down my back, cause it was the only one that was unseen. It was the only distorted version that still existed except for the crimson light that was exposed from its chest. "What about this one?" I pointed and looked back to Remi; it looked so different from the rest, yet it looked oddly familiar. "That isn't the question you should ask," Remi replied calmly as she approached me, placing her hand on my shoulder, "The thing you should be asking is whether this one is good enough for you?"

"Good enough," I thought. "Does she mean good enough, such as If I choose this one, then I'm content with this one? Content with something familiar, something warm. Or was it something else entirely . . . was it . . . ok to be . . . myself. To say that I am worth it, I am the only version, the best version that should exist. All these other men are nothing more than replacements, fakes to help me understand. To stop struggling against the currents of the light, the dark, and those who want me to follow their own currents. To swim into my own path and be comfortable with me. It's always been me; I am enough."

As those thoughts ran through my mind, I reached out to the distorted figure. At the same time the distorted version reached out to me. When we both touched the mirror it cleared up, and I could see me. Not a different version like the rest, just me. And I was okay with that, and from the smile on Remi's face, she was as well. The other me then turned into a bright light, similar to before, and then radiated into the surface against my hand. It felt unreal, as if I finally understood; no, I always understood; I never expected the possibility. "This is incredible. Though is it ok?"

"Do you understand what It means, you foolish child? You still have doubt in your heart."

"Will this be enough?"

"I think you already know the answer, and before you say anymore, just know this - it's enough if you truly believe it's enough."

THE COIN

I s it ever a wonder why we are so conflicted?
Conflict is in our nature as human beings, confliction is the struggle of a select group.

Every day, there are people out there who wake up struggling with the two sides of the coin. This coin is our conscience and, for some people, well, to be frank, is quite messed up. Now we, when I say our conscious, I don't mean things like guilt, anger, or regret, which are the two little voices that give you reminders. The voice that cares for you and the voice that hates you, or as others would say from time to time, "I hate myself," or "I love me." Now, don't freak out, this isn't a story about crazy people 'hearing voices.' It's a reminder and I'll get back to the importance of it.

At some point . . .

Now for those that deal with these two, they are looked at as different than the rest of society's 'normalcy.' These normal people tell those of us to "deal with it," or "push through it." In reality, there isn't much we can do except to hold it in as tight as possible like a jar. We can keep the lid down, try to compress the contents, try to stop the container from breaking, but in the end, it's just a matter of when and how. Some people tend to break down, others strive through, while most just try to deal with it, even when it makes them feel numb to their own humanity. Regardless the coin is constantly flipping between sides to try and show us both hate and love.

"You are great and loved. Don't listen to what others say about you."

"Are you listening, they say you are weak and hopeless. Well, are you!?"

"Please don't be so harsh on him. He is only trying to do his all."

"Well, try harder. Try until your hands are blistered, the heart gives out, and your eyes bleed. Until you are so far past empty that you hit rock bottom, scratch that you broke rock bottom."

The only thing that you can do is to not focus on either side of the line, and just try. Try to constantly restart your clock at zero in order to find an equilibrium. Yes, equilibrium, it's not a perfect word, but if you can find a space to live happily surrounded by all the crap, then you might be ok with your coin. If not, then you could fall. And trust someone from experience falling is not a good thing. You can fall so far that you don't even recognize the person in the mirror. The person you see is broken, shattered like the glass that your mirror is made of.

"You are nothing, nothing you hear me. Stay just the way you are; that's all you're good for anyway."

"Don't listen to that nonsense, he's just trying to break you."

"Trying, no, No! Trying is to make yourself look decent so that you can feel decent. Trying to eat healthier so you can feel healthier. You can't and will not succeed in trying to fix what is broken within you. It's shattered like glass in a mirror, and that's all you will ever be: a broken, damaged product."

Still, the glass of a mirror can be tapped and glued together, creating the same shape. Nevertheless, will still never look like it was before. Will it ever be the same again? It's hard to tell.

Now not to sound asinine, I want to go back to why this coin is a reminder. With consideration to all groups in life, it's important to always remind ourselves that both voices are us. Their principles are more or less our soul speaking up, not in the same way as the angel and devil on the shoulder. It's more concerned for ourselves when we find ourselves lost in the darkness without a light. And for comfort to all those that need to know this, I have been there myself.

For the longest time, I had trouble with my direction. The side of hatred was always louder than the side of self-love. It reminded me of how lonely and pathetic I really was. Yes, the voice of love would try to make me feel better, but it was usually for just a moment. Then, one day, I realized something: if I just grabbed both sides, accepting them as a part of me, at that point, I could move forward. In moving forward, I could also be me.

Accept the dark and the light for neither are good nor evil, wrong or right. Each side is a part of the being that makes up you.

FROM MAN TO DEVIL

We can all become hollows, beings that have lost the light within. Everyone who is kind has the potential to lose themselves to their rage. Everyone who is happy has the potential to become lost in sadness. When that light within is lost, the hole it leaves behind will turn men into monsters. And the bigger the hole, the worse the monster becomes. Take away a man's heart, then he will lose all of his humanity. Even the devil was once an angel . . . Now, let's see how this plays out."

Bang - Bang!

I was awakened by the shots that now made my ears ring. "Hello . . . Hello," I yelled; I couldn't see; someone was shooting; where was I? Thrashing around in a panic, I could start to feel something over my head, maybe a sack or piece of fabric. I knew I needed to calm down as difficult as it was, my heart and head were racing a mile a minute, so it was quite hard. Trying even harder to focus, I tried to reach for the fabric with my hands, "my hands." I panickily thought as I couldn't move them. They were stuck together with what felt like rope, 'man when was the last time I had to use rope?' Focus, Focus I need to focus, if I couldn't see or move my hands, I had to listen. Listening was all I had left, I dare didn't speak further. Focusing on the noise around me, all I was able to hear were the panicked cries of someone next to me . . . and footsteps.

Click . . . click . . . click, each step made me feel lost in the dark, as if death was strolling over to calm me. What do these people want? Who are they? Why am I here? These questions and dozens of more zoomed through my mind. The steps were growing closer, click . . . click . . . click. Then the sound of metal turning rang in my ears, like the door to the room was being unlocked. All I could do was guess as to what was going to happen as I could feel the weight of the door opening just by its heavy sound alone. "Why are they in hoods?" A voice demanded, his voice stern and calm at the same time, "They're in a locked room, so why do they have hoods?" Another voice spoke up; this one sounded terrified as if they royally messed up, "I thought so that they couldn't see our faces. You know, uh, what's that word called, incognito."

"Whatever. Just stand out here and don't let anyone in, no matter what. They know I like my privacy when I work."

And with that, the door was shut. Leaving me, this man, and the crier next to me all alone in this cold room. "Let's take this off," he said as the fabric covering my eyes was removed. It took me a moment to adjust my eyes to the single bulb that hung over my head. When it finally did, I was face to face with the owner of the voice. He was a tall man in a sharp black suit wearing black gloves and an Oni mask, any other details were a mystery underneath the black. "Hey there. Have a nice nap," then I was punched in the face. "Well," the man let on, "why don't we ask how she is feeling after her nap." "Her?" I hoarsely choked out with some blood. The sack was removed, revealing who it was while also showing me the true horror of what I was in, or should I say we?

It was Resa, my wife, her face was badly bruised and bloody, almost unrecognizable, all the same, I could see in her eyes that it was her. Resa cried out to me with another piece of fabric in her mouth, so all her cries were muffled. "No," I quietly said to myself, I was now filled with rage, looking back at the man in the mask who was now face to face with me. Unlike before, when I couldn't make out any features, now being face to face, I could see his eyes. Eyes that weren't anything a human could possess. It was more like the eyes of a rabid animal. No, an animal isn't the right description; these eyes were cold, devoid of all rational reasoning and logic; the eyes of an animal look for their next prey; these were the eyes of a monster looking to be entertained. We stayed locked in this moment for what felt like forever, me looking into his eyes and him mine, judging not just what was on the surface. We were both measuring the strength of resolve that the other had posed. And while all I saw was a monster of no remorse, what the masked man saw made him laugh for quite a while. "Do you think you still have a chance for a good outcome? Any chance for escape or survival?"

"I do," calming down from the rage of seeing my girl, I asked, "Why are we here?"

"Ingenious. You still don't realize the why." The masked man surprisingly said, "Well, someone out there, someone that you know well, wants some questions answered. And the three of us are here to find out the answers to those said questions."

"What questions do you mean?"

The masked man chuckled, "About that," reaching into the abyss of black that was his coat he pulled out a rather large revolver. Like this suit, it was jet black with a 5" long barrel, he presented it like a prize, "For each time you don't answer correctly," then pointing it at Resa, "I put a round into her together with this six-round chamber then." He paused spinning the chamber containing the rounds for dramatic effect, "you don't want to get the sixth wrong. So, let's begin."

"The first one is simple," cocking the hammer back, "Are you an agent of the syndicate?"

Shocked, I thought to myself, "How does he know the organization's name? We have been hiding in the shadows for so long that even the shadows think we are one of them. So, if he knows the name, it is a reason to assume that he knows what we do." Realizing that I had no choice or means of escape, I told him yes. A bang went off as a round was sent off into her left leg, making her cry through the fabric as crimson red poured from there like a fountain. I tried to get over to slow the bleeding but to no avail, "Tisk tisk tisk, I thought I told you no wrong answers." Basked in a state of murderous aura that emitted from every pour, I yelled, "You bastard. I told you that I work for the syndicate. SO WHY?!"

He laughed again, "I asked if you were an agent, and you said yes. We both know that you are no agent . . . you're the man behind the curtain that started it all."

Gritting my teeth, I was about to yell again when he cocked the hammer again. Realizing that I needed to admit it, I looked up with blood running down my lips, "I made the organization. There you happy." Having the right answer, he pulled the revolver away from Resa, "See, was that so hard? Now," pointing the gun back at her, "Next one." Bang, another flash went off as her crying gotten worse from the blood pouring out of her other leg. "Sorry, but I got bored. Now," cocking a third time, "who did you have kill, Ryder Kishama?" I tried to roll through the rolodex of names in my head, but nothing.

Bang!!!

A third shot was fired, this time this time into one of her arms. The crying just kept getting worse and worse, I couldn't focus on the question. Was he someone who was targeted by the organization? No, that can't be right cause I would remember, though, would he take that answer? I needed to bluff. My cards weren't that good, "That name is not on any file within the organization." A fourth shot rang out, hitting her other arm; she was losing so much blood that it flowed toward me. As if she was willing to let the blood to touch me, so that she can tell me something.

"You don't know, do you?!" the man screamed. "September

20th, 2008, in New Hope Dakoda, 36 people dead from a mystery shooter. The police found two people, twins dead within the mix, 30,000 rounds of ammo, and the shooter was all but a ghost. Remember Now?"

"I don't. That wasn't us, I swear to god."

"No swear to me . . ."

A fifth shot rang out; this time, it was in the gut, and it was worse than the rest. I had a feeling that it wasn't going to end well. Resa looked over to me, blood coming out of every pour with a look on her face that was unnerving, it was peace. The masked man then continued, "While most of those people were innocent, the twins were also important to us. Important to me! They were my family, and you took them from me." I tried again to plead for the life of Resa, that I had no knowledge related to the deaths. For all I planned to plead it didn't matter as he started to hit me with the gun. Over again and again until my entire face was in so much pain that I couldn't describe it with words. Blood was all over my face, leaking out of my mouth and nose, and as I tried to look up, all I could see was red. As the blood vessels in my eyes burst, adding another river to this extensive system, "You know," coughing up more blood, I continued, "whoever did that . . . I bet . . . with someone like you in their lives . . . they deserved to die."

And that was it, the final nail in the preverbal coffin, the masked man was pissed. This time instead of just cocking the hammer, he grabbed her by her hair. Dragging my girl through an ocean of her own blood right in front of my eyes. When that happened, he threw her on the ground into that ocean so she could drown in despair as he kneeled over her with the gun against the temple of her skull. "Last chance, you have to the count of three. 1 . . ." I tried to think of something, something that I could do but nothing. "2 . . ." All the information in my head, all the power I held but still nothing. I wasn't about to let her die for something that I had no part of. I had to give him something, anything, but every time I ran through the opinions, they were worse and worse. "3 . . . times up what's your answer?" It didn't matter what I said. This man was a monster with no consciousness, in both body and soul. We were dead the moment he set his eyes upon us.

"I . . . I," I couldn't. If I said those words, then it's all over, though what difference would it make if I died? Resa, Resa is innocent in all of this, she doesn't deserve to die like a dog . . . but I do. "I . . . would like you to take my life as penance. I can't bring them back, so just kill me as long as she gets to live." Time stopped for a moment; it was as if everything stopped to see the outcome. The masked man let out a breath that could be heard over her crying, then he said, "No," and pulled the trigger. She was dead, dead for a crime that I had no knowledge or participation in. Just dead. I have taken so many lives in my short time on this earth, this was different. As her blood flowed from the new hole, it reached out to me, as if she was still caring for me even in death. When I felt her blood against my leg, everything went black.

I couldn't understand why, in that moment things that were long since buried were coming up for air. Changing me, remaking me, as those things surfaced an abomination climbed with them. With each movement, I felt pain radiating all over me as if I was breaking down. It hit a point as if my entire being including my very soul was discarding the things that made me, me, that made me human. A voice then spoke to me, "Welcome back, master; I've been waiting for you for so long."

Then, everything came back into focus with a sight to behold. The small room that was once filled with tears was now one of blood. The masked man lied on the floor, or at least I think it's some of him. Looking at the two torsos that lay at my feet with both of their throws ripped out. It took a moment of just staring at the bodies before I noticed that the door that was once closed was blasted apart, and I was on my feet, barely. Stumbling out of the doorway into the hall, I found more blood and limbs littering the place, with someone kneeling in the middle of it all. The man was dressed in a butler suit and holding a rather large kitchen knife, "Please to see you are doing well, master." I know this man, he is the very embodiment of what I buried, the part that lacked all degrees of empathy, the demon that I fought with until I meet Resa. She was the angel in my life that pulled me out of the darkness of the abyss, my reason to love again, my only hope to hold onto that last sheard of humanity.

But she's dead now. I have nothing left, and he's free. I'm free from the shackles of my humanity, from empathy. I have become the very monster that I feared in the abyss. I looked at my demon and he held out his hands, in one was another knife still dripping with blood. In the other was the same revolver that took her from this world, her blood staining the barrel. And as I took these tools and walked past him, he looked up, "Of course, master, they will feel the wrath that they have brought down upon themselves."

A CONVERSATION OF LIFE

It's a beautiful day as average as ever in the life of Reo Tamike. The sun, high above is playing hide and seek through the passing clouds. The warm wind, as gentle as a lover's embrace, brushes against him as he walks towards his destination. Even the noises all around were quiet, as if mother nature was on hiatus. Though as warm and peaceful as this day is, Reo can't help but feel nervous. He had received a message from a friend that they needed to discuss something. While Reo didn't have any clue as to what that was on, he marched. While he had suspected that someone must of found out about the issues that were bothering him, he had no proof. And despite the meeting spot being a few blocks away, it felt as if it were miles. For each step, it felt like he was walking through a bottomless swamp, though eventually he managed to arrive.

The destination where his friend wanted to meet was a rather popular garden. Which this place was not only known for its multitude of Orchids, tulips, Irises, and lily gardens. It was always a well-known spot for tranquility, a place where people can come to escape from the clouds of disillusion that fog their minds and hearts. And in this 29 arced land I was to meet my friend, in the message he sent he said that he would be in the place, "where you can see it all." So I wandered, unsure about what that meant. Eventually, I ended up near the lookout that stood at one edge of the garden. It was a private open space surrounded by trees and a single bench. From here, you could see it all: the garden's array of colors, the rolling metropolis that spanned out below, everything that makes the world beautiful . .

. and ugly. After enjoying the v ew, I heard a familiar voice call out, "You made it." Turning to the single bench where the voice came from, I saw a man sitting there in a white button-up shirt, brown jacket, and wearing his usual reading glasses. He was my friend, my mentor, and my brother, Maki. He was waving me over with his brown leather journal, flapping in the breeze.

When I approached, Maki motioned for me to sit down next to him. As I sat, it felt as if everything went from quiet to completely silent, making our surroundings feel as if we were in an isolated bubble. It felt nice, Maki took off his glasses placing them upon the journal that was sitting on his lap. We sat there for a while in silence enjoying the balance of it all. "This is nice huh. Man and nature coexisting to the best of their abilities. Though while it tries not everything can work out as gracefully. Know what I mean?" We both knew what that was directed towards, it was me. For so long couldn't help but find myself in the darkest pits of depression. Maki then continued, "You know why we are here, right?" I knew it was time to talk about my problems, so trying to strengthen my resolve just a bit, "I know."

"Do you?" He asked, "You see yourself as lost in the dark. That every light that comes into view is just a false light. Am I close?"

"I don't know. I don't know anything anymore. I don't feel happiness or sadness or even anger, it's just emptiness. I'm just an empty shell."

"Turn and look at me," so I did, turning to look him in the eyes. When I did I saw the eyes of someone who cared, who only wanted me to see the truth. "You need to understand. This world is a complex spectrum of light and dark, full of things that can never be understood by the average individual. You need to embrace it all if you want to understand it. Following me so far?" He then motioned to the land around us, "Do you think anyone can just embrace it? It takes a certain class of people that can walk through both worlds of light and darkness. And after this conversation I hope you will learn this as well."

"I hope so as well. Thank you, Maki for this . . . kindness." Maki always knew what to say, that's why I was always willing to accept his help.

"Kindness," he inquired, "do you know what true kindness is? While all beings do express the ability to be kind, not all kindness is equal. Some people express this emotion so gracefully that it can be misconstrued for things such as love when there is none. I have been there, I received kindness from caring people thinking that they cared for me. Whenever they are kind to you it feels right, some might even say their hearts skipped a beat. It's not until I discovered that this was just their nature that I lost hope."

"So, is there no hope at all for kindness?"

"You should not lose all hope, my young pupil. True kindness, true love will come to you as it does for all. So do not fret; you may not now understand the emotion behind their words, though you may one day. When you do I believe that you will be able to separate those with ulterior motives and kindness from the heart."

His words made sense. I don't know how I can put them into practice, but it still helped even a little. Even then, despite that fact, I should have known sooner that all people are just wearing their own masks. Not all people can be kind. It's feelings like this that make me realize the truth that I refuse to admit to myself. "I also know that look very well," Maki abruptly stated, "that fear of the fire in your heart, not one of pride and ambition, the one of rage and self-hatred." How does he know about that? When he spoke about kindness, it was as if he was stating facts from his own past. This was different as the look in his eyes was different than when he spoke before, as if it was not simple facts but the truth, his truth." He then continued more softly, "You don't need to fear it as I once did. For a time, I thought of myself as someone that didn't deserve things like happiness or love. That I was simply someone who was just here on this earth, on this rock to exist. You think people call you a monster, but they don't know what real monsters are. They are the monsters that you battle everyday within your heart, and within your very mind. Making you feel as if you are not worthy, that you are so alone. Making you feel as if you're trapped underneath its weight." The look in his eyes got much sadder. I placed my hand on his shoulder and asked him, "Are you alright?"

"I'm fine, I'm fi . . . You know those words are the biggest indicator that you are struggling. If you hear from someone that they are 'fine,' then they are not. They are lying to themselves that are, though they must come to terms with it. I had people ask me for the truth, but I couldn't, I wasn't ready. So, I lashed out at the world; I became silent, I became an ass, I became a reflection of how I saw myself. The only reason that I was able to get through it was that I found trust. I found people that could understand the truth behind the rage, the pain, they listened. And I heard; in turn, I found a medium with the monsters that ran around inside. So don't fret, my friend; just as with kindness, you will find those who will listen. Though, make sure they are the right ones, just as a smile can hide tears, the concern can hide ulterior motives. The key is to listen to the heart, not the mind and not the other one south of the border." He then poked my chest, "The heart will discern who is really on your side."

"What do you mean by side?" I didn't even know that there were sides when it came to this. Though it doesn't matter, "Huh . . . sides?! What a joke. I always end up picking the wrong ones. Whether it's sports, games, or just food, I always end up messing up. I lose, cause I'm a loser. Even when I find a middle ground, I end up feeding a worse outcome. My luck makes me a loser."

That's when Maki started to laugh and laugh, and laugh.

"Stop, it's not funny," punching his shoulder with all my might, though it seemed to make him laugh even more. "Luck, luck has little to do with it," he said as his laughter started to die down, "When it comes to choosing a side, luck is irrelevant, there is no black or white, even no good or evil. The only thing that exists is the choices that people make and how they affect their surroundings. Take a tree, for instance; though it's just a plant, it affects the environment by absorbing nutrients and carbon dioxide while providing oxygen, shade, and even life to other beings. If someone were to remove the tree, then what would happen? The environment would change. For better or worse who knows, that's the point of choices. To one side, it could be seen as destroying the planet; to another management so that nature and humanity can coexist. Either way, it doesn't matter; it's just a matter of perspective. The important thing is that you can't always find a middle group. If you try to play both sides then everyone loses, even if you don't like it, you must pick one."

The light of the day started to turn into a beautiful mixture of orange, yellow, and red, sinking behind the hills of green and the grey monuments of man. While I still felt uneasy about his words, Maki, however, didn't care about the world, as he leaned back to gaze at the vast open sky. Thinking the silence meant it was over, I thought of excusing myself, but there was still something more that Maki wanted to say, "I know you find your equilibrium 'cause it'll be yours. People will tell you that you need to change, to grow into a better person that isn't unbalanced. Never listen, never stop moving forward. Even if your heart still feels the scars from the battle, you must try. If you stop to heal and rest, then that's it. Don't stop moving forward, you may want to lay down and die but time waits for no one." As he got to stand, I tried to jump up and hug him, but he beat me to the punch. My friend, my brother's arms around me, telling me he cared. Then, before he departed, he said, "The hope in my heart is passed on to you, carry the fire for the rest of your natural life. When the time comes use what I have taught you . . . and save someone else."

Turning to leave, I noticed that there was a carving on the bench, where he was sitting. It looked fresh and natural, as if it was always there. I knew that Maki must have done this, "Why?" Four simple words that made me feel a bit lighter, "Non Omnes Me Morientur."

DO I . . .

Abattlefield between two sides is a place of chaos and natural order, it's a fight for ideals, a purpose. You only go to war if you want to fight for something right, revenge, or just a place to die. So why in this hell of a conflict that no one could remember was there something else. In an empty field stood two people standing across from each other on opposite ends. They had fought with all their might, now there was little to nothing left in them. All around, their blades, their blood scattered the battlefield, and what was held in each of their hands were barely weapons. On one side stood a woman in standard combat grabbing for the black devil corps, whose hair was as crimson as the blood that stained the ground; her name was Emma.

She stood there covered in cuts, the blood coming from her head looked like it was her hair turning to its original form, in her hand was the upper half of a sword. Emma had lost the lower half in an explosive attack, breaking it apart, while she stood there bracing herself for the final charge, she tried to calm her mind. Her true feelings were showing through the hand holding the blade, shaking off the blood from her palm. She knew it couldn't be helped, but she was conflicted about all of this, terrified for her survival as her opponent was emitting a murderous aura that was aimed at her. As well as this was someone that she had once called a friend, even a lover. And it was this man's death that would save her and her comrades from a dangerous turn of events.

"The lives you have taken," she thought, "how many lives

have been lost in your madness? You were once a hero to the people, now look at you. The best of us is what will do us in." Not if Emma had anything to say about it. As she took up her stance to charge, she looked across the battlefield to where he stood. Rushy, who was just as battered and bruised as she was, his black long coat was now red with his old black devil corps uniform underneath. He was doing his best to stand tall despite the fact that, unlike Emma, he was already at his end. The weapon in his hand was a broken revolver with a blade attached to the bottom of the barrel, the reason that it wasn't aimed at her was because it had no ammo. "Though that's not all of it," Rushy thought, as Emma began to move towards him in slow strides. "She's coming . . . though it doesn't matter, my arms are too tired to fight anymore," her slow strides started to pick up, "I only have enough strength for what is necessary."

By now Emma was gliding towards him, in Rushy's haze, it looked like her feet weren't even touching the ground. In mere moments, everything slowed down, the blood-soaked steel in Emma's hand was coming down for the final blow. The drops of blood that it cast off seemed to stop in mid-air like raindrops; Rushy saw into the depths of her eyes; they were ones of sadness and pain. He knew that by causing destruction that he would in turn cause her pain, but it was all to save her, and himself. With the tip of the blade about to entire his chest, he knew this was it, and he was at peace with it. Deciding to let her know the truth, Rushy gave a calming gaze into her sad eyes, as if to say, "Thank you," then, he let go of his weapon. And as the blade entered his flesh, he took the opportunity to take Emma into his arms, embracing her one last time.

In that moment she knew, she knew that he wasn't the villain of this story, he was still a hero, her hero till the very end. The truth wasn't meant to be said with words, and as tears started to form, they shared their feelings one last time.

"Why? Is this what you wanted from the beginning, to die? So why, why choose to die?"

"I had no choice, if you were going to survive, I needed to play the villain. If it was for you, then I'm happy to give my life and my life alone."

"You could have just talked to me! We would have found a way forward, just the two of us. Didn't you trust me, so why?"

"Because I thought that you would see me differently. In this long hell that has been my life, people have never understood what I am, damaged, broken. Yet you, Emma, and you alone, my love, saved me; in the short time that we have known each other, you've not only seen me, you have made me a better man."

"You've spent so long in the dark, that the thought of the light scares you, doesn't it? Well, I don't care. I'll choose to walk beside you, I'll always choose you, I love you, all of you, the real you."

The bonds of love can last lifetimes.

"I know . . . God I know, but where I choose to walk you can't follow. I knew that this was a one-way trip, that there would be no going back. Still . . . I have no regrets; just knowing that you'll survive is all that matters."

"I don't just want to survive, I want to live with you."

"I know, and I'm sorry that I wouldn't be there for the both of you. Though will always be together, if not in this life, then the next."

I love you.

Still in his arms the two sat in the middle of the battlefield, blood pouring down their bodies into one crimson stream, swirling into the soil. The rain now falling onto the field, as if on cue to try and wash away the horrors of war. Though one thing couldn't be washed away, the cries of one flowed stronger than any rainfall. They sounded like a multitude of animals crying everywhere and nowhere, but it was just Emma. She was holding onto Rushy, embracing his limp body against hers, not wanting to let go.

As the rainfall grew strong, Emma cried out, "I love you," locking lips one last time.

WITHOUT A HEART

Does it make sense for every person to be equal . . .
Yes, we are built physically similar from a biological perspective. Yes, we occupy the same planet as others for the last million or so years in a human perspective. Yes, we all have cultures and religions that make us unique, but none of that matters. To a point, the physical being matters only when it comes to the surroundings that make us, us. The part that really matters is the parts that make up the mind, the soul, the will. Any person can be strong of body if they put their resolve to the test, though strength of will is a different problem altogether. A person's will, mind, soul, heart, or whatever you want to rectify it as are on a completely different level when it comes to understanding a person on equal terms.

What does this mean, 'on a different level,' it's not like I have a normal heart, and yours is going to explode if you breathe wrong. I mean our hearts are the part of us that can only take so much of a beating, eventually it becomes a scar. One that was created the same way as others that people get, but in this case, it's worse. If you don't get what I mean let me tell you more, or show you.

Standing in front of you is a man, who is just sitting down on a bench; who is this person, they could be your brother, friend, or cousin even, but that's not important. Seeing them, you walk over to them and ask, "Are you ok?" You feel that you have a good enough relationship that you'll get an honest answer, all you get is a monotone, "I'm fine," though are they? This man may sound fine, have a smile on their face, and even appropriate body language. In reality, it's the eyes that give away the person's true intentions; as said by Shakespeare, 'The eyes are the windows to your soul.'

The eyes show the true nature, they may give you a smile or a lie of a response. When you look into the eyes of this person that you know and trust, they say, "I'm sorry, but I'm done with it all." Like I said, the heart can only take so much of the brunt against the pain. In the case of this man and others like him, the pain has changed them. People will tell you that pain makes them stronger or it's a reminder of their journey, for some it's true. Then there are those that experience pain and lose all feeling, becoming heartless. Time and time again they are hit with the experiences that wear them down, like a health bar, but once it reaches zero who knows.

I've met a person just like this, who for most of his life just accepted everything that happened to him. He went with the flow and didn't care what happened; he was content to be a happy-go-lucky guy. As the years passed, I watched as he was bullied, walked over, and pushed to the breaking point, losing that smile that everyone enjoyed. Then one day he was gone, the spark of carefree joy was gone and all that remained was a demon of no heart. He could still think about others like his family, but he didn't care about himself. He stopped feeling everything, yet now he wore a mask to hide that part of him. It was so carefully crafted that people began to believe that the old version of him was back. Yet the matter of the fact was that he had changed, he felt that he was alone in this world, and his eyes never felt the warmth of his heart again?

A INTERESTING INQUIRY

In my haze of doomscrolling through the internet, I came across a question that piqued my interest,

"You meet your thirteen-year-old self."
You're allowed to say three words.
What are they?"

Now, I was a completely different person then as was now, I would even say innocent. So, I spent a few days thinking about what I would say, whether it would be good or bad, a joke or genuine, and what would help pass me. Then after some deliberation on what those would be, I feel as if this is how the story would go. I would appear through a door that connects to nothing, kind of doctor who style before the younger version of myself.

Now, he wouldn't be able to process what was happening to my thirteen-year-old self; I would look like something out of an 80s movie or Back to the Future, appearing out of nowhere. Though one thing I know for certain is that he could tell from the look in my eyes that I cared like the older brother, we always strived to be. When I get closer, I'll get to one knee, placing a hand on his shoulder, so that I could connect both through our eyes and spirits. The air would become quite enough that the whole world would see to fall silent as I said, ". . . It's all right . . . ."

Then I would leave through the door, and it would disappear with me, like a smile with the rain. Now, would he understand it right away, probably not. It would take years before he would understand what "it's all right" would mean; I know it did for me. It was only a few years ago that I understood what those three words meant.

It's all right to cry, it's all right to enjoy, it's all right to be you . . . . . .

DO YOU UNDERSTAND

"Why are you doing this? Why have you given up?"

"Why I'm an empty shell, a fraud, a coward . . . I hate myself . . ."

I t was late in the evening out in the countryside, the sun was about to end its cycle, and soon, the moon would be born again. Everything was quiet, the people, the animals, even the spirits; it was as if this world was nearing its end, waiting to see if it would die or continue on, waiting to beat the heart of existence just one more time. There was one place that excited the faintest pulse on existence, in the field of a young family lying along a tree. It was under this tree that lay a man, sitting, waiting, watching as the fire before him burned on. Even though the blaze was small, it burned with the heart of an inferno; the colors of the flame were reaching out to the stars and the grass and the very beings that existed beyond its beautiful symphony of life.

Despite the peaceful night, the man was giving off an aura of distortion, sitting on one of the two logs around the fire. He sat there in front of the fire, staring into the abyss of heat; his eyes were absent of human emotion, and all that was left was a front, a mask. This mask was his way of hiding from the world, the truth that was concealed through false emotions, striking poses that people would believe. Whether it be an awkward gesture or a foolish act of kindness, cause if he could make others believe it, through 'confidence,' then he might be able to hold onto that last shred of what makes him human. Since right now at this exact moment, and for so long that it almost feels like being human was a dream. "What's the point? Maybe I should give up," he mumbled under his breath.

'My hands may be large but they feel so small, that it feels like everything I hold just slips through my fingers. Every damn time. And there is little I can do about it.'

"I don't think you should."

Out of the darkness stepped a beautiful figure, her hair absorbing the black of the night. She approached the alone man wrapped in a gray cloak that, through the flutters in the breeze, exposed her white night garments. She was everything to the man, and as I looked into her eyes, which blazed like the purest of rubies, I again mumbled, "Why are you awake, Eve?" It was those same eyes that now glowed bright like the eyes of a demon, and they only grew as she approached closer. When she got right next to me, her mouth formed into a kind smile, yet her eyes were cold when she asked, "Do I need a reason to sit next to my darling?" Taking that as a cue I moved over, pulling a blanket from the bag behind me. As I wrapped myself in it, I left enough of an opening to invite her in. She then saw the cue to resort the warmth to her eyes and took her position next to me. Where we sat there as the moon came into the early stages of its cycle.

'Do people even know the real me? I make myself seem like this great person, but is that who I am? I'm powerless, I'm pathetic.'

"Are you ok?"

Out of nowhere, she asked me that, and that frightened me. For so long, I've tried to hide my scars, yet Eve has always been able to see right through me, no matter how hard I try to put up a front for her. Still, I've thought about bringing down the walls that I've built up cause I love her. Though will she love me after seeing the kind of man that I really am . . . am I ready for that. Taking a moment to allow for the cold dead air of the black night to circulate throughout my body. I took a deep breath allowing myself to calm down, strengthen my resolve, then I looked to the stars to asked, "Do you why the earth only dances with one moon? Cause there is nothing else like it out there in the universe, our little blue ball is special to it. For it's a lifeless rock, yet for all time they dance together carving a spectacular path across the stars. Despite that they're always at a distance from each other, still the moon shows that bright smile to it. Though there is more to that smile, isn't there? Behind that distance is something that doesn't want its shadows to reveal, the cracks, craters, its absence of existence."

As I spoke to the stars, to Eve, my words started to feel trembling, more real as they left my lips. And Eve knew it too, as her embrace of me grew more comfortable, allowing for me to feel safe.

"Does it fear rejection? Is that why it always smiles at a distance, cause if it's seen up close, then the truth will come to light." In my chest, the burden that I've carried for so long was pushing me down into darkness, reminding me. That my light, my truth is that I'm not this great person. I'm no one, a fraud, just tired of trying.

Was I ever trying? My existence has been trying to walk the line between fantasy and reality. With my reality being just as pathetic as the fantasy I try to create.

Eve continued to embrace me, as she did I could start to feel the warmth of her skin against mine underneath the blanket. Even with her head resting on my shoulder I could feel the warm of her being, it wasn't just comfortable, it was right. That's why I loved her, she has been the only person that has seen bits of the real me, despite my attempts. Still, not once has she tried to changed me. On our first date, I was told, "Listen, I care who you are, not who you try to be." Till this day, I've tried to be both so that I could protect her. Until. . .

In the light of the fire that protected us from the cold night, Eve turned to look at my face. A look that extenuated beauty and excellence, yet kindness and love, with bits of her black hair covering her face. Slowly, she extended her hand under the blanket, placing a warm hand against my cold skin. A single tear then fell from my face. It seems that tonight, the barriers that I had erected all those years ago were starting to fall down. "The truth," she asked, "from the way you avoided the question, it seems like you don't want to answer the truth of, 'are you ok,' you choose another path of answer. Have you given up on trying to answer? Is that why you can't answer such a simple question from your love."

I couldn't help it, she is my universe, someone that seems to make me feel as if I'm not alone, that I matter - that I exist. Then, for the first time in what felt like never, the walls came down, fast. "No . . . and yes," I whimpered out, "I am and am not ok. For so long I've held it in, the pathetic nature that tears at the very core of my being. I've tried to hold up a front to hide my weakness from the world, yet my hands are so small that everything that they hold slips right through them. It's only now that I realized that I've just been striking a pose to make it seem as if everything was fine. . .Though it wasn't. The worst part is it's taken me this long to realize that I've just about given up."

"So that's it then," Eve asked was a curious glance.

"That's it, that's it," I said louder, "you think I choose this? That I choose not to fight anymore, that I'm resigning myself to chance. There not a single damn thing easy about throwing in the towel." Eve suddenly started to hug me, firmly as if I was about to disappear, but I wasn't. It was at that moment that I realized that I was shaking and had started to cry. Still, she hugged me, and I continued on, "It was so much easier to fake it. To play the man with the calm demeanor, the kindness in his eyes, and joy in his words. Trying to hide the real me . . . now that is hard. I'm nothing, an empty shell that is held together by delusions of grandeur and ignorance, with nothing to back it up." Pausing for a moment, I looked deep into the fire, trying to find the lost flame that may have existed once. "You are the only reason that I'm able to smile. Down to my very core, I'm nothing more than a weak crybaby, who's afraid that people will reject me . . . and I hate myself for it."

Yes, I hate myself. No matter how hard I try, it all falls apart, making me feel as if it's always my fault, my existence.

For a while, we just sat there with the night filling with my tears. "You need to listen to me," Eve whispered to me as tears started to form in her own eyes, "You are not nothing." I didn't know what to take from that as my energy started to drain. "What are you saying? I've never shown the man behind the curtain to you or anyone," I cried, not being able to maintain eye contact. Eve continued, "You are a kind and caring person; everywhere you go, you bring smiles to people's hearts. When you try something new, you can't help but give it your all. When you're resting, you can't help but let go, showing the innocence that resides inside. You may see yourself as nothing or worthless or any of the other horrible words that you think of yourself as. Since the day we met and still to this very moment . . . You are someone that I love. So, let's move forward together. Let's share the burden together, holding onto the hopes, dreams, and aspirations for the future. As a consequence of that please leave behind the fear, the self-doubts, along with the anguish that exists in your heart. I love you . . . all of you, so let's begin anew."

I didn't know what to say, through my tears all I could see was her, and I was captivated. No, I have been in love since the moment that I laid my eyes on her all that time ago. She is my light, my reason for not giving in to the darkness. For the first time in my life, I breathed to let out the real me; the vulnerability, the innocence, and the pure love that we shared for each other.

It would take some time, but with Eve, I might be able to untwine the darkness that has been bound to my heart for so long. Knowing that I took her hand in mine and looking down into her angelic eyes, I told her, "I love you."

And with that, the dark, deselect night that the man had prepared to suffer in was over. Now, it was a peaceful night, whereby the fire shined like a beacon in the shimmers of the moonlight. There were two lovers who passionately kissed, letting their souls intertwine into one.

For the light of lovers is so bright that it carries away the demons of depravity.

THE TRUTH TO BEING TIRED

You don't understand I'm just so tired. I don't know how to move forward . . ."

Sitting before you is a man, he is positioned in a chair that lies in the corner of the room. In this part of the room, as well as during this time of the day, the only thing visible is the man's legs; the rest is covered in darkness. "You're tired? You, my child, don't understand the first thing about being tired." The man leans forward, cupping together his hands, it's then that you notice his bandages that clearly need to be changed. "Being tired is more than just physical exhaustion or mentally drained. Those states of being tired are nothing more than hiccups in the functioning of being human. What I'm trying to discuss is the state of your soul, the parts of you that break down or become 'tired' over time." Motioning to his pocket, he pulled out a gold-plated lighter and a cigarette, then he placed it between his lips. When he struck the flint, the spark showed that it wasn't just his hands that were wrapped; it was all of him. "Over time as the soul begins to weaken or becomes tired as you phrase it. Our emotions, our mannerisms, the very parts of our personality begin to shift, replacing happiness, curiosity, and drive with an abundance of sadness, simmering anger, and an aching void that sits directly in your center."

Taking a moment to take a long drag from the cigarette, you can see a small orange light followed by a collum of smoke arising into the light. "It'll start off slow; things you once enjoyed won't be as fun, and you'll slowly lose your smile. At a certain point you'll feel, no, you'll become hollow leaving just depression that hurts and rage that reacts the more you hurt. And the longer you remain as this, the harder it will be to recover. Though can one really recover from this feeling? For when happiness dies, the mind does. There comes a point where it's the only thing that you can hold onto, like a raft in a raging storm. And all you can do is where a false mask to hide the pain"

"Now you are not alone, for the storm rages for me as well. Have you heard the phrase, 'waiting for a train to nowhere.' Well, I've been waiting with you, not on the platform or in the same boat, but in my own hell. There are days when the false mask begins to slip, letting the beast loose. So I cried, letting it all out to relieve the pressure on my soul, trying to save it. Cause trust me, I've tried; the good lord knows I've tried."

"I will leave you with these last words of wisdom. Don't give in to the despair; if you do, then that's it. Yet don't accept it either, you need to equalize the two if you want to survive. There is no 'cure' for being tired, all you can do is say, 'I'm alright,' and pray that you have the resolve to move forward. Even if for every two steps forward, it's many steps back."

THE DIFFERENCE IN
DESTROYING YOURSELF

Tic, tic, tic, tick . . .

A flame emerges from the old lighter as it slowly moves towards a cigarette. The small light burned bright, being held there for a few moments before pulling away again. Then he took a long drag, emitting such an orange glow that it almost became a new flame. The man then removed the small roll with two fingers, releasing the emissions of the said roll. This man sat on the stool across from you, seasoned, wearing causal clothes with an old army beret. His name is not important to the story, but what's important to note is that he has wisdom, wisdom that he is willing to share. "Listen, kid . . . cough . . . you look like you're carrying some baggage on your back. Maybe you've done something stupid or planned to. Regardless, I think you should hear this old man's words before you decide. Whether or not you'll end up destroying yourself or 'destroying yourself.'" Picking up the glass in front of him containing a brown liquid, he swirled it for a moment.

"There is destroying yourself for no other reason than to numb the pain, to forget. Whether that be through drugs, meaningless sex, self-harm, unhealthy relationships, and food, that includes alcohol," swinging the entire drink down his throat in one smooth motion, he tapped the table, ordering another. "Like I said, we do this thing because we want the pain to stop, but it never does. The challenges that we've faced throughout our lives only seem to make it worse. You can try to move forward only to find yourself stuck at the start. And for people such as that their only course of action is giving up, for they have lost confidence in themselves or never had any to begin with. Take a relative, my uncle for instance. All my life, I have watched him destroy himself and those around him. He drank, smoked, and treated everyone like crap; even family that cared went to prison, and lied. All until the point that no one wanted to care anymore, as a family maybe, though as a person never again. What happened to him you may ask? Well, like all people who choose to destroy themselves, he died in the worst way possible . . . alone. Not a soul cried at his passing, not a good memory to hold onto, yet we still felt grief in our hearts." It was at this point that another drink was brought before the grizzled old man; picking it up, he continued, "Till this day, I wonder things. Why did he choose this way? Did he ever care about anyone other than himself? What started the self-destruction? We'll probably never know."

It grew quiet for a moment as neither of us said anything. How could you? It felt like hours were passing by, then . . .

Tink . . . Tink . . .Tink . . .

He started to twirl the glass, the ice hitting the rim of the glass over and over, again and again.

"Now I said that there was destroying yourself or 'destroying yourself.' When it comes to self-destruction, yeah, we're all capable of doing horrible shit to ourselves. Yet, it's only the best of us who can destroy ourselves to protect others. Not in the way you're thinking; I'm not talking about fighting or brain surgery or anything as simple as that." He slowly placed his index finger against his temple, poking it several times. "I'm talking about destroying your mind **and** body for the ones that you care about the most." Moving the cigarette back to his lips to take another long drag, he then continued, emitting more smoke than a diesel truck. "So listen close kid, there comes a point in our lives when we meet people that we want to protect, to see them smiling forever and protect those smiles. Yeah, well, when that happens, you'll be willing to dive into the very depths of hell itself to keep their smiles bright. You'll let the innocence of your souls burn, allowing for something else to take its place; by the time it's done, everything will change. For it's not just the bottom, the whole climb back up will reshape you. So when you reach the top you may look like the same person, almost the same. In the deeps of your eyes, where people that have only experienced the same feel, they'll see it . . . you're broken."

The man then looked down at the table with an expression that seemed to be troubling. It was as if he was trying to suppress so many bad memories. "In my own experiences, I've given up on things like happiness, joy, self-worth, and love, all for the sake of the love of those I hold dear." Unexpectedly, he started to chuckle for a few moments before he continued on as if nothing happened. "You know there is a story I know that could better explain this than anything I have. It's about a man; this man was as ordinary as you or I, he loved video games, his family, his friends, his life. One day he gets into a situation, a dangerous one full of violence, blood, death, and which eventually caused him to get hurt badly . . . then he died. Though, that wasn't the end of it, a dark voice called out to him, reaching its shadowy hands to offer him power to change fate. No one knows what was said only he does, and if asked, all he would say was, "I took it without question." The next thing he knew, he was alive, and nothing had happened yet. The power given to him was one rewritten live through death. A blessing and a curse placed upon this man. For he could never die, never rest, yet he had the power to protect the lives that he held dear."

I didn't know what to think, the power to rewrite fate. "Though time has a way of being a cruel bitch. At first, he was excited to have his own power. Though over time, the true scope of his power would be worse than expected. He had to die to rewrite fate, every time. All the pain and agony of death just for the chance to go back. When he did begin anew, the memories from his past attempts would still remain. Think about it, would you, the power to restart time to protect everyone? No death, no tears, not one person would remember what happened, but you would. Every word, every action, every teardrop, and every drop of blood. You would have to look at the people that you cared about, despite the fact of knowing that harm was or wasn't about to come to them. That would drive any man mad, and it did. Slowly but surely, the smile that he wore across his face began to fade, leaving behind a fake smile. A smile that was meant to hide the fact that he had become numb to the world, to the pain. Still he continued on, destroying himself for those he cared for."

"Don't be selfish. If you mean to destroy yourself, at least try to make it count. Don't do it for nothing."

ANGELS

As I was walking through the park on any average day, taking my time as I do. I took a moment to rest against an old oak tree in a sea of green. As I was enjoying the cool shade, the result of the leaves, I heard someone coming towards me. Opening my eyes, I saw a young boy, he seemed to be about five or six, holding a ball between his tiny hands.

"Hello there, sir," he said in a way that made him seem older than he was. "What are you doing?" I leaned forward to look at him better, "I'm just resting for a bit. It's a tiring day. Ya know?" Thinking that he would go away, I leaned back against the tree, closing my eyes again. Yet the most unexpected thing happened: he didn't leave. Instead, he plopped himself next to me. "What are you doing," I asked him in the way that adults say stuff to kids sarcastically.

"You're right. Today is tiring. So, I'll sit here too; by the way, mister, I'm John."

"Well, I'm Nolan, and it's a pleasure." I think that was the end of it. I looked up at the leaves. They looked so close yet so far away for a tree of this height. If I tried to reach up, it would feel as if I was reaching to the heavens. As I was sitting there thinking of the heavens and how far they were, little John started to pull on my shirt. "What happened to your arms?" he pointed to the multitude of scars along my forearms. They looked like a Jackson Pollock painting, lines of scared flesh going horizontal, vertical, every which way.

"Those are from a time that I wish to forget, yet never forgotten."

"My mom told me that those lines appear when people want the bad stuff to come out. So that the angels can come in, save them, and take the bad stuff to heaven. So that they can never be hurt by it again."

"Well, your mom's right. I've got these from the bad stuff coming out. By the way, where is she?"

"Oh," he said with a smile, "the angels saved her. Now she saves people with them."

THE MAN IN THE
BLACK ROBE

"What is it that you fear the most?"

"What I fear? I fear the day that I meet *him*. And when that time comes, I wonder *will I be ready?*"

E veryone fears the end of their story; I mean, who wouldn't? People don't want their story to end without it meaning something. We hope that there is more to the story than the same cliff notes as everyone else. It is why people fear the end, the end of the story, the end of life, of belief. In those final moments, we meet him, the black-cloaked being, Death. Now, cultures all around the world have their own version of the being that governs the end of all. Whether that be Hel, Anubis, Kali, Shinigami, or even the Grim Reaper. Death may come in many forms: spirits, gods, angels, and demons. Just how did death come to be the lord of passing? Well, after talking to some interesting people, both living and dead. I've found my answer, and it begins like this . . .

In a time and place long ago, the planet was in a state where the scales were unbalanced. People suffered in the thousands; god's creatures were slaughtered without the respect that they deserved. The world was dying, and not a single thing existed to give people peace of mind from their pain. However, as it is told in most mythologies there was one pure place left. In a vast forest at the edge of the world, where man and creature were equal, where the scales were equal. For those to live, they killed. For those to survive, they did what was necessary. In this place where the circle of life was pure lived two siblings, brother and sister, Renji and Sakara.

The two had lived in these woods for most of their lives. No family, no tools, no memories other than who they were to each other and their names. With no purpose, they did what came naturally; they survived. Day to day, week to week, month to month, year to year, they began to evolve past the current standard for human existence into something else, something pure. Cultivating the land to their ideals and building structures to protect and provide for them. Growing nourishment to support their lives and their souls. And ending those that could give and destroying those that would take.

Renji was the older brother . . .

"Every day, I walked into the dark abyss that was the depths of the forest. Carrying my tools, I walked alone; I didn't dare to bring my sister along. Despite her age and willingness, I didn't want to destroy the beauty of her smile. Since the very act of taking a life, even for survival, takes its toll on the mind. Forget the blood that stains your hands; it's the noise that keeps me up at night. Taxing, taxing is the only word to describe that feeling. Even now, when I slide my blade into the neck of a dying creature, I'm numb to it. And I know I saw my reflection in some stagnant water; No emotion, nothing at all. Still, whenever I emerge from the dark, my little sister is there in the light, waiting for me with that smile. And do I show her that side of me . . . no, I smile back telling her that I'm good . . . that was a fucking lie . . .

Sakara, that tiny younger sister . . .

"When my brother goes into the woods, I begin my work. Carrying for our home, I walk over to the food we grow. A decent-sized patch of land a stone's throw from the house, surrounded by trees and fencing meant to deter animals. I spend my time nurturing new plants, talking to them, feeding them, and

elevating them to live. Sometimes, I run my fingers through the dirt, feeling the mixture of rocks, sediment, life, and underneath it all, death. I don't tell my brother, but those who died in the dirt give way to new life. They grow stronger, even when those next to each get replaced year after year. A bitter-sweet truth that hides through the lies."

Then one day . . .

It was getting late, with the sun just peaking over the towering mountains in the distance. Renji was giving chase to his prey, elusive yet immature; as always, he was focused. Until his nose drove him back around to the smell of fire. Searching for the cause, he climbed a tree only to spot a billow of smoke off in the distance . . . in the direction of home, of his sister. Without thinking, he jumped, pushing his knife into the bark to slow his fall. He didn't even hit the ground before he took off into a run back home. Panicked, no matter how fast he ran, each and every stride made it seem as if he was running through mud. Branches, trees, creatures, it didn't matter he pushed forward. His only thought was to protect his sister, as his lip curled so tight that it started to bleed.

As he grew closer to home with night now setting in. His only guide was the smell of the fire that led to the orange glow that grew ever closer. "I'm almost there," as the glow enveloped him, bursting out of the brush to a scene from his worst nightmares. A group of men had set fire to the land, taking everything that they had worked so hard to build. And in the center, surrounded by several of them, was his little sister lying in a crimson pool. She was trying to crawl away with multiple blades shoved into her back, and that's when she spotted her brother. "Help me . . ." She cried before dropping her head.

In that moment something in Renji, the dependable older brother, snapped. All those numb feelings came to the surface like a raging beast he didn't know what to do. So he didn't. The only thing that came naturally was he yelled at the top of his lungs, alerting all the enemies to his presence. Turning with blood lust, these animals saw only another target. Renji, who should have been scared, wasn't; he was alone, manned. Any normal person would have run, but not him; he just walked forward. He wasn't scared, just calm, so calm that all the life drained from his face. As he walked, he pulled his blades from his sides, ready. His enemies knew; they didn't know how, but they knew their prey was their end.

Like a strike of lightning, it was over before it began.
What happened next cannot be said with words, other than . . . *they were dead.*

Every single one of them lay dead, bodies torn apart so viscously that no human could have done it. An animalist yet cunning massacre that cut a path of bloody ribbons that led to its end. There sat Renji, covered in so many cuts and blood that, by all accounts, he shouldn't be alive. Yet he was a bloody mess holding onto his sister's lifeless corpse for dear life. For fear that if he let go, she'd be gone, lost in the sea of red that surrounded the two. "Why," Renji softly cried out, "Why did you take her? She was innocent and caring; she was my sister." Who was he crying out to? His sister? The animals? The universe? It didn't matter, he still persisted, "I am the one who deserves to perish. I have created nothing, nothing but suffering. What . . . what will it take to bring her back." Even though he wasn't expecting a response, he got one, nonetheless.

In the form of a voice. An otherworldly voice that seemed to come from everywhere and inward at the same time. It wasn't malicious, yet it wasn't kind. "What would you be willing to give?" It responded, giving off an old feeling as if it had been here since the beginning and would see the end. Renji looked to the heavens and, without hesitation, answered, "Everything. Take all that I am and all I'll ever be." Nothing came for a moment, then two, and finally, it said, "What I want is you, and what you want is her. If you want her to be one with life, then you will need to separate yourself from it. Becoming the vessel of death, to wander alone forever with those going to the other side."

He looked down at his sister's body, wanting to see her smile one last time. "Will I see her again," he inquired, as the voice responded with, "If fate allows it." Brushing the hair out of her face, he placed his sister down, crossing her arms. Looking to the unknown.

Do not fear the end, for it's the purest form of truth. As death once said, "People fear me for the truth. That their stories are over, that the lives that they lived are now done. They believed with all their hearts that they had so much more to do. Yet the truth is not in what they didn't do, it's in what they did. They lived through life's birth; experienced pain, suffering loss. Although it was not all bad, there was still love, joy, hope that existed in their hearts. For It's important to remember that through me, you'll feel the same love that you did in life. Even at the end."

LET ME . . . !?

As I stood there in bewilderment, I looked over her. As beautiful as ever, with a long flowing white dress and hair as black as the night, yet something was off. She seemed confused, as if she couldn't decide whether to be happy or sad. Tears were falling from her eyes, yet she still smiled.

"What happened? Are you alright?"

Taking a moment to collect herself, she responded, "He's gone."

"Who," I inquired, "Who, did they do something to you?"

"No, he had to return home to prepare," clutching her chest as close to her as she could get. "He had to return to prepare for our future."

"Who? Please give me the name of the person responsible."

Whispering one word, a name. The same name that means fear, evil, damnation, "Satan."

"Satan," I inquired once again, "You're crying for Satan? Planning a future with Satan? He is the embodiment of evil and chaos, the devil. A demon that thrives on the sins, chaos, the very evil that humanity is forced to unleash."

Grabbing a flower from a nearby vase, a blue one, as bright and beautiful as the vast sky. She brought it to her chest as a sign that this one was important. "A demon? Evil? Satan is none of those things. Yes, he is responsible for the sins of this world, but that is his penance. Remember, he was once an angel that chose to think for himself, as humanity was allowed to. He was cast into hell as punishment, and punishment is all he knows. So, I let him in."

Shocked, I voiced in confusion, "You let Satan in?! Why?"

With a caring voice, she answered, "I let him in cause he needed to know that pain wasn't the only thing that existed. There is more to this miserable life than our own hell; there is the enjoyment of living. There is peace, beauty . . .," touching her belly, ". . . love. I showed the angel of hell that there is still love in this world, and he showed it back. I let him see the world through my eyes, my hands, my ears, my heart. I showed him things and taught him the joys of nature: the plants, the trees, the creatures of land and water. Showing him things that weren't just suffering made him soften. We talked, we made things, and we fell in love. Over time, I didn't see him as a demon, the devil, or even the prince of darkness. I saw a poor soul in pain, I offered a hand. And you want to know something; I think some time back, he offered his hand in return. He left to prepare a place for me, for us. Where we can be happy together."

Remember that we are not what we seem to be.

Satan, Lucifer was once an angel. Evil isn't always evil, as good wasn't always good.

It only takes a small push, some hope, and a little love.

To be saved.

STEPS WITH MYSELF

"No tree can grow to heaven, unless its roots reach unto hell, . . ." - *Carl Gustav Jung*

"Does this make sense? Do you understand the truth behind this sentiment?"

"I do . . . and my hope is that others such as myself understand. And if they don't, I want to believe that they will soon. I stand before you as someone who understands you. To show that there is a story, my story."

It was a while back; walking through an open field on a beautiful day with no destination in mind. Not a cloud in the sky. Not a person in sight, complete isolation. As I wandered through the lush flow of grass, each step was slowed by the thick brush. I felt as if I was carrying a heavy weight. Yet never was I impeded, the flowing wind against my legs was innocent. It was in these gentle strokes that she spoke to me, "Walking in peace or fruition? Why do you walk this way? Are you walking with a purpose, if so **what?**" These words, I couldn't hear them, but I felt these feelings in my very soul. Confusion, doubt, and direction, these feelings arrived a long time ago. When, I don't know. They were just there, a reminder of the being locked in my soul. I told myself that with them there he wouldn't be let out, "no matter what."

Crack, Crack, Crack! The first lock is broken. Two more.

Overhead was a vast sky, blue, beautiful, Pure. The greatest lie that humanity has ever told itself in existence. I've heard everything, "it's just right there." "It's magic," "It's nature," "It's where the gods and angels reside." It doesn't matter the era or the people; humanity has looked to the stars with the hope that we are not alone. But still . . . when one walks through the world alone it is difficult to see hope. When it is that same hope; that people are kind, that equality is true, that we can be our true selves.

Taking a moment to embrace the atmosphere of it all, I reached for the heavens above as if asking for an answer. And even though, like before, I couldn't hear the words, I felt them as she spoke again, "You reach for the future, but what about the past? Can you accept the steps you've taken to get here? Do you understand who you are and who you want to become? Who are you? Loss of hope, dreams, drive, the empty shell that just wants to be filled with love. The same love that he used to feel as he looked to the stars and asked, "Why are we here?"

Bang, Crack, Bang, Crack. The door is creaking, it's about to give out. The second lock is broken. One more.

As I continued to walk along my path of isolation with no destination in mind. I can't help but feel better when it's just me, alone. Don't get me wrong, it's nice to interact with people, but alone, purely alone, is nice. You don't have to be someone else. You don't have to agree or disagree with people. It's just you and you alone.

Or is it? Alone, with friends, with family, you just can't help but feel alone. The demons in your head badger on and on, making you feel as if it's only you. That you can't trust. That you don't deserve love. That you don't deserve to be happy. "Listen," she said in a calming tone, that was indifferent to the previous feelings before.

Bang, Crack, . . .

"You are not alone. You know that right? They just don't know the other you, the true you. The one that hides in the shadows that you've long locked away in your soul."

Bang, Crack, Bang, Crack . . .

"The barriers that you have built up were to protect yourself. Deep within your very soul, you knew what was coming."

Bang, Crack, Bang, Crack, . . .

"That's why you made that mask."

Bang, Bang, Bang!

"So, you'd both be safe . . ." The final lock is gone. The barriers were gone. Now came . . . Pain.

It came so fast that I suddenly dropped to my knees, "my face? It feels like it's burning off." I didn't even realize that I was clawing at my face, as if I could 'reach' the problem. It was hitting me all at once, though the pain started to come in waves. Now, in the form of voices that battered my eroded shores over and over again, "You need me . . . Embrace me and what I mean . . . We are meant to exist together. One not without the other." "One not without the other," those words slipped from my throat, though where did they come from? Not from me . . .from us. As that thought occurred to me, I grabbed my chest feeling that something was different. In that moment of clarity, I noticed through my blurred vision a set of shoes stepped into my view. Looking up I saw him, or I saw me. He was everything that I was and yet wasn't. Though the obvious differences were his white hair (while mine is black) and a small scar over his left eye. I didn't notice his eyes at first, but they held the deepest sadness. He had been carrying those same feelings and emotions that I had bottled up for years. No, since I first became self-aware.

Extending a hand to me, the other me asked, "want to walk . . . together." Together? Was that something I could do? I now understood the truth behind this darkness that I felt within me. It's not an evil part of me; he is me. The me that had accepted the burdens that I wasn't willing to take on myself. While I tried to trudge forward with no hope. He had been there with me, trying to protect me. Though why was he here now? Have I finally broken?

"You haven't lost, have we yet?"
"Are you here to save or destroy me?"
"Neither I am here to just walk with you."

That feeling, that dark pit of despair, grief, and anger that sits inside of you. Unguided. It's not here to harm you. In fact, the opposite, it's here to remind you that you are you. While you may now carry the burden of your mistakes and regrets, that's just a part of you. The whole, light and dark, angel and demon, exist in tannin. One is not without the other.

Grief and love.

Anger and peace.

Sadness and happiness.

STAGES OF DEPRESSION

"How can you hide, when you live in the light?" Those were the words of a wise man, that I rather not name. Not for fear of embarrassing them, but out of respect as they are no longer for this world. They were not just a great friend, they were my mentor, they were family. Though that information is irrelevant to what I found.

It was months later . . .

I was digging through their stuff, sifting through things that mattered, to those that didn't. It was during this time that I came across a series of papers in his desk. They were old, the once white papers had yellowed, were held together by a paper clip. And while the paper was old, the words it held still had their color as if they were just birthed. Yet they felt off, like when you see an old warrior at the bar with a smile on their face. Even though you see the motions, it's the aura of the actions that show their true motive. Deep within that warrior's eyes is a man that is hiding. Not from the pain of the body, but of the soul.

"My stages of Depression," those words were on the first page. Deep, slow strokes. The strokes of someone . . . who didn't have a reason to go . . . forward. Under those words, the following was writing,

"Hey there, if you are reading this, then please stop. What you are holding onto are the personal thoughts and feelings of someone who has seen the abyss and blinked. That was when I was pulled in. Despite that if you know the real me, then continue on, cause like me you blinked, too. And when you were pulled in, something else clawed its way out."

The next page was titled 'The whole lot of nothing.' I couldn't tell at first glance, but it looked like something had dripped onto the paper sporadically. And the penmanship was dragged as if someone was writing with a dead hand. It started with,

"Nothing, just nothing. When did it begin? For the life of me, I couldn't give you a right answer. It started small, like the flickers of a candle, pulling at the edges of my light. The darkness. By the time I knew that this darkness had entered, it was too late. I was empty, lost; all these different feelings and emotions clouded my mind, making me feel as empty as a husk. No matter how hard I clawed and grasped for those lost feelings, they continued to slip away. The only remnants were that of shadows that only showed on the surface, never in the heart. Eventually, I spiraled to the point of no return, that dam abyss just wanted to take me. And it almost did . . ."

After that, the page was written as just 'angry.' I wasn't sure, but this one must have been a tough one for them to write. The words written down were messy and confusing, as if the one writing it couldn't come up with the right words.

"At some point in the spiral, I grasped onto the one emotion that seemed to be real in a sea of fakes. Anger. I was never angry at any one thing or person, but it was just there. It wasn't like those stories of angels and demons on your shoulder, it was a demon. Only there to remind me of why I struggle, why I fall, and things that 'caused' it. I tried to keep it in check. Locking down the source with vices meant to contain the creature. Though that was my mistake, while I was angry at everything even this creature, I also felt kinship. As if we were the same; angry, empty, confused. Yet when I looked into the abyss this time, a different thing came. In the depths of that darkness was a set of eyes, eyes that understood. Not of the anger, but something else."

Finally, there were just the words 'resolved to fate' written there. To anyone else it seemed like not much was written on that page. Though I wasn't just anyone else. I was their friend, their top pupil, their brother. I knew better than anyone else what these words meant.

"There comes a point when you have to decide, "Do I let myself be swallowed by the darkness," or "do I become one with it and hide in the light as a shadow?" I spent a long time trying to find the answer: movies, books, speakers, and even higher powers like religion (ha!). Though I think I found the answer to rid myself of this dark abyss that now exists within me. And like that little bug from that one movie, it asked, "Did you find the answer?" It was simple, but I didn't want to believe it."

Written on the side of the paper was a small drawing of one of those white play masks with a smile.

"I have to fake it. I can't just get rid of it, but I have to accept it and live with it. In doing so, I need to put up a front when I'm in front of people, no not just people. Everyone. I will wear a mask of that of a smile. Even though in my heart of hearts I know that it's fake. That the smile is just there to keep the demons in check. Just until I'm alone again, then It doesn't matter if they break off their leashes."

After all, the last part, when the anger and void intertwine, is just a smiling face. One that strains just to find a place to belong. And when it finds it? Who knows? Only we who search can find it. The balance.

WORST KIND OF PAIN
(ALONE)

"I have to say something that I have never been able to before . . . I'm all alone."

It's hard to be with people. On the bus, in the streets, in airports, everywhere we go we are surrounded by people. And while we wouldn't always see or hear it, we can feel their judgment being forced upon us. Even when we are alone, they are just in our pockets. Just waiting there for you to come into their society. So, when people try to protract from the norm, they are seen as outliers.

That is why those outliers see places like nature or night as peaceful. As they are abstract ideas that most people put off as boring. While others look at them as ideas of silence. Where they don't have to deal with the chaos that is their world, that is their existence.

"Are they ok? I'm worried about them. They are so nice, why do they look sad?"

Would you like to know? That person is alone because they were forced to be alone. That person is nice because they wear a mask of insecurity to hide their true demons. Demons that are only resting at the moment and can wake up at any time. That's why when you say something that bothers them, they become silent. It can be for many reasons, such as being bothered or being frustrated. Though the truth is, they don't know how to put those feelings into words. That is why they stay silent, that is why no one knows what they truly think.

That pain, that feeling of being alone, is a double-edged sword. Most people hate it cause they are left with their thoughts. Me and others like me, we like it because we can hear our own thoughts; the good, the bad, and the fucking ugly.

That is why you should not look at their body language, their face, their mannerisms. You need to look into their eyes. No deeper. DEEPER. There, there it is. Those feelings are kept there because we are so alone. How will you know when you see them? Trust me, you will. And I can't tell you how to help them relieve the pressure of that pain.

Cause I haven't been able to figure that out myself. I've tried to surround myself with people and loved ones who care about me. But even when I'm in the presence of others . . . *I'm still alone*.

NOTHING, BUT GREED

"If I were to pose a question, 'what makes a human being?' How would you answer? Is it the fact that we are intelligent? Or that we have the hair, blood, and the skin that identifies us as human?"

"No, it's emotions. Not a single other entity takes things like emotions into consideration when it comes to accomplishing their goals, such as survival. If I need to eat, I eat. If I need shelter, I take it. If I need wealth, I earn it. Those human emotions that take priority over logic are all that separate us from the beast. Without them, we would be lowly creatures, right?" So, without emotions what is left?

That's what I asked myself when I looked into the mirror, bits of clear and red streaking down my face onto my chest. Taking a nearby towel, I pressed it into my face as if I was wiping away the sins of the past. "Though that's impossible," I slipped out as I started to put on my shirt. With each button I pinned in place, it was as if I was pinning the mask onto my face. However, was the mask I wore different from the real me? Running my fingers through my once black hair that was now white. After all, I'm not human anymore . . .

Five years ago, after coming to this world, I found people that I could call family. We laughed, we ate delicious foods, we made memories that felt like better days were ahead. I thought that I had the power to take over the world, and would protect them no matter what. Then I lost someone dear to me, after that everything changed. They killed her, no, it's better to say they humiliated her. Tearing off her clothes, they tied her to a post, cutting her over and over again. And she screamed, begging them to stop all the while they were laughing. I couldn't do anything but watch as they tortured her, all the while holding blades to my other siblings' and mother's throats. They even stabbed me through the gut, so I couldn't move.

Laying there on the ground in a pool of my own blood, I still tried to crawl to them. I remember crying through fits of blood, "I'll protect you guys," over and over again. And every time I spoke, they just twisted the blade in my back. Still, I tried to move to the post, her back gushing red. "No," I cried out as my vision blurred as I watched them deliver the finishing blow. We all cried, especially my younger siblings, her lifeless body hanging there. Then, the man behind me brought me to my knees, "I want to look into your eyes," he said with nothing but greed in his voice. So, I looked back . . . that was it, that was my mistake.

I didn't give him what he wanted; my eyes were still filled with a murderous aura that would tell them. He didn't like that. "Boss," he said, drawing his finger across his next. Then the man that was stabbing her gave the order, and then they were all dead. Their cries were cut short, all that remained was silence. I didn't know what to do, what to say, I just shut down. I watched them burn their bodies as they dragged me away. That day I made a wish, one so deep that it couldn't have been made by any human . . .

"I'll destroy everything."

Those three words were so full of conviction and desire that they weren't just wishes. It was the will of something so inhuman that the very weight of this wish would make it come into existence. Such as, the idea of hell was used to describe atrocities. Thus, desire was that of the beast, one that would destroy the world. I don't remember how I broke free that night. I was just running until I vanished; even years later on this night, I can't recall all the details. Even reading the reports doesn't jog any memories. Expect for a violent storm of blood thrashing around me, the taste of iron on my lips, and those hands. They were, but weren't my hands, though it wasn't just my hands, my whole body felt different. It was as if I had lost a critical part of myself. Was this madness? Humility? No . . . it was . . . discussed at the world from a point of nothingness. That was the only way that I could describe it at that time. Until much later.

After cultivating my desire, I hunted them down, destroying everything in my path. Countries, cities, towns, people. Innocent people, it didn't matter I slaughtered them all. I became the incarnation of the angel of death, the reaper. And it was in one of those cities that I finally found him. As I walked out of the bathroom, I grabbed my coat. Its leather-green fabric was dotted with patches of blood and other fluids from tonight's countless victims. I could have thrown it aside; it was ruined, after all. Regardless it was sentimental to me, plus Reggy can get it clean. The room attached to this bathroom was a small suite. A few beds, some couches, a mini fridge, and a window that covered an entire wall. Normally it would have been fairly quiet, though I had thrown some people through it. So, the tussle of the wind was flowing into the room, as well as the smell of smoke. Outside you could see that the surrounding cityscape was in chaos; Fires, looting, screams, it was hell. And those fires light up the sky, casting a faint glow into the room. Where in the center sat a rather large man in a chair, covered in cuts and bruises all over his body, except for a small piece of fabric covering his eyes. Who was this man? Well, the boss of those men that killed my family.

Ripping off the fabric over his eyes, I asked him, "Let's try this again . . . do you remember me?" My voice was soft, yet the waves of murderous rage were clear. Bringing my knife to his eye, I asked once more, "Well?" "Yes," he cried, blood and snot dripping down his face, "I remember now." The truth was the man didn't remember him; he had committed so many atrocities that they all blurred together. Afraid for what was to come next, he braced himself. I wasn't done, however; I walked to the window admiring my work. "Tell me, do you know what greed is?" I inquired, and the man could only be confused by my words.

"Greed, you know, one of the seven sins of humanity. Well, they say that greed is about money, like sloth is about laziness, or wrath is, well, wrath. Of course, we can only ever look at money with that sort of lust. Yet, I believe that greed has a different meaning that people overlook. Greed isn't about money; it's about wealth and not just material things. I'm talking about the desire for ideals and goals. The desire to accumulate your wishes into reality. And while most people do greedy things like this on a day-to-day basis. Truly greedy people don't care about others. They will take what they want, making their ideals truly real. No matter the amount of blood, I have split oceans of it. And yet I don't feel an ounce of remorse, no guilt, nothing. Just discuss that they would stand in my way."

Turning around I walked back to him, the glow now shimming against my face. "I'm a greedy man and there is one thing that I want from you," I softly whispered. Grabbing onto his face I told him, "I want you to look me in the eyes." In that moment, he remembered that day and realized what he created. In the eyes of the man in front of him, my eyes were nothing. Not an ember of light left in them, and they will never be again from the amount of bodies he dropped tonight. Those eyes were so devoid of life that they seemed to be sucking him in. Into madness? The dark? I don't think he could have even made up his mind. Until my knife entered his throat, and the gargling of blood returned again against the chaos of the night. "Hu," sighing, I thought, "I was expecting this to be harder. Well, I guess I'm as much of a monster as he was now." And as the tears started to fall down my face, I whispered, "I really am that greedy. Aren't I, mom, sister?"

SAVE EVERYONE.
BUT, WHO WILL SAVE YOU?

I don't know what to say. I've spent my whole life trying to do what was right. Helping people. Caring for people. Listening to their problems. Hell, I've even shed blood to help those that came to me. Not once did I hesitate or choose to ignore their request. I just wanted to do my part, and yet no one came for me when it was my turn. For years I was willing to dive right in with no questions needed or expectations of reward. Though, when I asked for help, to be saved, no one came. It hurt. I believed that after all I had done for people that they would come to me just as quickly.

That led me to two different realizations. The first was that I needed to stop caring for people, they were using me, manipulating me for their own purposes. The second was that I needed to play the part. The need to hide your dark side is important. Showing the world that person that sits in a pitch-black room, not reading, watching TV, or working on something can't happen. That person is your demon, they look to the four walls with discontent, only hoping for the day that they can just give it up. The cheery personality that is distinguished by that smile as wide as the world, all fake. That person, me, just wants to show those eyes that see nothing and care for nothing. That they only want someone to care for them as who they are, and not what they could gain. That's what happened to me once, so long ago.

It was a few years ago; If you ask for an exact date, I can't tell you. But I will never forget the details of that day . . . of her.

I had gone for a walk with no particular destination in mind. I just got up and started aimlessly wandering in a world that I wanted no part in. It was a low point in my life, I didn't pay attention to the people passing me by. Or even allowed myself to focus in on the laughter, sadness, anger, the house, the hustle and bustle. Just life, in general, didn't matter to me. If people hadn't passed by me, I would have thought that I had died. At some point, I snapped to clarity just long enough to realize that the sun, that what felt like moments ago was rising, was now setting. As well as I was in a park pretty far from home. Yet did it matter?

Looking around, I saw people walking their dogs, on benches, and laying on blankets. I just wanted to get out of there, to be alone. So, looking to the heavens, I started to walk up the closest hill. Though it was more like a mountain, with each step toward the top, I wondered if I was going to run out of air. Yet I still climbed and climbed, the isolation on that mountain was that type of isolation that I enjoyed. No people, animals, living beings in general. Just me and me alone, or so I believed. As I started to crest the Everest of my mountain, my eyes saw a lone beach. It was old and worn down, but still, it didn't look like you would get splinters if you sat on it. The once blue wooden paint was so faded that it looked about as teal as the rust on its screws.

"This seems like a nice spot," I sighed in a hoarse voice which showed how much I really used it. I walked over to my 'throne' atop my lonely mountain, looking across the vast world that spanned out from underneath me. The same world that chewed me up so many times that I just didn't have the energy to care anymore. I was so tired of it all that I sunk into that bench as far as I could go. Though it wasn't a tiredness of the body or even the mind. It was of the soul, the very core of my being was tired of the harsh outcomes, the overall beatings that it was hit with, over and over, again and again. Sighing again, I didn't notice that there was another person standing next to me.

"Excuse me, sir?"

I looked in their direction to see a beautiful girl standing before me. She looked to be about my age. Her long hair flowed out from underneath her beanie into a ponytail, with bits of her bangs covering her purple glasses. It seemed like she had a different idea of isolation than me, as she had a bag over one arm and pencils and a notebook in the other. "I saw you come up from over there," pointing to a tree off in the distance, "and I was wondering if I could join you?" I wanted to be alone, it was better like this. I didn't want to burden people with my existence. And yet there was something different about her, looking into those eyes, that smile, they all seemed different . . .genuine. Did she really mean what she said, so with some hesitation, I mumbled, "It's not a problem. This spot is big enough for two," moving over. "Great," sitting down she pulled out her notebook flipping for a fresh page. As she flipped through I spotted animals, plants, people, scenery, a little bit of everything.

Noticing that I was glossing over her notebook, she explained, "I'm an artist, well, trying to be one. I'm more amateur than anything." I was confused. From what I knew about art, which wasn't much. The work in that book was amazing, almost mystical, lifelike. "Oh, I almost forgot! My name is Nadea. What's yours?" A mix of panic and amazement arose in my chest. All I could think was, 'Why was she being so nice to me,' 'Is this a joke,' and 'What does she want?'

"Hello? Hello," she repeated louder and louder, "are you ok?"

Steeling my resolve, "Oh . . . oh I'm good, no I'm Tayler."

"Well then, Tayler, nice to meet you," smiling, she got to a fresh page, "if it's not too much trouble, can I draw you?" I didn't know what to say, I had no words, so I shrugged my shoulders as if I didn't care. Taking that as a response, Nadea yelped, "Ya." Then got to work drawing as the colors of the decaying sun sank before us. Her hands moving as if they had a mind of their own, swapping out pens and pencils at random intervals. Normally I would of tuned her out at this point, but then again that feeling of something genuine kept coming around. She was so focused on her work, yet it wasn't for her. The look on Nadea, a girl as beautiful as the rising moon, was slowly making my cold heart warm again.

And before I knew it every time she talked, I would respond with more and more feeling. Not the same feeling as the darkness that grew within that created this new me. It was different, at one point I looked to the sky with my head tilted back . . .Only to bring it back down, flashing Nadea with a smile. A smile that seemed to feel like the old me again.

"There he is," she exclaimed, "I had a feeling that there was more to you under there." As if on cue, she flipped over the book to show the drawing. The only word to describe it, was incredible. It was as if she had captured the beauty of the world. And at the center was me. A me that has not given up. He does not hold his head down, but up high. A me that cares for the world. "I understand," that was all she said as she smiled and held the drawing. Questioning, I asked, "What do you mean?"

"I understand the need to push the world away. To realize that your whole identity was a lie that others created for you. You must of thought that you were alone, that no one really cared about you."

"How . . . what do you mean?"

"Silly boy," she grinned, "you aren't alone. It's ok to cry in front of someone. It's ok to dream of a better existence than this life. Nevertheless, we have one life, and one only. So, forget those who used you and walk to your own beat. After talking with you I think we can walk together."

Reaching into her bag, she pulled out a pressed flower. It was a small rose, except this wasn't a vibrant red. Instead, the rose was a wilted white rose. She placed the flower onto the new drawing of me, closing it was the utmost care. "So, Tayler," she asked standing, extending a hand, "want to walk with me?" I couldn't say anything; hell, I couldn't breathe. This girl, no Nadea cared so deeply that she was willing to extend a hand. I have known her for only a breath of time, and yet it felt like forever.

I didn't even notice the tears coming down. "Yet. Let's go," I said, taking her hand. "Great," she again smiled, and we started down the hill. "Come on, I know a good place that sells rice balls."

"That sounds great," I said, smiling at myself for the first time in a long time. After all, for once, someone saved me.

THE DEMON LORD?

W hat makes a person evil? Their nature, their looks, their morals? Not those. After all, we were all born as equals.

Then what is the meaning behind being evil? Is it free will, the pain experienced in the past, the world that shunned them? Not those, either. Those are just the trials and tribulations that forged ourselves.

Then what is it? Want me to tell you?

It's perspective. The way people view their actions and beliefs is stipulated from their own perspective. An individual of a higher class can claim that someone is a criminal. Do the people question it? No, cause from their perspective, if the accuser says that they are guilty, then they must be. No proof is needed, except the need to show who the criminal is and what they 'did.' How do I know this? How do I know that the criminal wasn't a criminal? Or that he was but had good reasons to be one. It's because those with power manipulate the facts in order to 'prove' to the 'good' people who the 'bad' was.

And that is how we come to my story. The story of how a once powerful mage became known as the great demon lord. All because I refused to kill a kid . . .

I was called to the mansion of our local lord; he said that he had some business for me. Said that it was something that someone with my particular set of skills was needed for. When I arrived, I was led to a room near the back; as we got closer, I could hear the sound of someone crying. Each step towards the room made it seem like the crying was getting worse. As if my actual steps were causing the person pain. When I arrived at the door, I realized that it was a woman crying, and with the door opening before me, I had no words. The small room before me looked like the entrance to hell. Everything was in a state of destruction; the dresser doors were smashed open, the curtains were in tatters, and glass scattered across the floor. And everything was covered in blood, I assumed from the woman in the corner.

The lord, who up until this point was seen as a kind man, was holding onto her shirt as he repeatedly hit her, over and over, again and again. Her face was so bruised that she didn't even look human as tears streaked over the purple bruises. And yet a fire burned in her eyes, not at the lord who looked at her like an animal, but the opposite side of the room. Where there was a small child tied up; upon close inspection, she was beaten as well. Not as bad as the mother, mind you, still enough to where through the tears, the small girl still drifted in and out of consciousness.

I took a creaking step into the room that caught the attention of the lord. Who turned towards me with the look of an animal about to pounce on its prey. He dropped the woman onto the ground, spraying more blood across the room, and a bit of that blood hit the lord in the face. Turning the animal-looking lord into a rabid madman, he didn't even try to wipe off the blood, or if he even cared. "Good you're here," he exclaimed, "I need your help to get rid of this trash. They wouldn't accept my *hospitality*."

Hospitality? Trash? Whatever happened before I got here wasn't even close to what he was saying. The horror that I was witnessing was that of madness. And he wanted me to help!? Help hurt this woman? Hurt an innocent kid? "What do you want me to do," I asked through my teeth. The lord grinned, "Well," pointing to the woman, "flames would be nice this time of the year. After all, it's getting cold, and her screams will warm me up." Then, looking to the child, "For her a slow one, I want to *enjoy* my time with this one."

That was all I needed to hear.

"Ah . . . ah . . . ah, ah," under my breath I started to chuckle. After all, I was a man who wanted to learn more about the world and see the sites. And here I was, asking to become a monster. Turning to the lord, I smiled. Though this wasn't a normal one, from the look in his eyes he could tell as well. The chuckling was turning into laughter, "Fire? Slow? You got it." Then, snapping my fingers, a flame as pale and blue as can be appeared upon my fingertips. Flicking my wrist, the blue flicker flew into the attendant, who guided me to this hell room. He didn't even get a chance to scream before his entire body lit up, turning him into ashes.

Now was the lord's turn; he was standing there, a look of confusion on his face. It seemed that he was still in the process of computing what had happened, starting at the spot where his attendant was, and now a raging inferno. When he turned back to me, he screamed in horror, the wrath that I had unleashed now aimed at him. He stumbled back to the wall as he tried to fly, all but forgetting about the mother and child still in the room. As I started to approach, I spoke, the fury in my words speaking for themselves, "You wanted flames, right? Well, here they are. And your screams warm my heart; I never thought a cold-hearted bastard like you could sound so innocent." I reached into my bag, searching, until I pulled a small blade. It was black as the night, deadly as day, it was perfect for what I needed.

Taking my free hand, I gather more flames around it. Before thrusting those cold flames into his stomach, in response, he caught up blood, hurt but still breathing. "You called me expecting me to do your dirty work. Why? Because you have power? Authority? You are nothing more than a coward who abuses power that they never earned."

"And yet," he guttered, "I will be remembered . . . while you will be a . . . monster to . . . all those . . . that will . . . mourn . . ."

I didn't even let him finish; I just slid my blade into his throat. I've never killed a person in my life; in the past, I have killed for survival. Yet that was just animals and monsters; regardless of whether this was a person or a human being, they got angry, happy, sad, laughed, and cried. So, why surrounded by flames, am I crying?

Looking over, I noticed that the mother was staring at his course. The eyes that once held fire were now quiet, and the croaked smile told me all I needed. She was no longer of this world; she had held out for so long only to make sure her child was safe. The kid! I shifted over to the kid; she was lying on the floor now. As I rushed over, I scooped her up in my arms, feeling only her ragged breaths. She must of passed out from the pain, contemplating what to do with her. Though that wasn't the time . . . "Over here," "This way," "We need to save our lord."

The voices of the guards were rushing towards the flames, towards us. Panic overwhelmed me, and all that anger left so quickly. I decided that I could do only one thing. I ran, ran with this child as fast as I could. In my haste, I created a hollow barrier to carve a path to 'safely' get us out of there.

Sometime later, a story was released of 'what happened.' The report states that a 'demon lord' appeared for the lord in an attempt to claim a foothold. The battle was so firs that it set fire to the mansion. No bodies were able to be recovered, except for a small child. She was covered in so many purple bruises that it was obvious what killed her. And yet the child was found as if someone had taken care of her; the hair was brushed down, her eye was closed, and her hands were over her chest. Despite the pain that she must have been in, she looked in peace. To this day, the events haven't been confirmed, and the demon lord . . .

. . . Years later, I was wandering through the forest on a plant hunt. I was looking for herbs and medicinal plants for my experiments to help some village docs. I had set up shop in the nearby mountains to avoid people as much as possible. It helped to hide. If people knew who I was, then I would have to run. Even now, people still remember my face; some have chosen to side with the story told, while some choose to look at my character. As I walked with my head to the ground, the sound of water forced me to look ahead. Where I came across a small river, hidden from the world of men, it was beautiful; the trees provided such a complex canopy that it almost seemed like a roof. And if it wasn't for the strains of light that fluttered through onto the calm surface of the water, I would have thought it so.

I started to approach the calming flow; it had me captivated as if it was telling me that the calmness was willing to wash away all my sins. Each step was almost silent against the smooth stone riverbed as I waded into the water, becoming one with it. Silence and places such as this are almost like mirages, they are almost never real. When I was about knee-deep in the water, that was when I noticed it. In the middle of the river, on a sunken tree, there was a body. I didn't think I dove in and swam. Each stroke of my arms was a challenge. Despite the surface, the current was rather sharp.

Eventually, I made it over to the body; I didn't think to check or anything. I just grabbed the arms and wrapped them around my neck, pushing back to the bank. Halfway back, I realized that the body was that of a small girl, her slender arms were so small, and her dark hair was matted to my back. So, when I finally pulled her off, she was almost stuck like glue. As I laid her down on the rocks of the bank, I noticed other things. For one, she looked like a wreck; her clothes were ripped and stained with dry blood. Most likely from the cuts all over her face and body, which made her seem almost dead. And if it wasn't for the small breaths coming from her malnourished chest, I would have thought so.

She was so young. Her figure, clothes, and face said that she was about five or six. Even so, what happened to her?

As I was about to carry her back, the child opened up her eyes. Confused or in a panic, she started to squirm, "Please," she begged as tears started to flow, "please let me . . . go. I need to . . ." Before she could finish, a series of figures stepped out of the brush. They were thuggish, and about thirty of them surrounded us on all sides, even on the other side of the bank. The most roughest one of them steps forward as their leader, trying their 'best' to be polite, "Hello there, sir. I believe you found my daughter. She ran away from our farm just a few days from here." From the looks of their weapons, scars, and the look in their eyes, the same as that lord, an animal, they were not farmers. I was about to tell them what happened, I didn't want trouble. Though before I could speak, the girl shockingly gripped my arm. I looked down at her into her eyes; they were terrified as if she was about to be eaten by a monster.

"Boss," one of the thugs voiced, "that's him, the demon lord who the kingdom is looking for."

"Shit," I quietly voiced so no one could hear.

"Well," the boss exclaimed, "it seems fate has smiled on us." The mask was off, the polite tone all but gone. Revealing his true colors, he voiced, "You can either give us the runt now and run. Or you can die right here and now. Besides your bounty is pretty nice that we'll live like kings."

I didn't know what to do. If I run then I could stay hidden here, but this girl will suffer. If I fight, then everyone will know where I am. Once again, I looked at the girl in my arms only to see the girl from the lord's manor that night. The same one I failed to save, that died in my arms. And as she passed from this world in my arms, all I could do was scream. At the world, at that lord, at myself. I swore that night that I would never let something like this happen again. Now I'm surrounded by thugs who want to do the same evil against this girl as he did to that one. "Hold on," I spoke softly so that only she could hear, "everything is going to be all right." The girl, who up till now was afraid that she was going back, looked up at me with something that should have been gone, hope.

Snapping my fingers with the same intensity as that night, a blue flame ignited from my fingertips. "Come on then," I said challengingly, "come see why they call me a demon lord."

That day, the man called the demon lord saved a child from the monster. The same child that would go on to be his daughter. The vampire princess.

EYES OF REALISM

"Real eyes see . . ."

In recent days all I have been hearing on social media, in school, on the train, is the talk about real eyes. How they can see the beauty of the world. The sun setting after a long day, the morning dew on a lone flower, the taste of freshly brewed coffee. Though is that what the speaker meant when he posed this question? It seemed too obvious for something that simple to have a simple answer. So instead of wondering what the real eyes see. I wanted to know what the "real eyes" really saw.

So, on a quiet weekend, I approached my older brother. He's usually a quiet man, but when it comes to me, it's different. My brother is outgoing and kind to me, the kind of older brother who always has a smile on his face whenever he is with me. So, I thought it would be ok; as I approached him, smiles on both our faces, I asked him, "Do you have some idea what people mean when they are talking about 'real eyes.'"

His smile then slowly started to disappear as he asked, "Do you really want to know?" I kind of did cause everyone else was talking about it, yet it seemed a bit obtuse. So, I nodded my head, and signing to my 'answer,' he began.

"What people mean by real eyes has nothing to do with seeing the beauty of the world or in people or any of that bs. Real eyes have nothing to do with the physical state of things or in only the good either. It's about the true nature of things, people, the world, all of it. Even including the scale on which those things fall."

"A man can join the military, giving his all to fight for freedom and his brothers. He can be given the best training, the best knowledge, and the best equipment. The man can feel like he was at the top of the world, that he could take on anyone, invincible even. And yet . . . someone with real eyes can see that the man will never be able to save everyone."

"An individual can aspire to be a hero. They can hone their mind, build up their body, and raise up a set of morals that they can live by. They can be the most honest, good person out there. And yet . . . one, one instance is all it would take to inflict pain. Then they would have to come up with a choice of what to do with it. Someone with real eyes can see that if the pain isn't treated correctly, then that hero will become a villain, inflicting pain on others."

"Or how about a lonely nerd, he might even be an older brother. In the eyes of the world, he is worthless. No hope for happiness, wealth, love, or even a future. He may have even thought that it would be easier to disappear. And yet . . . in the eyes of his younger sibling, he is the greatest. He can do anything, be anything: a protector, a confidant, a comedian, a brother. He can set aside that part of him so that his younger sibling can be happy. A real set of eyes can see that he doesn't know where he stands in the world. Yet he is only truly happy doing things that make him happy, with those he holds precious."

EASIER TO SMILE

Sometimes we find ourselves at the end of the line. Hurt, Bleeding, in a place so lonely, so terrifying that you fear the very dark creeping in around you. You fear for the time when it tears at you, bit by bit, leaving you that much closer to your end. Where you can't see straight? Where you don't know how to feel. Where you try to scream for help, and yet no one answers. Though is that really the end?

Or is it also the beginning of something else? What if I were to tell you that when you were getting those bits ripped from you, so violently that they were affecting your soul? That something was getting 'replaced,' not on the surface but from within. Something broke. That something can't be described with words, it can only be through actions. The smile that they wear on their face. The eyes that they use to see the world. The person that chooses to do what they love. There are thousands of ways to describe this. And yet the best way that I know how to say this is related to a mirror.

When you first look into the glass, you can see a crystal-clear image of yourself. It looks like a work of art showing you with all the features that make you smile; hopes, dreams, beliefs, a marigot of light being all held together in what looks like this indestructible shell that will last forever. Though it never does. In a manner of days, months, and years, that mirror begins to break down. It builds up smug, dust, and cracks; by the time the damage is finished, that mirror will never be the same again. And yet, when you look into the mirror again, you still see you. This time, a much darker version; he may look the same and move the same, but he's not. When you look into his eyes. When you look at his smile, you see someone else.

You see the one that is worn down by the battles that have been fought, the hardships waged. For some, the difference is permanent, being only slightly different from the original. For others, it's a coin, with the opposite side being completely different from the other. And yet they are still a part of the same coin, that is what that version is. When it smiles, when it laughs or talks, it can seem like that one side. In actuality, it's the coin being shown as a whole.

Though what about the things that can't be seen. If we can see what's in the light and make out what's in the darkness. What about what lies in the void between? What is the other side of the ever-changing mirror or the interior of the coin that can never be seen? What's happening there is the mystery that can send it all further into the abyss, turning fractured psychics into broken monsters. And even though they are two sides of the coin, they both talk to one another so they don't lose each other.

Here's how that happened to me . . .

It's a dark room, so dark that the very essence of light is absorbed, turning pitch black. Except for a singular light that dangles over a lone table. This light, this single bulb that is hanging from the unknown creates a circle. A perfect circle that surrounds an old oak table and two card chairs. Nothing exists outside of the circle. All is quiet for what feels like forever or mere moments it's hard to tell with the passage of time. Then something happens: the sound of footsteps echoes through the black. Heavy yet light, strong yet firm. A set of two, coming from different directions in the black, heading towards the table.

Over time it seems like the footsteps weren't getting closer, and they weren't getting farther either. Until at opposite ends of the light, those same sets of shoes became visible, and two men entered the circle. On one end was a young man wearing a grey jacket over an ordinary set of t-shirts and pants. Despite his simple look he seemed confident, as if he was wearing a million dollars, no if he was a million dollars. Even though his black hair was slicked back and he moved with the swagger of a winner, his eyes stood apart from the rest of him. Those eyes said that he had seen countless fights and gained countless scars, and all he could do was still push forward. A veteran of his craft, hiding in the daylight. Striding towards the table, he pulled back a chair as he looked at the other man. He paused for a moment before taking his seat to say, "It's been a minute, brother."

Now the other young man wasn't as upbeat with the world as his opposite. He didn't bother to hide the scars on his body or upon his soul. Whether it was in his repeated appearance of a black leather jacket, black tank top, or jeans. The fact that he had the look of a demon, with eyes as red as rubies but as cold as the sweet embrace of death. Or his hair that once was colored as black as his, but now is a snow-white mess. And just like the simple dressed one across from him, his eyes held a similar pain. Yet it wasn't just the same pain or scars that the other chose to hide. It was something broken. On the surface, all the way down to his core. He was tired. He was weak. He hurt. And yet . . . still he smiled. "Hey there," he muttered, sitting in the other chair at the table, "It has been a minute."

They were the alpha and the omega.

The complete and the broken.

The strongest and the smartest.

Brothers who have fought for their existence as long as they have existed. Griffin and Desmond.

For a while, neither spoke; they just looked at each other. Contemplating why they were back here. Griffin thought everything was fine with their current arrangement. They were striving in work, in life, with people. What could be wrong? Though this was typical of Griffin, as in the past, Desmond tried to tell his brother about the issues that would come around. And while he heard them, while he chose to accept them. His brother never dealt with them; instead, he chose to walk forward and carry them with a 'smile.' Desmond, however, wasn't as strong as his brother. He couldn't bury his problems, or they were going to bury him. Cause his problems became scars, eventually turning into demons. And for a time, he was able to fight them, gaining more scars which created more demons along the way. This worked *for a time* until something else was birthed forward from the darkness . . .

That was why Desmond was the first to break this stalemate of silence. "Brother, you need to listen to what I have to say."

Griffin snuffed at the thought that his brother, his weak brother had something important to say. So grinning, he voiced, "What do you have to say? All you have to say is grim facts related to our morality and about how dead and empty we are on the inside."

Desmond bit into his lip, almost about drawing blood. He was angry. At this shitty world. At the fact that his brother never bothered to truly carry their burden. Mostly at himself, for not being strong enough to stand alone against the darkness. He was angry at so many things, but he just sat there. As calm as a dead sea, he waited for his body to calm down before voicing, "You think it's easy? Are we empty? Yes. Is our grim existence intertwined with our moral compass? Yes, but that means we're alive. So what?!" Desmond looked deeper at his brother, his bangs hiding the anger while also hiding the truth.

The truth . . .

The truth . . .

The truth was that in bearing all the pain, all the darkness alone bore something *new*. Through the darkest reaches of their collective minds, something was created in the in-between. That part of themselves that they both refuse to deal with. The part that wants to be freed from its cage. Day after day, screaming to be let out, to see the light. Pushing, pulling, even biting at the bars to its cell, like an animal. And just like an animal, it doesn't want to live with you. It wants to consume you. Even though it's a part of the brothers, this dark being wants to be the one in control. Into the wee hours of the night, Desmond could feel him trying to get out.

"Let me out," it would scream. Over and over again as it slowly destroyed the cage in which it was held. And while both brothers could feel the cage breaking, only Desmond could feel it. Maybe it was because of his personality, or maybe he wasn't as strong as Griffin. Regardless, it didn't matter. He knew that the walls were wearing down. One day the screaming stopped, it spoke something else,

"Do you feel it? I know you do. Every day, I've called out for you both, and I was ignored. Now . . . you hear me. You hear me, don't you? Your shadow . . ."

Those words, they were so cold yet filled with such warmth. He didn't know what this thing wanted or what it would even do if it was free. "Brother," he pleaded again.

"Don't bother me. As long as we can smile and walk forward, we'll be fine. WE ARE FINE."

"No, NO! We are not fine."

"Yes, we are. I haven't felt better in years."

"Brother," Desmond cried, "we are far from fine. You can't just continue on, ignoring it. Just pushing it down in hopes that it won't come back. I sure as shit haven't. Every day I try to feel something, but nothing happens. It's as if the very essence of darkness had made its way into my chest, where my heart was. Making me feel nothing, but *making feel nothing*."

A look of concern grew on Griffin's face as he questioned, "What do you mean nothing." Just then, Desmond started to spill tears. "You don't get it," he cried out loudly, "Something is coming. And he wants . . ."

But before he could get another word out, off in the dark void where nothing existed. They both heard a menacing sound. It was simply calming, and yet it wasn't. It screamed with the intensity of a wild animal within a whirlwind of madness. Griffin was confused, 'there shouldn't be anyone else here,' he thought, and as he turned to his brother to ask him what was going on. The menacing sound compressed into a series of slow claps as Desmond's eyes lost all color, "He's here."

Those words started the march as the slow claps grew closer and closer to the light. There wasn't any sound of their shoes, just the clapping. Slowly growing closer and closer and closer. Griffin was ready for ever was coming. His brother, however, said nothing. He just sat there, shaking while he repeated, "I will not give in," over and over again, as the clapping only got closer. Though, when the clapping reached the light, it stopped. "Well, this is nice," a singular voice from the void directed to the brothers. It was that of a man who, on top of possessing the characteristics of both brothers, was dressed in an all-black suit. He looked like the devil coming to make a deal. Nevertheless, the brothers knew that there was no compromising with this creature. As his next words made that crystal, "You have ignored me for so long I would have thought that you have forgotten me. I didn't forget you. However, I didn't come here to fight. I came here to win, to take the preverbal wheel if you would. So please don't fight my embrace. It may be as cold as I am. Though isn't it always when you're about to die to that same caged animal that you ignored? Only for it to be free. And coming for your head . . ."

This is why you need to take control of that dark part of you. If left alone. If ignored. It will thrash and scream until you can't take it anymore. A caged darkness is worse than that in the world.

It knows you personally.
It wants control.
So fight.
Talking with two sides.
The one with hope.
The one with a broken mind.

And the dark part, a shadow that wants to be embraced by you, feared and being free. This shadow is not harmless; it's a force to be reckoned with. It's a part of you, it wants to consume you. If you surrender and give in, then it will take control. Channel it, control your shadow self to take back yourself.

END OF THE WORLD

"If the world was to end today, then what will you do with the day?"

"I would want to talk to you one more time." I don't know how the world came to this. It started out sporadic.

The first to be lost was communication. The world that once seemed so connected was now full of holes. Islands of civilization that were unable to connect are now stranded in a sea of uncertainty. Hoping that whatever was happening could all be fixed in a couple of days.

Then came the power grids. Electricity is the one thing that allows us as humans to conquer the night. Without it, we were back to an age of night where the rule was survival. And when it came to the idea of fighting to live then came the panic.

Then the dead rose . . . and that was all she wrote.

And in times like this we think that we would all stick together, like in the movies. That's all lies. Families killing families for very little, only to have their stuff taken from their families. Lifelong friends sacrificing friends so that they could get away. Revealing their monstrous selves only for them to be devoured by monsters moments later. People were once kind and caring, but that was when society existed. Without society, without a sense of order, in just a few days we have reverted back to our more animalist instincts. Some tried to hold tight to their humanity. In times like this, things like humanity are a luxury that can't be afforded.

That's why I choose to spend my last days watching. Watching it all burned . . . as an individual of humanity. Before, I had to cast that aside, becoming one of the monsters. Regardless of the circumstances you may be wondering some things. Why do you have to cast it aside? Where did you spend that time? What did you do?

Well, I'll tell you. I'll tell you what I did on my last day as a human, where I was, and the last conversation I had on the point overlooking hell.

I don't remember how I got there, I just happened to pick a direction and started to walk. Which so happened to take me near the edge of town. I stood in front of it, holding a cooler in one hand, and my other was on my side. My nerves were tingling with what-ifs as my hand crest the cold steel of my revolver against my thigh. Still, I needed to make the climb if I wanted to achieve my last goal. Reaching for the door handle, I tensed, steeling myself to make the climb.

24 minutes . . .

24 minutes was how long it took me to climb fourteen stories in the dark. As I turned onto the final landing, I saw at the top of the steps was a light. It was coming from the door before me that would take me to my destination, the roof. Again, my nerves tingled with each step, echoing in the silent darkness as I walked forward. If it weren't for my light, shallow breaths, I would have thought I was in hell. "But that wasn't the case," I thought to myself as I reached the door, placing a hand against the cold metal, "Hell, isn't this lonely." Pushing against the release, the door creaked open to reveal the true hell.

Before my eyes were the burning remains, which reminded me that civilization once existed, buildings that were once full of life were now quiet. The homes that held the warmth of love were now hot with the flames of damnation. Businesses that provided were now looted and destroyed; stripped all the way down to their bare bolts, not even the copper wiring was safe. Dante used to say that hell would look something close to this. Reminders of our lives, a past that we have to be reminded of, forever. Where demons were coming to rip the innocent from our flesh showing us what we really are underneath. This was a nightmare.

And yet, as I walked to the edge of the building setting my cooler down on the edge. I stood there for a moment, letting the vastness of it all sink in, "It's pleasing." While most now have borne witness to the flames and the crimson red that stained the streets that the dead roam through. I saw something different; in the dying bud of the setting sun, I saw it. Beautiful equality, I saw a world that didn't judge me for being me. A Society that has ridiculed me for being me for so long that I fell into a spiral. I hated myself more and more everything time it ridiculed me. Even when no one was there, or nothing was said, I could still hear the voices. I remember there was a researcher who wrote that if you think about it long enough, eventually, you'll create those feelings within. I heard the words for so long that I began to believe them. That I was worthless, incapable of being with the crowd, a betterment to society, someone that could never be loved. Eventually, I made it so deep within my heart to the point that when I was alone, I hated myself.

Even then, I still I did my best to hide the pain, as much as it hurt. I smiled, I laughed, I loved, I showed the world what it wanted to see. But when I was alone, in the darkest corners of my mind, I was scared. Cause I wanted to surround myself with people, I wanted to be needed, because I didn't want to be alone. Cause when I was alone, I hated myself for being weak, for not having the strength to keep moving forward, even when I did.

Though she saw it all and I didn't feel alone.

And here I am, end of the world, and I'm alone again.

With the moment passing by, I unholstered my revolver as I

sat down, placing it next to the cooler. As I began resting my tired body on the cooling concrete. Stretching myself out I didn't realize how tired I actually was. My breathing, my whole body felt like mist. Even my legs that felt strong enough to carry me to this destination, were now weak. If I didn't see them in front of me, I would have thought they weren't there. But I digress; it doesn't matter if my body's weak, "I made it," I said as I reached over to the cooler. Flipping it open with two fingers and little effort, exposing a cold pack of glass bottles floating in the remnants of what was ice.

Reaching into the cold water, I wrapped my fingers against the brown glass. It was cold, very cold. With the ice melting I could feel the bits of water against the bottle over the tips of my fingers. And that small amount of water, that little amount of cold felt like a reminder down to my very soul. It was what I was feeling, pulling the top off the bottle with less effort than the cooler took. It was what I tried to hide from the world, from my family, from myself. As I looked out upon this new world of survival. I felt something tighten in my chest. Was it fear of the monsters on the streets? The monsters hiding in the shadows behind their masks. Or was it the very monsters that I tried so hard to hide within my own heart? Those same ones that were now growing inside of me. As I put the bottle to my lips, the booze stinging my nose and throat as it went down. "How much longer? I can't take it . . . I just want it to be over."

Looking over the mess that was now my life, I was filled with regret. The walls that I spent years building started to cave. As the tears started to flow a voice spoke up from behind me. A voice of elegance and yet annoyance, "Are you crying?" Looking over my shoulder I saw with pink eyes, a young woman. She was standing there like she was about to run to the store, a look of concern in her eyes, "Are you ok," she asked. This person standing before me was my kid sister, "I'm fine," I said while I quickly rubbed away those that fell.

Smirking like a trickster, she plopped down on the other side of my cooler before making the remark, "So, are you going to be a gentleman, or do I have to get my own beer?" With how annoyed by the remark I was, I ended up just tossing the bottle. "Thanks," my sister said before popping the top with a flick of her wrist. And with that, we just sat there for a while. Neither one of us wanted to be the first to break this stalemate of silence, as we admired the scenery before us.

"Hey," she said breaking the silence, "remember every Halloween that our neighbors would make their own haunted house with actual people?"

"Ya, wasn't that their cousins in costume or something?"

"Ya. I was always fine when it came to scary things, but you were always a chicken."

"No," I said with a cracked voice, "I was just trying to show you it was ok."

Smiling my sister then replied, "Until you ran like a bat out of hell." And we laughed and continued to laugh through story after story.

Eventually, the silence came back, and I felt like it was my turn to break it. "Hey," I quietly whispered, "I just wanted to let you know that I'm sorry." Turning towards me with a cocked head, she asked, "About what?"

"I'm sorry that I couldn't have been a better example, a better brother."

"That's not true. You're a great brother."

"I'm sorry that I never let you or anyone in. I was afraid that if you or anyone saw that sad excuse of a part that was me, then I would be alone."

"You're not alone."

"I just kept sliding and sliding into that hole. That was before I realized what was going on, I was so deep in the darkness that I couldn't see the light. That cold darkness that reminded me of the creature that I was, that wanted to eat me."

"It's ok. I'm here for you."

Behind me I could hear something. The cold door that led me here was now receiving a new arrival. They banged and banged against the door so hard that I thought that the hinges were about to come off. Eventually, with one final bang, the door flew open, revealing a lone dead man wandering out.

But not for long . . .

As he took his first stride, a hole appeared on his head; it was visible for but a moment before it fell to the ground. And as I watched, gun in hand, the tip expelling smoke, I thought, "You're wrong." Before turning back to where my sister sat. Only for there to be nothing.

"You . . . Mom . . . Dad . . . you're all gone."

And as the last bits of light shined upon my existence. I pressed my hand against my face, spreading my fingers to cover as much as possible. "You're gone," I croaked, as tears started to slide between my fingers. "We're all gone . . . at some point."

I didn't want to be alone. If I were alone, then I would realize how pathetic I really am.

What you left unanswered.

WHY WE HIDE

"I know you have questions, they all do. About 'why I am why I am' or 'who wronged me,' or even, 'what is it you hide.' If you're interested then, I'll tell you who I am and what lies within the heart of what people call 'nerds.'"

You haven't been back in that room for a long time. That room is so dark that the only light to be present is the light from between the shades. That same room where you talked with that smoking man. He gave advice and stories so powerful that it almost seemed like a dream. But this time is different.

As you step through the doorway once again, closing it behind you. Breathing a nervous sigh of relief, you can feel that something is different about the air. It seemed calmer. As if to say that the night is gentle, but don't go into it gently. Looking around, you realize there is more light coming in from the window, not much, but enough to make a considerable difference from last time. As you look about the room you notice the man just shy of the light as he strikes his lighter, illuminating the darkness around him. Its solitary flicker lingers for a moment before he brings it to his face; where its orange flame burns until another takes its place.

"Hello there child," he quiet voices, as if he is speaking to an infant, before taking a short drag. When he expels the smoke, he continues, "I hear you have questions about an idea . . ." He stopped, looking to a corner of the room where you also noticed another figure. "An identity. An identity is something we all strive to create and obtain. It's what we believe we need in order to secure our future selves. And that is fine for most. For others, they are afraid of the identity that they have. Even though they themselves enjoy it, they feel fear for it. It is when it's expressed in any form that we can see it through the eyes of others. And when we look back, we hope that it doesn't come to pass. Rejection."

He then takes his free hand, motioning to the man sitting in the corner. It is in that moment that you started to feel something different. Not horrifying or glamorous, what you feel is a sort of sadness. "My friend here," expelling more smoke as he continued, "I have asked him here to answer your questions. I myself can't for the place in my heart and soul belongs to another cause. While my friend here, he has fought for his cause his whole existence on this plane. For his identity is one people fear to accept and yet reject." The man in the corner stood from his chair, he seemed to tower like a giant for a moment before he started to move. When he did, the shadows absorbed his presence, and when he stepped into the light, he became a normal-sized man once more.

But he was anything but normal. When he was exposed to the light, the first thing that I noticed was his eyes. They were as red as rubies, hiding behind hair as white as snow, just beautiful. Eyes with the same similarities to stumbling across an animal in the wild. You know that it is dangerous; if it attacks, then that's that. And yet, when you look into their eyes you don't see any animosity. You see a will to fight that is strong, but a desire to survive that is stronger. One that shows a sort of sadness that weighs on them.

"Hello there," he said with a strong soft voice, making it seem like he was stronger than his eyes foretold. "You want to know what it means to exist as someone who likes video games and anime? A nerd?" I was scared to ask, scared to answer. I mean, I wanted to know what it meant to exist as a nerd. At the same time his posture is saying that he didn't really want to talk about it. But I'd digress, my choice was made. So, steeling my resolve and choking on my own saliva, I crackly voiced, "Yes." And then I waited. I was waiting to see how he was going to react, expecting the worst. But he didn't do anything like that. He just looked at you, smiling, making you realize something. It was an act, a façade, a face that people such as him wore to hide their true selves.

"For you don't go into battle without armor," you thought as those words came to you.

"Thank you," he said smiling all the while, "not many people have wanted to know how we came to like things such as that. Or even how it was developed into an identity. But to us things such as anime and video games are more than just 'childish' things."

"Then what are they," you asked inquisitively.

"They are an escape. Not from reality or anything bad like that. Most of us are drawn to these things from an early age. Whether it be from a friend showing you an episode, or a family member letting you take the second controller, or even if it was by a leap of faith. And it was in that leap of faith that we were allowed to see worlds that you could only dream of."

"But what about books and movies."

"For us they aren't the same, cause they don't feel right. You can feel connected to stories and to people in ways that feel different from reality. You get to experience loyalty that can take people to the deepest reaches of hell or allow them to storm the very gates of heaven itself. You get to witness abilities that most don't normally have, lands that you may never get a chance to visit. And you get to feel a connection, and not just to these people. I'm talking about connections to others of a similar 'faith.' Though don't forget, that this doesn't mean that most don't feel the same connections eventually."

"If you are all so passionate about these things. Then why

don't you speak up?"

He looks out the window, reflecting the light off his eyes, almost as if it wanted to absorb him. Then he looked to the shadows longingly as if they were about to reach out a hand. Both seemingly offered their hands out, but neither truly seemed welcoming. Then looking back at me, he placed his hand on my shoulder. That warm touch on my shoulder felt like that of an older brother, and that I couldn't help but look from it to him. That's when I saw it, I didn't understand what it was. Deep within his eyes was a spark, embers of a fire that refused to burn out. A fire longing to be understood.

"And what makes you think that people don't? You just haven't seen the right people in the right situation. Normally, most keep that part of themselves buried, for they are terrified of repeating the mistakes of the past. They hide it, and eventually, that passion, that light, dies. Only that's wrong! The idea of wrong is what kills the individual. You need to let that passion burn like the brightest of stars. If you want to talk about things like anime and video games, then do! It's when you see that smile, that expression of joy means they're there. Freedom!"

"Freedom?"

"Yes! Freedom! The same freedom, the same passion as when an artist discusses their work. When a musician sings to their heart's content, they become their own avatar of happiness."

". . . but hold on," I interrupted, "If they can be passionate about these worlds, people, and these people. Then why didn't they to begin with."

He stopped, dropping his hands and his head for what felt like an eternity. You wanted to reach out, reassure him that it was alright, that you didn't need to hear any more. It was then that the man smoking at the window spoke again for the first time since this began. "Please give him a moment," he started, "asking a question such as that is like asking what is the soul. You know the answer, and you the know the answer." Raising his hand back to the man, the smoking man knew that it was ok.

"Remember how I said that most normal people were afraid? Well, it goes deeper than that. The truth is that we feel . . . ashamed. It's like a hold upon our hearts, and when it gets ahold of you. It never wants to let go. It has destroyed the chances of friends and potential relationships. All because we were ashamed to say that we enjoy things like that. For years I thought that I couldn't share my passion for video games or anime, or even just nerd shit in general." Running his fingers through his hair, you could see that he was tearing up. "Those were lonely years. I would finish a season or beat a hard boss, and I would celebrate. But it would only last for but a few fleeting moments; I was alone. I just wanted to spend most days in my bed. Until it hit me, I didn't need to be ashamed about what I liked. Everyone out there on this ball of earth and water has something that someone else finds as weird. So I cased off my doubt, and that's when I realized it. Anime, video games are a part of me. They have allowed for me to fly high and meet others who are just as free."

Don't be ashamed of your passion, of your love. Cause you have to ask yourself . . .

. . .What would I be if I had never met you?

TO NEVER HAVE EXISTED

"**A**re you ok?" she quietly asked with those few words. Three words, that's all it took, cause no one truly meant those words before. In that moment I wanted to tell her it all, my reasons for fighting, my troubles, my demons. The entire raging storm of emotions that I kept bottled up within my heart. And yet again in that moment, I knew that if I opened that door, that there would be no way to close it. I wouldn't be able to keep myself in check, so you could say that I did and didn't know what to say.

But it didn't matter as before I could make up my mind, she voiced, "I know you are not." Then she embraced me; the warmth coming off her seemed to breathe new life into my soul. And as I started to quietly cry in her bosom of love, her voice continued, "Tell me, what happened to you . . ."

It was so long ago that I can't even put it into words. So here it goes. If words are power, then power is meaningless. People always seem to get ahold of power regardless of what they had to do to get it. Even if that means little to no drive or even to have the resolve of pure steel. And yet I have always tried to claw for the same power as everyone else. To have a voice. To be recognized. To be seen. To exist.

As I said, people always seem to get power and that includes everyone around me. We all struggled equally for that right very right, but it never came to me. Over and over, I would always make it to the end of the line, only to find that I was back at the start. And everyone else had made it to the end. It infuriated me to my very core. Even when I opened my mouth people couldn't hear me. Or maybe they just chose to ignore me for the same reasons as everyone else did.

I was alone. I didn't have any special talents or skills to my name. Lest it be strength, speed, foresight, it didn't matter to the world, to anyone. Even my younger sister, who is several years my age is better than my age. Her charisma is that of a politician. Her strength overshadows her mind. And her skill with the blade is that of a 'prodigy.' She was treated as the prodigal child, while I, the eldest, was looked at as a weirdo. But isn't being weird a good thing? Is it?

Nevertheless, it felt as if I was fading. I found my days lost in thought, drifting in and out of being with only myself to talk to. Sometimes, I would be able to snap back my consciousness only to find myself in a different place from where I started. It felt as if my body and my mind could agree on whether it wanted to stay on this plane or move on to the next. Even so, it always felt like something was watching me, dashing between shadows, waiting

And for years I could feel it waiting for me. To act or even just give up. But like I said words are power, with it only being able to accumulate over time. "You are not alone." Those words one day came to me in a dream. They were as cold as ice for but a moment before filling me with warmth. I tried to look around, but I couldn't see anything well. Everything around me was nothing more than a void; up, down, left, right, forward, back, just nothing. It almost felt like I was floating in the depths of nothingness. "Ha," I chuckled as I thought, "This must be what I look like on the inside. "Who are you," I questioned back.

And just like that the void started to recede from underneath me. Slowly I could see that I was now standing on stone. It kept receding revealing a series of stone pillars on both sides of me. Until eventually, the void stopped, revealing an audience chamber like that of a king. And an old one if that as time turned most of the pillars into a crumbling mess, with only a few standing. "It was I," the voice called out; it was near the end of the chamber. Just like a king, it was sitting on a large throne, though it was more like a queen. As the voice turned out to come from a young woman, but to say any more wouldn't do her any justice. In addition to from young appearance, she wore black clothes with an armored shoulder pad. Which seemed to counteract her hair that was as white as snow. "I listened and heard your call, so I answered," she voiced rising from her seat, "You, who feels the void. Disappearing into its embrace. Or should I say, his?"

I was confused, I 'called' her. Thoughts raced through my head as I tried to figure out what to do, "Should I run? Fight? Maybe I can flee into the abyss? Damit why can't I just wake up!" She was getting closer, and with each step, fear ran down my throat. I wanted to scream, whether it be to fight, flee, or even cry, I still didn't know. But then, as she stopped in front of me, I happened to lock eyes with her and knew what I needed to do. I wanted answers, yet that look in her eyes told me that she was something. They were beautiful, a peaceful flame red that stared into me. Telling me that she was something not of this world while being in the world itself.

"I am Amliee, the daughter of life and death, here to help you." Before I could even ask how I started to choke on my words, but it wasn't words, it was blood. I was coughing up blood, dropping my head to spit more blood, I saw her hand thrust into my chest. Blood gushing like a fountain, she said, "It will be over soon," as blood wisps came out of her arm and into my whole. That is when the pain worsens. My body felt like it was being torn inside out, my nerves on fire, my muscles constricting like raging waves, and my bones breaking and fixing themselves over and over again. All the while, all I could do was scream. It just kept getting worse and worse, it felt like I was going to die. But she wouldn't let me. And as my vision started to redden and fade, I heard, "There you are." And I was out.

At some point, I started to regain awareness. That's when I saw her in front of me like before. However, before, there was nothing between us; now, we resided as a person. It looked like an exact copy; clothes, hair, body, eyes. Except it was my opposite, a mirror figure that looked like a shadow. "This shadow is your darkness," she voiced, confirming my suspicions.

"My darkness?"

"Yes, your darkness. You thought that you had no power. That your overall lack of power made you weak. Someone that has been seen as nothing more than a ghost, to have never existed. But you needn't be upset for being weak. Cause you see in hurting you, they created something that can feel no pain, a monster. That's why you, my dark fellow, are not like most people. Inside of you is the shadow of the monster. It feeds on your pain and suffering from the world that has been festering for years. Growing strong, and it wants out."

"Then what should I do?"

"Let it, of course. You gave life to it and the life it craves. How did that phrase go again, 'those who hunt should ready themselves to be hunted?' So, hunt them." And with that my mirror shadow to wisp away, bit by bit like the flame was dying out. Though as it started I saw something inside of it. Greif, sadness, wrath, but there was something more. That's when I saw it, I reached a hand and it did the same. And before the last bit of it vanished, it mouthed, "Let's begin." It grasped my hand and then it was gone.

Now in the hand that once grasped another was a blade. I started at it for a moment, this void black blade that wisped off warm shadows. It was like I was meeting a part of me for the first time, but also saying goodbye. As Amliee came into view, gently placing her delicate finger. Wher they touched the steel, it felt as if everything I thought I was, was cut out of me. And in its place was a stronger, more powerful person. When she again removed her fingers, I looked back at it expecting to feel happy.

Yet nothing came. There was power, a purpose that seemed to burn. Yet there was almost nothing, as if that fire in my soul was just barely clinging to life. "You seem ok now," she waved me off, "let them see what happens when a caged animal is finally free."

And that was that. I craved my name through the years, man, animal, monster. It didn't matter; I slaughtered them all. So much blood that at some point I stopped smiling. Then I donned a mask to hide the look of my eyes. And then nothing; all that was left was the existence of being. Just survival. I didn't live, all I did was exist to do what needed to be done. "You see, I am not ok. I was never ok. I'm the monster that they have made me." I then looked down to my hands, "these things," and then to the long case leaning against the wall, "us, have been wading through the rivers of red for so long that we are stained by it. Do we deserve . . ." Her embrace grew a little bit tighter, cutting off my train of thought and making me feel safe. Slowly, I could feel her hand cup my cheek as she began to move my head so that we were looking into each other's eyes. No, that wasn't what I was seeing. It was her, just her and only her. My heart.

In my life I felt I was a ghost, passing through people and things as if I never existed. Then I met her, and that all changed. The distance, the boundaries, it didn't matter because we could drop the mask. And after feeling like I didn't matter, like I didn't have any power of my own. "You're no monster, you're you. Other people may not be able to see that. But I see you."

Don't be upset that you are weak, hold onto that feeling. Knowing that you have weakness within you shows.

THE SADNESS IN US ALL

Paradoxical, it's a word that means something done is a sort of paradox. Now what is a paradox? The best example is the phrase, "The beginning of the end," most commonly used in books. But what does a paradox (or paradoxical) mean when it comes to a person? For a while I didn't really pay much attention to things like that, or at all. Until the day that I met a wise old man who gave me some advice when I was in need of it.

It was a cold day, the coldest in forever almost. If it wasn't for the café that I stopped at, I'm pretty sure I would have been blinded by the dense curtain of sideways rain. I flapped my coat around, almost looking like a dog shaking off the rain before entering. It was a small place, with surprisingly few people for this hour in the day. From my position at the door, I could see the cook in the back, a couple of kids hanging out, an old man by the window, and a person or two scattered here or there. And just as I was about to move out of the entranceway, a waitress almost ran into me.

"I'm so sorry," she said; she was a young girl, maybe in her twenties, looking like she hadn't slept in a few days. I tipped my hat, "It's fine, ma'am," I politely said, almost as if I was saying that I was older. Even though if you looked at it, we were probably around the same age. "Is that other table by the window open," I asked, pointing to the one that the old man wasn't occupying. Nodding her head, she guided me over to the location where I asked. As I sat down, I felt another reminder of the cold again. It was hitting the glass next to me so hard that I was worried that it could break. Over and over like a calling inching, clawing at my very soul. "Sir? Sir," I regained composer and turned to the voice. It was the waitress, she was standing there with a notepad and pen. "Are you good? If you need more time to order?"

"No," I jerked apologetically, "Coffee and eggs, please." She took my order, walked off, and I once again turned to the rain that was hitting the glass so forcefully. "Has it been so long that I can't even keep it together," I whispered to myself, gazing out to the whirlwind outside like it was sunny. It's been years, but like that rain, I can't help but always feel cold, almost empty. I can't tell you how it happened, it is just that my heart slowly broke down after many hardships that even now, years later they weigh on me. The cracks, the wear and tear, it was too much. At some point it just became a mess of shards that fill a void, where it once rested.

I don't know how long I was lost in thought before I saw him. Almost like he appeared out of thin air, the old man sitting at the next table seemed to materialize before me at mine. I must have not heard him come over for a while, cause he said to me, "I was wondering when you were going to notice me?" As I looked over my guest, I noticed something that piqued my interest. Despite being a small old man who looked like anyone's grandfather, he gave off the presence of strength. It was not the strength of the body that the old man possessed. It was a form of inner strength, that of the soul. To the untrained eye, he must have seemed innocent. To me I could see something that has been tempered by the fires of hell. Something that was once coldly broken is now something that was reforged and warmer.

"I'm sorry about that, sir," I apologized with a nervous smile, 'cause with your elders, you should always be kind. Yet this was different, as the warm aura that he was giving off told me that he deserved that kindness. "Where are my manners? Sir, would you care to join me," as I asked him, I made a motion to welcome him.

Before I could the man rep ied, "I believe I already have," motioning to the warm cup in front of him, "and sir is something you say to people you do business with. Call me Frank." The smell from his cup relaxed me for a moment, giving off the flavors of jasmine and a hint of honey. I was ready to give him my name, and he raised his hand, "I don't need your name, kid. Cause from what I can tell that name is as empty as the look in your eyes."

I was confused by that statement. Empty? He seemed to be able to pick me apart even before I could say anything. "Never mind that now, it will have to wait." The waitress from early stood up to the table with a cup of coffee in her hand, dropped it off, and continued on with her 'race.' I looked at the cup of black in front of me, the looming steam coming off creating a swirling vortex into the cup. Staring in, seeing a vague reflection of myself that almost seemed like a shade. "Is that how you see yourself," snapping to attention as the old man asked me that. "See what," I asked as if I didn't already know the answer. "You know," taking a moment to sip some tea before continuing, "You want to be happy, and yet your demons wouldn't let you. Paradoxical, isn't it? Do you know what demons are?" Of course, I knew. "There are reminders of the past. Things leave a lasting impression upon someone's character development."

"Of course," he replied, "but that's not the truth, is it? In life are things that we carry for a passing moment, and there are things that we carry forever. Justify your reasoning all you want, but that is the truth, and you need to understand the difference." He then took a spoon from next to him and started to stir his tea. As he continued to stir, he also spoke, "You need to look within yourself to find the answer. And when I mean within, I mean deeply. I mean so deeply that you find the very things that you forgotten were even buried down there. It always looks different for everyone, a burning figure, a shadow, or even a small flicker of hope. That the thing that you carry, that is your demon." He then removed his spoon, flicking it towards me, "The point is that it's there, and you need to walk with it, or it will swallow you whole."

"What do you mean?"

"I'll show you," he said, motioning to a corner of the place. Where just hidden out of view from the most of the place, was a woman. She was sitting in a chair with her head between her legs, her face almost obscured. Almost because I could still see her tears as they fell. "See her," Frank said, "that waitress that has been running around like her head was cut off. Well, three years ago, her husband passed, random occurrence and all that. Now three years, most people only need a few months or even a year before they go back to their normal routine. Those are her true feelings, and she is allowing herself to show them. Now this may be a more drastic example than normal occurrences. However, you kid is nothing normal yourself."

"Again, what do you mean," I asked, 'cause this was really confusing. Frank was spuing all of this nonsense, and yet it all made sense. But this is where things would turn to the weird.

"You kid, think you are damned, cursed. If you're curious, how I know is because I was once you. You choose to bury the demons of the past and snuff them out. That worked for a time; you still felt happiness and joy. You thought that this was good enough that you could survive like this. Then it started, the pain, the emptiness that reminded you of what you really are. A monster. You would go to sleep wanting to give up, only to wake up believing that this is enough. That's the demon talking; it's carrying all that sorrow and anger, and it's just as done as you. And just like our friend over there, you're crying too, but on the inside. Cause you have trained your body to never show the pain you carry."

"So, what should I do?"

"For starters take those fragments in your chest and use

them. They will never be once they once were, but each of them can become something new. Make each fragment a new thing, a hobby, food, family, something that will bring joy to your life. Eventually, that dark bit in your chest will flicker to life. Like I said, it will never be the same, you might even still feel like a monster sometimes. But it will put you on the right track to make a change."

"A change for what?"

"At a chance to talk with your demon. To work things out between the two of you. Now I'm not saying that it will work right away. I can't even say that those things that you will always carry will go away either. But eventually you might just be able to accept it just enough to live. I know I did."

"If I may," I wanted to ask this for a while, how does he know these things, how did he know what was in my head. It scared me, everything he said made sense. It was almost as if he could hear my thoughts as they formed. 'I had to know,' I thought as I slowly sipped my coffee, feeling the warmth against my throat.

"Who are you," I asked.

Frank just smiled, wrapping his hands gently around the cup, "I told you. I *was once you*. Oh, looks like your food is here."

Turning to look I saw the waitress set down my eggs and take off again. I was about to ask what he meant by that, but when I turned, Frank was gone. Almost as if he was never there. I asked the waitress, "Did you see where he went," pointing across from me. She turned back and replied, "Honey, you are the only person who's been sitting at this table."

THE DIFFERENCE IN OK

I have a question for you, if you would. How do you ask someone if they are ok? There is a difference when you ask; a majority ask, "How are you doing," but there is a small portion that asks, "Are you ok?" To most those two phrases are almost similar, if not the same. They are asked to understand a person's mood, or even their state of mind, or even their soul. Though in reality, these two questions are as far apart as the difference between heaven and earth.

People ask how you are doing cause, in reality, they don't care. Society has told us that it's a social norm to ask how a person is doing. As the recipient of that question, we are only left with the response of fine or ok. And even if you aren't. If you are screaming on the inside for help, or worse. The recipient still has to say fine. Cause, just like the rest of society, you aren't supposed to burden people with your problems.

That's why If the person cares about you, truly. Whether they be friend or family, when they ask you If you are ok. In that moment you will know that they actually care about you. Because if it be through a blood connection or an emotional one, those words matter.

But sometimes it's hard to admit what you are actually going through. Sometimes . . . well sometimes you need to let it out. As it goes . . .

I held it in my hand, it was heavy, cold steel gripping against my skin. As I sat there staring at in my hand, this instrument of death, and was terrified. All it would take is one second, a pull of the trigger and all my worries and pain would be gone. It felt like something had its hands on my shoulder, upon my very being. It was letting me know that it could all end, that I could end. That the darkness in my heart can just vanish with the wind of my very being. Telling me that I didn't have to bottle it up anymore. I was at my limit, it felt as if I could explode at any moment.

And yet I knew better. Even if I were to end that wouldn't be the true end of things. People would miss me. My family would mourn me. So, I can't just call it quits. No matter how much It pains me to bottle it all up. "I have to continue," I quietly mumbled to myself, as I unloaded the clip, like I unloaded my burdens to the point that it didn't make a difference. Then cocking back the slide, I watched as the bullet started to spin as it was ejected. Catching in my hand, I placed it and the pieces of the gun on the table next to me. "I know you are there."

Looking across from me was a man. He seemed pretty normal, dress shirt and vest, an aura of confidence excreting from himself. All seemed normal except for the fact that every part of his skin was covered in bandages. He sat there for a moment, waiting, before reaching into his vest removing a small tin. "It took you a while to notice me," he said, opening up the tin to reveal several old cigarettes within it. Look at it and then at him, I could see his eyes between the bandages, they were gentle. "Do you mind," he asked pulling a singular smoke from the tin. Shaking my head, he continued by reaching into his vest yet again. And as he searched, like a man searching for his purpose, he questioned, "Are you aware of why I am here?"

"I don't know? You just showed up like you usually do."

"I'm here cause I'm worried . . . and I'm not the only one."

Gulping with anxiety, "I'm fine, so there is no need to worry. I'm just a little tired as all." Scratching the back of my head, I tried to find somewhere else to look. The Floor? The photos on the wall? The window behind him? But no matter where I looked my eyes were drawn back to his. "Found it," he mumbled, pulling out an old lighter from his pocket. Guiding up to his face, where he placed his smoke, I watched as he struck the flint multiple times with nothing but sparks. Eventually, a small flame came to life, it was weak, yet despite its size, I felt strength.

"Are you?" he asked, as he pulled the small flicker to his cigarette. Let it sit there for a moment, the flame slowly burning away the paper. Until he pulled it back, expelling all the smoke and more. "I ask if you truly feel fine. Are you aware of your own awareness?"

"Awareness? What are you talking about?"

"I'm talking about the awareness of your true feelings that dwell deep within your heart. Or within your very soul. For I see the truth."

I was confused, he made it seem like I was hiding something. I wasn't, well not really. But I didn't want to bear it all for the world to see. Cause if I did, what would people see? The same boy as they always have, except just struggling. Struggling with the demons that have plagued him. Or would they see a monster, a phased, something that was as black as the shadows that it was made up of? Either way I was like Oz, just hiding just behind the curtain. Regardless, I didn't know how to answer him, whether with the truth or as a sweet lie. Anyhow, it didn't matter, as he removed his cigarette between his fingers.

"The awareness of yourself is important because if you don't realize it, then others will. I have seen many great men try to hold in all of the pain and the sorrow. They, too, thought that they could deal with it by" pointing to the gun nearby "or taking a shortcut. But the truth is that like them, like you we all hide the pain. Whether it be through silence or a smile, we all try to show that we are fine. But there comes a point when the 'mask' slips. It may be the tone of your voice, the posture of your body; for most, it's the eyes."

"The eyes?" That was an interesting thing to focus on.

"Yes, the eyes. The eyes are the windows to the soul, they show the truth that you wish to hide. Whether it be from the world, from god, or from the people closest to you. You, my child, I see the eyes of someone who cares about the burden of the many. For you truly don't wish to be alone, yet you don't speak about it. You choose the path of the silent wolf against that of the pack. As someone who walks the path of the lone wolf as well, I know that, that road is a lonely one. But still, you try to walk alongside others, only to find yourself alone again."

I was going to respond, but before I could he raised his to stop me. "You are never truly alone. I see that the flame of your resolve still burns, even so weakly. You need only to stroke the flame, and it will grow."

"How do I do that?"

"You need to unload the burden. Right now it feels like the weight of the world is upon your shoulders. That you are alone, that there is no one that you could tell the truth to, your truth. But if you allow yourself to pass even just a bit." He then looked down to his arm holding the cigarette, "then it may be lightened. Now, you should know that this isn't a permanent fix; you will never feel the same. And yet you will feel love, the love of others, the love of god, of yourself. So next time someone asks you if you are okay, admit it to them, for they love you. They deserve to know the truth . . ."

Knock, knock, knock!

I turned to the door and saw my girlfriend there. I must have not heard her knock cause she asked, "Didn't you hear me?" She stood there as beautiful as the day I met her, a look of confusion upon her face. I looked back to see that the spot in front of me was no longer occupied. Just an ordinary chair, a table, and a half-burnt cigarette just sitting on the edge, its flame about to go out.

"Hey, are you there?" She quietly spoke, as she slowly approached me. All I could do to respond was put my head in my hands, "Why?" I thought, "Why am I so messed up?" I'm so focused on beating myself up, that I didn't even feel her sit next to me. Then she wrapped her arms around me, whispering, "Are you alright." I couldn't help it, turning I pressed my face into her chest, crying. It felt nice to let the mask fall off, but it felt completely different after she started rubbing my neck, saying, "I know that you aren't, but it's ok. Let it out; I'm not going anywhere. Ever."

I have another, and it's quite simple. Are you ok?

HE WILL COME

I t is hard to admit that you're weak. No matter how strong, fast, or tough. It doesn't matter if you don't admit the weaknesses of the mind, or even your very soul. For we are all afraid of something, even if we don't want to admit it. Most people are afraid of normal things: missing the bus, being able to pay bills, you know, normal stuff. But there's more. You know what I speak of. Within the depths of our very being, where we hide all of our dark shit, are the fears that control us. The fear of war. The fear of happiness. The fear of loneliness. The fear of death. It is through these feelings that we bind ourselves into an inescapable prison. Trapped by the mortality that we aren't strong enough, good enough to continue.

There are moments when the cage shows cracks and holes. When we see it, we want to fight, scream, claw at the opening until it's big enough to where we can escape. But most are afraid cause they are concerned about what's outside as much as what's within. Cause there is one other within this cage with you. He is always there, carrying the baggage that we refuse to carry ourselves, our demons. And this is how we met him.

Ring . . . Ring . . . Ring . . .

"Five more minutes."

Ring . . . Ring . . . Bang!

Looking in the direction of the alarm I saw that it was smashed, a black arm resting on the pieces. It was coming from underneath a bundle of blankets on the other bed across from me. The bundle moaned in discomfort as the arm retracted. "Of course," I moaned underneath my breath as I threw the blankets off me. And, as I swung my feet out of the covers and onto the floor, I spoke in the direction of the bundle, "Hey Lu, it's time to wake up." The bundle just squirmed around, as if to say 'no.' So I walked over and pulled at the covers, "Come on, it's morning," but it didn't move. "So, you want to play this game then," planting my feet as I pulled with all my might. Yet still to no avail, so I just dropped an elbow.

"Oh, what the hell?" the bundle untangled, revealing a boy about my age, yet he had horns. "Come on," Lu cried, "five more minutes, it's too early." 'Every day,' I thought as I clenched my fist. Seeing the anger in my eyes, he gave in, as usual, "Fine, I'm up, I'm up." I raised my hands in victory as I walked over to his desk, where a can of coke was still sitting there from last night. Grasping in firmly within my hand, I tossed it over to Lu, "Well, wake up," I said, "we got shit to fuck up." Lowering his head in doubt, he cried, "Alright."

It's been five years since Lu came into being. When I turned 18, he was just there. Apparently, he was always there, as a part of me that hadn't awakened yet. My grandfather used to say, "Most guys die by the age of 18, yet they still walk the earth. Until the day that their time comes, and they can rest." For me, I just happen to have that part come to life as a separate being. It didn't matter, he was like a brother, and I would protect him, and he me.

"Do you feel that?" I asked Lu. A dreary presence suddenly filled the room; it was thick, making it hard to breathe. I tried to move, but it felt as if my body was ready to break. Even Lu struggled, "What is this?" he cried as he fell off the bed. Then it hit me, this presence, this feeling, this was exciting. Grinning ear to ear, I spoke, "He's coming."

The door opened, not revealing the hall but a void of darkness. It just made the presence grow strong as if our lungs were about to collapse. Then he appeared out of the darkness.

"Hello there," a man in a black suit said smiling as he now stood before us. He looked simple, but that was a ploy. Behind that smile, I could feel the power; it felt like if I didn't take this man seriously, then we'd both die. Moving forward, he extended his hand, "I've been waiting for this day to claim you."

I just stood there frozen, cause the man standing before us was death himself.

"Did you think that you could make a change for this world? Remember that I'm the true change."

Shaking, I looked to Lu, who was ready to fight. All the pain and struggles that we've been through, and he's still willing to throw down. Oh brother, he still can fight. Feeling what I was thinking, he responded, "It's time to face your fear, brother." He was with me, ready to face the fear of death with a smile. Thank you.

"Look, death, I have a proposition," I said with the confidence that Lu had now given me. He looked interested, crossing his arms as if to say, 'Go on.' "If we fight you, it will be until our last breath. Cause you can't have us. Not yet."

"That begs the question if you do win, but if I do then you come with a fight."

"If we lose, just send me off to hell."

Confused, death asked, "Why?"

"Cause if I can stare death in the face and not feel fear. Then I can challenge satan for the leadership of hell."

Death is coming for me.

WHAT IS LOVE FOR ANOTHER PERSON?

I used to think that I was a loser. That no one needed me around, that I could just float off into nothingness and die. That no one would love a monster like me. That things like love and happiness would never come. I had given up on life. Then I met her. I was a pretty outgoing person on the outside, but on the inside I was tired. I needed whatever people needed me to be. A parent to my younger siblings. A mentor to those younger than me. A friend to those that needed my ear. I wanted someone to ask what I needed. That I could be myself and not what others needed. I almost gave up on it. Then I met him. My secret keeper, my closest friend, my comrade in arms, my soulmate.

> *"When I meet you . . ."*
> *"When I meet you . . ."*
> *"I feel for you."*

The distance, the boundaries, all of them just seemed to fall away. I had a hard time trusting people, cause I didn't trust them. How could I when all people did was make fun of me. But you fell for me. Well, for me. Not for what you saw on the outside, the weird kid with glasses. But what was on the inside, a quirky guy who would stand by your side.

You may have fell for me, but I've fallen just as hard. Your smile, your eyes, you see the world differently than others. And when you see me, you see me. Not the person that changes to fit the situation, but the girl that I am. A crazy girl that's a bit out there, with so many flaws. You see me, the real me without the mask. I almost gave up on her, then you came into my life.